THE DROWNED LIFE

THE
DROWNED
LIFE

JEFFREY FORD

HARPER ⬤ PERENNIAL

NEW YORK • LONDON • TORONTO • SYDNEY • NEW DELHI • AUCKLAND

HARPER ● PERENNIAL

Page 291 constitutes an extension of this copyright page.

P.S.™ is a trademark of HarperCollins Publishers.

THE DROWNED LIFE. Copyright © 2008 by Jeffrey Ford. All rights reserved. Printed in the United States of America. No part of this book may be used or reproduced in any manner whatsoever without written permission except in the case of brief quotations embodied in critical articles and reviews. For information address HarperCollins Publishers, 10 East 53rd Street, New York, NY 10022.

HarperCollins books may be purchased for educational, business, or sales promotional use. For information please write: Special Markets Department, HarperCollins Publishers, 10 East 53rd Street, New York, NY 10022.

FIRST EDITION

Designed by Laura Kaeppel

Library of Congress Cataloging-in-Publication Data

Ford, Jeffrey.
   The drowned life / Jeffrey Ford.—1st Harper Perennial ed.
      p. cm.
   ISBN 978-0-06-143506-5
   I. Title.
   PS3556.O6997D76 2008
   813'.54—dc22

                                                    2008013181

08 09 10 11 12   OV/RRD   10 9 8 7 6 5 4 3 2 1

FOR JACK GALLAGHER,
who, over martinis late one night
on his screened-in porch,
the surf sounding just beyond the dunes,
told me, among other things,
about a guy who dragged a wheelbarrow
full of bricks with his eyelids

CONTENTS

THE
DROWNED
LIFE

• ONE •

It came trickling in over the transom at first, but Hatch's bailing technique had grown rusty. The skies were dark with daily news of a pointless war and genocide in Africa, poverty, AIDS, desperate millions in migration. The hot air of the commander in chief met the stone-cold bullshit of Congress and spawned water spouts, towering gyres of deadly ineptitude. A steady rain of increasing gas prices, grocery prices, medical costs, drove down hard like a fall of needles. At times the mist was so thick it baffled the mind. Somewhere in a back room, Liberty, Goddess of the Sea, was tied up and blindfolded—wires snaking out from under her toga and hooked to a car battery. You could smell her burning, an acid stink that rode the fierce winds, turning the surface of the water brown.

Closer by, three sharks circled in the swells, their fins visible above chocolate waves. Each one of those slippery machines of Eden stood for a catastrophe in the secret symbolic nature of this story. One was *Financial Ruin*, I can tell you that—a stainless-steel beauty whose sharp maw made Hatch's knees literally tremble like

in a cartoon. In between the bouts of bailing, he walked a tight-
rope. At one end of his balancing pole was the weight of financial
ruin: a mortgage like a Hydra, whose head grew back each month,
for a house too tall and too shallow; taxes out the ass; failing ap-
pliances; car payments. At the other end was his job at an HMO,
denying payment to people with legitimate claims. Each conversation with each claimant was harrowing for him, but he was in
no position to quit. What else would he do? Each poor sap denied howled with indignation and unalloyed pain at the injustice
of it all. Hatch's practiced facade, his dry "Sorry," hid indigestion,
headaches, sweats, and his constant, subconscious reiteration of
Darwin's law of survival as if it were some golden rule.

Beyond that, the dog had a chronic ear infection, his younger
son, Ned, had recently been picked up by the police for smoking pot and the older one, Will, who had a severe case of athlete's
foot, rear-ended a car on Route 70. "Just a tap. Not a scratch," he'd
claimed, and then the woman called with her dizzying estimate.
Hatch's wife, Rose, who worked twelve hours a day, treating the
people at a hospital whose claims he would eventually turn down,
demanded a vacation with tears in her eyes. "Just a week, somewhere warm," she said. He shook his head and laughed as if she
were kidding. It was rough seas between his ears and rougher still
in his heart. Each time he laughed, it was in lieu of puking.

"Storm warning" was a phrase that made surprise visits to his
consciousness while he sat in front of a blank computer screen at
work, or hid in the garage at home late at night, smoking one of the
Captain Blacks he'd supposedly quit, or stared listlessly at *Celebrity
Fit Club* on the television. It became increasingly difficult for him
to remember births, first steps, intimate hours with Rose, family
jokes, vacations in packed cars, holidays with extended family.
One day Hatch did less bailing. "Fuck that bailing," he thought.
The next day he did even less.

As if he'd just awakened to it, he was suddenly standing in water up to his shins and the rain was beating down on a strong southwester. The boat was bobbing like the bottom lip of a crone on Thorazine as he struggled to keep his footing. In his hands was a small plastic garbage can, the same one he'd used to bail his clam boat when at eighteen he had worked the Great South Bay. The problem was Hatch wasn't eighteen anymore, and though now he was spurred to bail again with everything he had, he didn't have much. His heart hadn't worked so hard since his twenty-fifth anniversary, when Rose made him climb a mountain in Montana. Even though the view at the top was gorgeous—a basin lake and a breeze out of heaven—his T-shirt jumped with each beat. The boat was going down. He chucked the garbage can out into the sea and *Financial Ruin* and its partners tore into it. Reaching for his shirt pocket, he took out his smokes and lit one.

The cold brown water was just creeping up around Hatch's balls as he took his first puff. He noticed the dark silhouette of Captree Bridge in the distance. "Back on the bay," he said, amazed to be sinking into the waters of his youth, and then, like a struck wooden match, the entire story of his life flared and died behind his eyes.

Going under was easy. No struggle, but a change in temperature. Just beneath the dark surface, the water got wonderfully clear. All the stale air came out of him at once—a satisfying burp followed by a large translucent globe that stretched his jaw with its birth. He reached for its spinning brightness but sank too fast to grab it. His feet were still lightly touching the deck as the boat fell slowly beneath him. He looked up and saw the sharks still chewing plastic. "This is it," thought Hatch, "not with a bang but a bubble." He herded all of his regrets into the basement of his brain, an indoor oak forest with intermittent dim lightbulbs and dirt floor. The trees were columns that held the ceiling and amid and among them skittered pale, disfigured doppelgängers of his friends and family. As he stood at the top of the steps and shut the door on them, he felt a subtle tearing in his solar plexus. The boat touched down on the sandy bottom and his sneakers came to rest on the deck. Without thinking, he gave a little jump and sailed in a lazy arc, landing ten feet away, with a puff of sand, next to a toppled marble column.

His every step was a graceful bound, and he floated. Once on the slow descent of his arc, he put his arms out at his sides and lifted his feet behind him so as to fly. Hatch found that if he flapped his arms, he could glide along a couple of feet above the bottom, and he did, passing over coral pipes and red seaweed rippling like human hair in a breeze. There were creatures scuttling over rocks and through the sand—long antennae and armored plating, tiny eyes on sharp stalks and claws continuously practicing on nothing. As his shoes touched the sand again, a school of striped fish swept past his right shoulder, their blue glowing like neon, and he followed their flight.

He came upon the rest of the sunken temple, its columns pitted and cracked, broken like the tusks of dead elephants. Green sea vines netted the destruction—two wide marble steps there, here a piece of roof, a tilted mosaic floor depicting the Goddess of the Sea suffering a rash of missing tiles, a headless marble statue of a man holding his penis.

· TWO ·

Hatch floated down the long empty avenues of Drowned Town, a shabby but quiet city in a lime green sea. Every so often, he'd pass one of the citizens, bloated and blue, in various stages of decomposition, and say, "Hi." Two gentlemen in suits swept by but didn't return his greeting. A drowned mother and child, bulging eyes dissolving in trails of tiny bubbles, dressed in little more than rags, didn't acknowledge him. One old woman stopped, though, and said, "Hello."

"I'm new here," he told her.

"The less you think about it the better," she said and drifted on her way.

Hatch tried to remember where he was going. He was sure there was a reason that he was in town, but it eluded him. "I'll call Rose," he thought. "She always knows what I'm supposed to be doing." He started looking up and down the streets for a pay phone. After three blocks without luck, he saw a man heading toward him. The fellow wore a business suit and an overcoat torn to shreds, a black hat with a bullet hole in it, a closed umbrella hooked on a skeletal wrist. Hatch waited for the man to draw near, but as the fellow stepped into the street to cross to the next block, a swift gleaming vision flew from behind a building and with a sudden clang of steel teeth meeting took him in its jaws. *Financial Ruin* was hungry and loose in Drowned Town. Hatch cowered backward, breaststroking to a nearby Dumpster to hide, but the shark was already gone with its catch.

On the next block up, he found a bar that was open. He didn't see a name on it, but there were people inside, the door was ajar, and the muffled sound of music emanated from within. The place was cramped and got narrower the farther back you went, ending in a corner. Wood paneling, mirror behind the bottles, spinning seats, low lighting, and three deadbeats—two on one side of the bar and another behind it.

"Got a pay phone?" asked Hatch.

All three men looked at him. The two customers smiled at each other. The bartender, who sported a red bow tie, wiped his rotted nose on a handkerchief, and then slowly lifted a finger to point. "Go down to the grocery store. They got a pay phone at the deli counter."

Hatch had missed it when the old lady spoke to him, but he realized now that he heard the bartender's voice in his head, not with his ears. The old man moved his mouth, but all that came out were vague farts of words flattened by water pressure. He sat down on one of the bar stools.

"Give me something dry," he said to the bartender. He knew he had to compose himself, get his thoughts together.

The bartender shook his head, scratched a spot of coral growth on his scalp, and opened his mouth to release a minnow. "I could make you a Jenny Diver . . . pink or blue?"

"No, Sal, make him one of those things with the dirt bomb in it . . . they're the driest," said the customer nearest Hatch. The short man turned his flat face and stretched a grin like a soggy old doll with swirling hair. Behind the clear lenses of his eyes, shadows moved, something swimming through his head.

"You mean a Dry Reach. That's one dusty drink," said the other customer, a very pale, skeletal old man in a brimmed hat and dark glasses. "Remember the day I got stupid on those? Your asshole'll make hell seem like a backyard barbecue if you drink too many of them, my friend."

"I'll try one," said Hatch.

"Your wish is my command," said the bartender, but he moved none too swiftly. Still, Hatch was content to sit and think for a minute. He thought that maybe the drink would help him remember. For all of its smallness, the place had a nice relaxing current flowing through it. He folded his arms on the bar and lowered his head, resting for a moment. It finally came to him that the music he'd heard since entering was Frank Sinatra. "The Way You Look

Tonight," he whispered, naming the current song. He pictured Rose, naked, in bed back in their first apartment, and with that realization, the music stopped.

Hatch looked up and saw that the bartender had turned on the television. The two customers, heads tilted back, stared into the glow. On the screen was a news show without sound but the caption announced "News from the War." A small seahorse swam behind the glass of the screen but in front of the black-and-white imagery. The story was about a ward in a makeshift field hospital where army doctors treated wounded children. Cute little faces stared up from pillows, tiny arms with casts listlessly waved, but as the report obviously continued, the wounds got more serious. There were children with missing limbs, and then open wounds, great gashes in the head, the chest, and missing eyes, and then a gaping hole with intestines spilling out, the little legs trembling and the chest heaving wildly.

"There's only one term for this war," said the old man with the sunglasses. "'Clusterfuck.' Cluster as in 'cluster' and fuck as in 'fuck.' No more need be said."

The short man turned to Hatch, and still grinning, said, "There was a woman in here yesterday, saying that we're all responsible."

"We are," said the bartender. "Drink up." He set Hatch's drink on the bar. "One Dry Reach," he said. It came in a big martini glass—clear liquid with a brown lump at the bottom.

Hatch reached for his wallet, but the bartender waved for him not to bother. "You must be new," he said.

Hatch nodded.

"Nobody messes with money down here. This is Drowned Town. . . . Think about it. Drink up, and I'll make you three more."

"Could you put Sinatra back on?" Hatch asked sheepishly. "This news is bumming me out."

"As you wish," said the bartender. He pressed a red button on the wall behind him. Instantly, the television went off, and the two men turned back to their drinks. Sinatra sang, "Let's take it nice and easy," and Hatch thought, "Free booze." He sipped his drink and could definitely distinguish its tang from the briny sea water. Whether he liked the taste or not, he'd decide later, but for now he drank it as quickly as he could.

The elderly customer stepped around his friend and approached. "You're in for a real treat, man," he said. "You see that little island in the stream there?" He pointed at the brown lump in the glass. Hatch nodded.

"A bit of terra firma, a little taste of the world you left behind upstairs. Remember throwing dirt bombs when you were a kid? Like the powdery lumps in homemade brownies? Well, you've got a dollop of high-grade dirt there. You bite into it, and you'll taste the life you left behind—bright sun and blue skies."

"Calm down," said the short man to his fellow customer. "Give him some room."

Hatch finished the drink and let the lump roll out of the bottom of the glass into his mouth. He bit it with his molars but found it had nothing to do with dirt. It was mushy and tasted terrible, more like a sodden meatball of decay then a memory of the sun. He spit the mess out and it darkened the water in front of his face. He waved his hand to disperse the brown cloud. A violet fish with a lazy tail swam down from the ceiling to snatch what was left of the disintegrating nugget.

The two customers and the bartender laughed, and Hatch heard it like a party in his brain. "You got the Tootsie Roll," said the short fellow and tried to slap the bar, but his arm moved too slowly through the water.

"Don't take it personally," said the old man. "It's a Drowned Town tradition." His right ear came off just then and floated away, his glasses slipping down on that side of his head.

Hatch felt a sudden burst of anger. He'd never liked playing the fool.

"Sorry, fella," said the bartender, "but it's a ritual. On your first Dry Reach, you get the Tootsie Roll."

"What's the Tootsie Roll?" asked Hatch, still trying to get the taste out of his mouth.

The man with the outlandish grin said, "Well, for starters, it ain't a Tootsie Roll."

· THREE ·

Hatch marveled at the myriad shapes and colors of seaweed in the grocery's produce section. The lovely wavering of their leaves, strands, tentacles in the flow soothed him. Although he stood on the sandy bottom, hanging from the ceiling were rows of fluo rescent lights, every third or fourth one working. The place was a vast concrete bunker, set up in long aisles of shelves like at the Super Shopper he'd trudged through innumerable times back in his dry life.

"No money needed," he thought. "And free booze. But then why the coverage of the war? For that matter, why the Tootsie Roll? *Financial Ruin* has free rein in Drowned Town. Nobody seems particularly happy. It doesn't add up." Hatch left the produce section, passed a display of anemone, some as big as his head, and drifted off in search of the deli counter.

The place was enormous, row upon row of shelved dead fish, their snouts sticking into the aisle, silver and pink and brown. Here and there a gill still quivered, a fin twitched. "A lot of fish," thought Hatch. Along the way, he saw a special glass case that held frozen food that had sunk from the world above. The hot dog tempted him, even though a good quarter of it had gone green. There was a piece of a cupcake with melted sprinkles, three French fries, a black Twizzler, and a red-and-white Chinese take-out bag with two gnarled rib ends sticking out. He hadn't had any lunch, and his stomach growled in the presence of the delicacies, but he was thinking of Rose and wanted to talk to her.

Hatch found a familiar face at the lobster tank. He could hardly believe it, it was Bob Gordon from up the block. Bob looked none the worse for wear for being sunk, save for his yellow complexion. He smoked a damp cigarette and stared into the tank as if staring through it.

"Bob," said Hatch.

Bob turned and adjusted his glasses. "Hatch, what's up?"

"I didn't know you went under."

"Sure, like a fuckin' stone."

"When?" asked Hatch.

"Three, four months ago. Peggy'd been porking some guy from over in Larchdale. You know, I got depressed, laid off the bailing, lost the house, and then eventually I just threw in the pail."

"How do you like it here?"

"Really good," said Bob and his words rang loud in Hatch's brain, but then he quickly leaned close and these words came in a whisper: "It sucks."

"What do you mean?" asked Hatch, keeping his voice low.

Bob's smile deflated. "Everything's fine," he said, casting a glance at the lobster tank. He nodded to Hatch. "Gotta go, bud."

He watched Bob bound away against a mild current. By the time Hatch reached the deli counter, it was closed. In fact, with the exception of Bob, he'd seen no one in the entire store. An old black phone with a rotary dial sat atop the counter. Propped next to it was a sign that read: FREE PAY PHONE. NOT TO BE USED IN PRIVACY!

Hatch looked over his shoulder. There was no one around. Stepping forward he reached for the receiver, and just as his hand closed on it, the thing rang. He felt the vibration before he heard the sound. He let it go and stepped back. It continued to ring, and he was torn between answering it and fleeing. Finally, he picked it up and said, "Hello."

At first he thought the line was dead, but then a familiar voice sounded. "Hatch," it said, and he knew it was Ned, his younger son. Both of his boys had called him Hatch since they were toddlers. "You gotta come pick me up."

"Where are you?" asked Hatch.

"I'm at a house party behind the 7-Eleven. It's starting to get crazy."

"What do you mean it's starting to get crazy?"

"You coming?"

"I'll be there," said Hatch, and the line went dead.

He stood at the door to the basement of his brain and turned the knob, but before he could open it, he saw, way over on the other side of the store, one of the silver sharks, cruising above the aisles up near the ceiling. Dropping the receiver, he scurried behind the deli counter and then through an opening that led down a hall to a door.

· FOUR ·

Hatch was out of breath from walking, searching for someone who might be able to help him. For ten city blocks he thought about Ned needing a ride. He pictured the boy, hair tied back, baggy shorts, and shoes like slippers, running from the police. "Good grief," said

Hatch and pushed forward. He'd made a promise to Ned years earlier that he would always come and get him if he needed a ride, no matter what. How could he tell him now, "Sorry kid, I'm sunk." Hatch thought of all the things that could happen in the time it would take him to return to dry land and pick Ned up at the party. Scores of tragic scenarios exploded behind his eyes. "I might as well be bailing," he said to the empty street.

He heard the crowd before he saw it, faint squeaks and blips in his ears that eventually became distant voices and music. Rounding a corner, he came in sight of a huge vacant lot between two six-story brownstones. As he approached, he could make out some kind of attraction at the back of the lot, and twenty or so Drowned Towners floated in a crowd around it. Organ music blared from a speaker on a tall wooden pole. Hatch crossed the street and joined the audience.

Up against the back wall of the lot was an enormous golden octopus. Its flesh glistened and its tentacles curled, unfurled, created fleeting symbols dispersed by schools of tiny angel fish continually circling it like a halo. The creature's sucker disks were flat black as was its beak, its eyes red, and there was a heavy, rusted metal collar squeezing the base of its lumpen head as if it had shoulders and a neck. Standing next to it was a young woman, obviously part fish. She had gills and her eyes were pure black like a shark's. Her teeth were sharp. There were scales surrounding her face and her hair was some kind of fine green seaweed. She wore a clamshell brassiere and a black thong. At the backs of her heels were fan-like fins. "My name is Clementine," she said to the assembled onlookers, "and this beauty beside me is Madame Mutandis. She is a remarkable specimen of the Midas Octopus, so named for the radiant golden aura of her skin. You see the collar on Madame and you miss the chain. Notice, it is attached to my left ankle. Contrary to what you all might believe, it is I who belong to her and not she to me."

Hatch looked around the crowd he was now part of—an equal mixture of men and women, some more bleached than blue, some less intact than others. The man next to him held his mouth open, and an eel's head peered out as if having risen from the man's bowels to check the young fish-woman's performance.

"With cephalopod brilliance, nonvertebrate intuition, Madame Mutandis will answer one question for each of you. No question is out of bounds. She thinks like the very sea itself. Who'll be first?"

The man next to Hatch immediately stepped forward before anyone else. "And what is your question?" asked the fish-woman. The man put his hands into his coat pockets and then raised his head. His message was horribly muddled, but by his third repetition Hatch as well as the octopus got it: "How does one remove an eel?" Madame Mutandis shook her head sac as if in disdain while two of her tentacles unfurled in the man's direction. One swiftly wrapped around his throat, lurching him forward, and the other dove into his mouth. A second later, Madame released his throat and drew from between his lips a three-foot-long eel, wriggling wildly in her suctioned grasp. The long arm swept the eel to her beak, and she pierced it at a spot just behind the head, rendering it lifeless. With a free tentacle, she waved forward the next questioner, while, with another, she gently brushed away the man now sighing with relief.

Hatch came to and was about to step forward, but a woman from behind him wearing a kerchief and carrying a beige pocketbook passed by, already asking, "Where are the good sales?" He wasn't able to see her face, but the questioner, from her posture and clothing, seemed middle-aged, somewhat younger than himself.

Clementine repeated the woman's question for the octopus. "Where are the good sales?" she said.

"Shoes," added the woman with the kerchief. "I'm looking for shoes."

Madame Mutandis wrapped a tentacle around the woman's left arm and turned her to face the crowd. Hatch reared back at the sudden sight of a face rotted almost perfectly down the middle, skull showing through on one side. Another of the octopus's tentacles slid up the woman's skirt between her legs. With the dexterity of a hand, it drew down the questioner's underwear, leaving it gathered around her ankles. Then, wriggling like the eel it had removed from the first man's mouth, the tentacle slithered along her right thigh only to disappear again beneath the skirt.

Hatch was repulsed and fascinated as the woman trembled and the tentacle wiggled out of sight. She turned her skeletal profile to the crowd, and that bone grin widened with pleasure, grimaced in pain, gaped with passion. Little spasms of sound escaped her open mouth. The crowd methodically applauded until finally the object of the Madame's attentions screamed and fell to the sand, the long tentacle retracting. The fish-woman moved to the end of her chain and helped the questioner up. "Is that what you were looking for?" she asked. The woman with the beige pocketbook nodded and adjusted her kerchief before floating to the back of the crowd.

"Ladies and gentlemen?" said the fish-woman.

Hatch noticed that no one was too ready to step forth after the creature's last answer, including himself. His mind was racing, trying to connect a search for a shoe sale with the resultant . . . what? Rape? Or was what he witnessed consensual? He was still befuddled by the spectacle. The gruesome state of the woman's face wrapped in ecstasy hung like a chandelier of ice on the main floor of his brain. At that moment, he realized he had to escape from Drowned Town. Shifting his glance right and left, he noticed his fellow drownees were still as stone.

The fish-woman's chain must have stretched, because she floated over and put her hand on his back. Gently, she led him forward. "She can tell you anything," came Clementine's voice, a whisper that made him think of Rose and Ned and Will, even the stupid dog with bad ears. He hadn't felt his feet move, but he was there, standing before the shining perpetual motion of Madame's eight arms. Her black parrot beak opened, and he thought he heard her laughing.

"Your question?" asked Clementine, still close by his side.

"My kid's stuck at a party that's getting crazy," blurted Hatch. "How do I get back to dry land?"

He heard murmuring from the crowd behind him. One voice said, "No." Another said, "Asshole." At first he thought they were predicting the next answer from Madame Mutandis, but then he realized they were referring to him. It dawned on him that wanting to leave Drowned Town was unpopular.

"Watch the ink," said Clementine.

Hatch looked down and saw a dark plume exuding from beneath the octopus. It rose in a mushroom cloud, and then spiraled into a long black string at the top. The end of the string whipped leisurely through the air, drawing more of itself from the cloud until the cloud had vanished and what remained was the phrase "322 Bleeter Street" in perfect, looping script. The address floated there for a moment, Hatch repeating it, before the angel fish veered out of orbit around the fleshy golden sac and dashed through it, dispersing the ink.

The fish-woman led Hatch away and called, "Next." He headed back along the alley toward the street, repeating the address under his breath. At the rear of the crowd, which had grown, a woman turned to him as he passed and said, "Leaving town?"

"My kid . . . ," Hatch began, but she snickered at him. From somewhere in the last row, he heard, "Jerk," and "Pussy." When he reached the street, he realized that the words of the drowned had pushed the street number from his thoughts. He remembered Bleeter Street and said it six times, but the number. . . . Leaping forward, he assumed the flying position, and flapping his arms, cruised down the street, checking the street signs at corners, and keeping an eye out for sharks. He remembered the address had a three in it, and then for blocks he thought of nothing at all but that last woman's contempt.

• FIVE •

Eventually, he grew too tired to fly and resumed walking, sometimes catching the current and drifting in the flow. He'd seen so many street signs—presidents' names, different kinds of fish, famous actors and sunken ships, types of clouds, waves, flowers, slugs. None of them was Bleeter. He passed by so many storefronts and apartment steps and not a soul in sight. At one point a storm of tiny starfish fell like rain all over town, littering the streets and filling the awnings.

Hatch had just stepped out of a weakening current and was moving under his own steam when he noticed a phone booth wedged into a narrow alley between two stores. Pushing off, he swam to it and squeezed himself into the glass enclosure. As the door closed, a light went on above him. He lifted the receiver, placing it next to his ear. There was a dial tone. He dialed and it rang. Something shifted in his chest and his pulse quickened. Suffering the length of each long ring, he waited for someone to pick up.

"Hello?" he heard; a voice at a great distance.

"Rose, it's me," he screamed against the water.

"Hatch," she said. "I can hardly hear you. Where are you?"

"I'm stuck in Drowned Town," he yelled.

"What do you mean? Where is it?"

Hatch had a hard time saying it. "I went under, Rose. I'm sunk."

There was nothing on the line. He feared he'd lost the connection, but he stayed with it.

"Jesus, Hatch . . . What the hell are you doing?"

"I gave up on the bailing," he said.

She groaned. "You shit. How am I supposed to do this alone?"

"I'm sorry, Rose," he said. "I don't know what happened. I love you."

He could hear her exhale. "Okay," she said. "Give me an address. I have to have something to put into MapQuest."

"Do you know where I am?" he asked.

"No, I don't fucking know where you are. That's why I need the address."

It came to him all at once. "322 Bleeter Street, Drowned Town," he said. "I'll meet you there."

"It's going to take a while," she said.

"Rose?"

"What?"

"I love you," he said. He listened to the silence on the receiver until he noticed in the reflection of his face in the phone-booth glass a blue spot on his nose and one blooming on his forehead. "Shit," he said and hung up. "I can take care of that with some ointment when I get back," he thought. He scratched at the spot on his forehead and blue skin sloughed off. He put his face closer to the glass, and then there came a pounding on the door behind him.

Turning, he almost screamed at the sight of the half-gone face of the woman who'd been goosed by the octopus. He opened the door and slid past her. Her Jolly Roger profile was none too jolly. As he spoke the words, he surprised himself by doing so—"Do you know where Bleeter Street is?" She jostled him aside in her rush to get to the phone. Before closing the door, she called over her shoulder, "You're on it."

"Things are looking up," thought Hatch as he retreated. Standing in the middle of the street, he looked up one side and down the other. Only one building, a darkened storefront with a plate-glass window behind which was displayed a single pair of sunglasses on a pedestal, had a street number—621. It came to him that he would have to travel in one direction, try to find another address and see which way the numbers ran. Then, if he found they were increasing, he'd have to turn around and head in the opposite direction, but at least he would know. Thrilled at his sense of purpose, he swept a clump of drifting seaweed out of his way and moved forward. He could be certain Rose would come for him. After thirty years of marriage they'd grown close in subterranean ways.

Darkness was beginning to fall on Drowned Town. Angle-jawed fish with needle teeth, a perpetual scowl, and sad eyes, came from the alleyways and through open apartment windows, and each had a small phosphorescent jewel dangling from a downward curving stalk that issued from its head. They drifted the shadowy street like fireflies, and although Hatch had still to see another building number, he stopped in his tracks to mark their beautiful effect. It was precisely then that he saw *Financial Ruin* appear from over the rooftops down the street. Before he could even think to flee, the shark swooped down in his direction.

Hatch turned, kicked his feet up, and started flapping. As he approached the first corner and was about to turn, he almost collided with someone just stepping out onto Bleeter Street. To his utter confusion, it was a deep-sea diver, a man inside a heavy rubber suit with a glass bubble of a helmet and a giant nautilus shell strapped to his back, which fed air through two arching tubes into his suit. The sudden appearance of the diver wasn't what made him stop, though. It was the huge gun in his hands with a barbed spear head as wide as a fence post jutting from the barrel. The diver waved Hatch behind him as the shark came into view. It hurtled toward them with a dagger-toothed lunge, a widening cavern, speeding like a runaway train. The diver pulled the trigger. There was a zip of tiny bubbles, and *Financial Ruin* curled up, thrashing madly with the spear piercing its upper palate and poking out the back of its head. Billows of blood began to spread, staining the watery atmosphere. The man in the suit lowered the gun and approached Hatch.

"Hurry," he said, "before the other sharks smell the blood."

· SIX ·

Hatch and his savior sat in a carpeted parlor on cushioned chairs facing each other across a low coffee table with a tea service on it. The remarkable fact was that they were both dry, breathing air instead of brine, and speaking in normal tones. When they'd both entered the foyer of the stranger's building, he had hit a button on the wall. A sheet of steel slid down to cover the street door, and within seconds the sea water began to exit the compartment through a drain in the floor. Hatch had had to drown into the air and that was much more uncomfortable than simply going under, but after some extended wheezing, choking, and spitting up, he drew in a huge breath with ease. The diver had unscrewed the glass globe that covered his head and held it beneath one arm. "Isaac Munro," he'd said and nodded.

Now dressed in a maroon smoking jacket and green pajamas, moccasins on his feet, the silver-haired man with a drooping mustache sipped his tea and held forth on his situation. Hatch, in dry clothes the older man had given him, was willing to listen, almost certain Munro knew the way back to dry land.

"I'm *in* Drowned Town, but not *of* it. Do you understand?" he said.

Hatch nodded, and noticed what a relief it was to have the pressure of the sea off him.

Isaac Munro lowered his gaze and said, as if making a confession, "My wife, Rotzy, went under some years ago. There was nothing I could do to prevent it. She came down here, and on the day she left me, I determined I would find the means to follow her and rescue her from Drowned Town. My imagination, fired by the desire to simply hold her again, gave birth to all these many inventions that allow me to keep from getting my feet wet, so to speak." He chuckled and then made a face as if he were admonishing himself.

Hatch smiled. "How long have you been looking for her?"

"Years," said Munro, placing his teacup on the table.

"I'm trying to get back. My wife, Rose, is coming for me in the car."

"Yes, your old neighbor Bob Gordon told me you might be looking for an out," said the older man. "I was on the prowl for you when we encountered that cutpurse leviathan."

"You know Bob?"

"He does some legwork for me from time to time."

"I saw him at the grocery today."

"He has a bizarre fascination with that lobster tank. In any event, your wife won't make it through, I'm sorry to say. Not with a car."

"How can I get out?" asked Hatch. "I can't offer you a lot of money, but something else perhaps."

"Perish the thought," said Munro, waving a hand in the air. "I have an escape hatch back to the surface in case of emergencies. You're welcome to use it if you'll just observe some cautionary measures."

"Absolutely," said Hatch and moved to the edge of his chair.

"I take it you'd like to leave immediately?"

Both men stood and Hatch followed Munro along a hallway lined with framed photographs that opened into a large space, like an old ballroom, with peeling flowered wallpaper. Crossing the warped wooden floor scratched and littered with, of all things, old leaves and pages of a newspaper, they came to a door. When Munro turned around, Hatch noticed that the older man was holding one of the photos from the hallway wall.

"Here she is," said Isaac. "This is Rotzy."

Hatch leaned down for a better look at the portrait. He gave only the slightest grunt of surprise and hoped his host hadn't noticed, but Rotzy was the woman he'd last seen at the phone booth, the half-faced horror who'd been mishandled by Madame Mutandis.

"You haven't seen her, have you?" asked Munro.

Hatch knew he should try to help the old man, but he thought only of escape and didn't want to complicate things. He sensed the door in front of him was his portal back. "No," he said.

Munro nodded resignedly and then reached into the side pocket of his jacket and retrieved an old-fashioned key. He held it in the air, but did not place it in Hatch's outstretched palm. "Listen carefully," he said. "You will pass through a series of rooms. Upon entering each room, you must lock the door behind you with this key before opening the next door to exit into the following room. Once you've started you can't turn back. The key works only to open doors forward and lock doors backward. A new door cannot be opened without the previous door being locked. Do you understand?"

"Yes."

Munro placed the key in Hatch's hand. "Then be on your way and Godspeed. Kiss the sky for me when you arrive."

"I will."

Munro opened the door and Hatch stepped through. The door closed and he locked it behind him. He crossed the room in a hurry, unlocked the next door and then, passing through, locked it behind him. This process went on for twenty minutes before Hatch noticed that it took fewer and fewer steps to traverse each succeeding room to the next door. One of the rooms had a window, and he paused to look out on some watery side street falling into night. The loneliness of the scene spurred him forward. In the following room he had to duck down so as not to skin his head against the ceiling. He locked its door and moved forward into a room where he had to duck even lower.

Eventually, he was forced to crawl from room to room, and there wasn't much space for turning around to lock the door behind him. As each door swept open before him, he thought he might see the sky or feel a breeze in his face. There was always another door, but there was also hope. That is, until he entered a compartment so small, he couldn't turn around to use the key but had to do it with his hands behind his back, his chin pressed against his chest. "This has got to be the last one," he thought, unsure if he could squeeze his shoulders through the next opening. Before he could insert the key into the lock on the tiny door before him, a steel plate fell and blocked access to it. He heard a *swoosh* and a *bang* behind him and knew another metal plate had covered the door going back.

"How are you doing, Mr. Hatch?" he heard Munro's voice say.

By dipping one shoulder Hatch was able to turn his head and see a speaker built into the wall. "How do I get through these last rooms?" he yelled. "They're too small and metal guards have fallen in front of the doors."

"That's the point," called Munro. "You don't. You, my friend, are trapped, and will remain trapped forever in that tight uncomfortable place."

"What are you talking about? Why?" Hatch was frantic. He

tried to lunge his body against the walls but there was nowhere for it to go.

"My wife, Rotzy. You know how she went under? What sank her? She was ill, Mr. Hatch. She was seriously ill but her health insurance denied her coverage. You, Mr. Hatch, personally said *no*."

This time what flared before Hatch's inner eye was not his life, but all the many pleading, frustrated, angry voices that had traveled in one of his ears and out the other in his service to the HMO. "I'm not responsible" was all he could think to say in his defense.

"My wife used to tell me, 'Isaac, we're all responsible.' Now you can wait, as she waited for relief, for what was rightly due her. You'll wait forever, Hatch."

There was a period where he struggled. He couldn't tell how long it lasted, but nothing came of it, so he closed his eyes, made his breathing more steady and shallow, and went into his brain, across the first floor to the basement door. He opened it and could smell the scent of the dark wood wafting up the steps. Locking the door behind him, he descended into the dark.

· SEVEN ·

The woods were frightening, but he'd take anything over the claustrophobia of Munro's trap. Each dim lightbulb he came to was a godsend, and he put his hands up to it for the little warmth it offered against the wind. He noticed that strange creatures prowled around the bulbs like antelopes around waterholes. They darted behind the trees, spying on him, pale specters whose faces were masks made of bone. He was sure that one was his cousin Martin, a malevolent boy who'd cut the head off a kitten. He'd not seen him in more than thirty years. He also spotted his mother-in-law, who was his mother-in-law with no hair and short tusks. She grunted orders to him from the shadows. He kept moving and tried to ignore them.

When Hatch couldn't walk any farther, he came to a clearing in the forest. There, in the middle of nowhere, in the basement of his brain, sat twenty yards of street with a brownstone situated behind a wide sidewalk. There were steps leading up to twin doors and an electric light glowed next to the entrance. As he drew near, he could make out the address in brass numerals at the base of the steps—322.

He stumbled over to the bottom step and dropped down onto it. Hatch leaned forward, his elbows on his knees and his hands covering his face. He tried to weep till his eyes closed out of exhaustion. What seemed a second later, he heard a car horn and looked up.

"There's no crying in baseball, asshole," said Rose. She was leaning her head out the driver's side window of their SUV. There was a light on in the car and he could see both their sons were in the backseat, pointing at him.

"How'd you find me?" he asked.

"The Internet," said Rose. "Will showed me MapQuest has this new feature where you don't need the address anymore, just a person's name, and it gives you directions to wherever they are in the continental United States."

"Oh my God," he said and walked toward Rose to give her a hug.

"Not now Barnacle Bill, there're some pale creeps coming this way. We just passed them and one lunged for the car. Get in."

Hatch got in the front passenger seat and turned toward his sons. He wanted to hug them but they motioned for him to hurry and shut the door. As soon as he did, Rose pulled away from the curb.

"So, Hatch, you went under?" asked his older son, Will.

Hatch wished he could explain but couldn't find the words.

"What a pile," said Ned.

"Yeah," said Will.

"Don't do it again, Hatch," said Rose. "Next time we're not coming for you."

"I'm sorry," he said. "I love you all."

Rose wasn't one to admonish more than once. She turned on the radio and changed the subject. "We had the directions, but they were a bitch to follow. At one point I had to cut across two lanes of traffic in the middle of the Holland Tunnel and take a left down a side tunnel that for more than a mile was the pitchest pitch-black."

"Listen to this, Hatch," said Ned and leaned into the front seat to turn up the radio.

"Oh, they've been playing this all day," said Rose. "This young woman soldier was captured by insurgents and they made a video of them cutting her head off."

"On the radio, you only get the screams, though," said Will. "Check it out."

The sound, at first, was like from a musical instrument, and then it became human—steady, piercing shrieks in desperate bursts that ended in the gurgle of someone going under.

Rose changed the channel and the screams came from the new station. She hit the button again and still the same screaming. Hatch turned to look at his family. Their eyes were slightly droopy and they were very pale. Their shoulders were somehow out of whack and their grins were vacant. Rose had a big bump on her forehead and a rash across her neck.

"Watch for the sign for the Holland Tunnel," she said amid the dying soldier's screams as they drove on into the dark. Hatch kept careful watch, knowing they'd never find it.

ARIADNE'S
MOTHER

Her name was Ariadne. She was in her early twenties, and she sat, tilted in her wheelchair, her arms folded up at the elbows and wrists like she was a praying mantis. No matter what happened, she wore an expression of surprise—mouth an "O," eyes wide, nostrils flaring for air. There was a white diaper on the tray of her chair to be used to wipe the drool from her chin. When I first met her, I asked her to tell me about her writing. A short time passed and then there came a series of breathy and brief high-pitched squeals like some kind of machine giving a warning. I couldn't make out a word. Her mother, who came with her every week to class, always spoke for her. She told me that Ariadne had been a brilliant writer in high school, had gotten a scholarship to college, and then took ill. I never found out what the disease was. The mother proposed that they sit in the back of the classroom, that the girl dictate to her the essays and stories, and that she would type them for her onto the computer. What could I say? Whenever the girl made noises, I tried to parse out the words but never could. Not so the mother—she nodded at Ariadne's bird song, typing like mad. And the papers, when they were done, were ingenious and grammatically perfect. One was a languorous ghost story in which the spirits of the departed, a mother and daughter, lived a quiet life in an abandoned mansion. By mid-semester, I was certain the girl wasn't actually speaking at all.

THE
NIGHT
WHISKEY

All summer long, on Wednesday and Friday evenings after checking out from my job at the gas station, I practiced with old man Witzer looking over my shoulder. When I'd send a dummy toppling perfectly onto the pile of mattresses in the bed of his pickup, he'd wheeze like it was his last breath (I think he was laughing), and pat me on the back, but when one fell awkwardly or hit the metal side of the truck bed or went really awry and ended sprawled on the ground, he'd spit tobacco and say either one of two things: "That there's a cracked melon" or "Get me a wet-vac." He was a patient teacher, never rushed, never raising his voice or showing the least exasperation in the face of my errors. After we'd felled the last of the eight dummies we'd earlier placed in the lower branches of the trees at the edge of town, he'd open a little cooler he kept in the cab of his truck and fetch two beers, one for himself and one for me. "You did good today, boy," he'd say, no matter if I did or not, and we'd sit in the truck with the windows open, pretty much in silence, and watch the fireflies signal in the gathering dark.

As the old man had said, "There's an art to dropping drunks." The main tools of the trade were a set of three long bamboo poles— a ten-foot, a fifteen-foot, and a twenty-foot. Each had a rubber ball attached to one end that was wrapped in chamois cloth and tied tight with a leather lanyard. These poles were called prods. Choosing the right prod after considering how high the branches were in which the drunk was nestled . . . crucial. Too short a one would cause you to go on tiptoes and lose accuracy, while the excess length of too long a one would get in the way and throw you off balance. The first step was always to take a few minutes and carefully assess the situation. You had to ask yourself, "How might this body fall if I were to prod the shoulders first, or the back, or the left leg?" The old man had taught me that generally there was a kind of physics to it but that sometimes intuition had to override logic. "Don't think of them as falling but think of them as flying," said Witzer, and only when I was actually out under the trees and trying to hit the mark in the center of the pickup bed did I know what he meant. "You ultimately want them to fall, turn in the air, and land flat on the back," he'd told me. "That's a ten-pointer." There were other important aspects of the job as well. The positioning of the truck was critical as was the manner with which you woke them after they had safely landed. Calling them back by shouting in their ears would leave them dazed for a week, but, as the natives had done, breaking a thin twig a few inches from the ear worked like a charm—a gentle reminder that life was waiting to be lived.

When his long-time fellow harvester, Mr. Bo Elliott, passed on, the town council had left it to Witzer to find a replacement. It had been his determination to pick someone young, and so he came to the high school and carefully observed each of us fifteen students in the graduating class. It was a wonder he could see anything through the thick, scratched lenses of his glasses and those perpetually squinted eyes, but after long deliberation, which involved the rubbing of his stubbled chin and the scratching of his fallow scalp, he singled me out for the honor. An honor it was, too, as he'd told me, "You know that because you don't get paid anything for it." He assured me that I had the talent hidden inside of me, that he'd seen it like an aura of pink light, and that he'd help me develop it over the summer. To be an apprentice in the Drunk Harvest was a kind of exalted position for one as young as me, and it brought me some special credit with my friends and neighbors, because it meant that I was being initiated into an ancient tradition that went back further than the time when our ancestors settled that remote piece of country. My father beamed with pride, my mother got teary-eyed, my girlfriend, Darlene, let me get to third base and partway home.

Our town was one of those places you pass but never stop at while on the way to a vacation in some national park; out in the sticks, up in the mountains—places where the population is rendered in three figures on a board by the side of the road; the first numeral no more than a four and the last with a hand-painted slash through it and replaced with one of lesser value beneath. The people in our town were pretty much like people everywhere, only the remoteness of the locale had insulated us against the relentless tide of change and the judgment of the wider world. We had radios and televisions and telephones, and as these things came in, what they promised lured a few of our number away. But for those who stayed in Gatchfield, progress moved like a tortoise dragging a ball and chain. The old ways hung on with more tenacity than Relletta Clome, who was 110 years old and had died and been revived by Dr. Kvench eight times in ten years. We had our little ways and customs that were like the exotic beasts of Tasmania, isolated in their evolution to become completely singular. The strangest of these traditions was the Drunk Harvest.

The Harvest centered on an odd little berry that, as far as I know, grows nowhere else in the world. The natives had called it *vachimi atatsi*, but because of its shiny black hue and the nature of its growth, the settlers had renamed it the deathberry. It didn't grow in the meadows or bogs as do blueberries and cranberries, no, this berry grew only out of the partially decayed carcasses of animals left to lie where they'd fallen. If you were out hunting in the woods and you came across say, a dead deer, which had not been touched by coyotes or wolves, you could be certain that the deceased creature would eventually sprout a small hedge from its rotted gut before autumn and that the long thin branches would be thick with juicy black berries. Predators knew somehow that these fallen beasts had the seeds of the deathberry bush within them, because although it went against their nature not to devour fresh meat, they wouldn't go near these particular carcasses. It wasn't just wild creatures either; even livestock that died in the field and was left untouched could be counted on to serve as host for the parasitic plant. Instances of this weren't common but I'd seen it firsthand a couple of times in my youth—a rotting body, head maybe already turning to skull, and out of the belly like a green explosion, a wild spray of long thin branches tipped with atoms of black like tiny marbles, bobbing in the breeze. It was a frightening sight to behold for the first time, and as I overheard Lester Bildab, a man who foraged for the deathberry, tell my father once, "No matter how many times I see it, I still get a little chill in the backbone."

Lester and his son, a dim-witted boy in my class at school, Lester II, would head out at the start of each August across the fields and through the woods and swamps searching for fallen creatures hosting the hideous flora. Bildab had learned from his father about gathering the fruit, as Bildab's father had learned from his father, and so on all the way back to the settlers and the natives from whom *they'd* learned.

You can't eat the berries; they'll make you violently ill. But you can ferment them and make a drink, like a thick black brandy, that had come to be called Night Whiskey and supposedly had the sweetest taste on earth. I didn't know the process, as only a select few did, but from berry to glass I knew it took about a month. Lester and his son would gather all the berries they could find and usually returned from their foraging with three good-size grocery sacks full. Then they'd take them over to the Blind Ghost Bar and Grill and sell them to Mr. and Mrs. Bocean, who knew the process for making the liquor and kept the recipe in a little safe with a combination lock. The recipe had been given to our town forefathers as a gift by the natives, who, two years after giving it, with no provocation and having gotten along peacefully with the settlers for more than a decade, vanished without a trace, leaving behind an empty village on an island out in the swamp . . . or so the story goes.

The annual celebration that involved this drink took place at the Blind Ghost on the last Saturday night in September. It was usually for adults only, and so the first chance I ever got to witness it was the year I was made an apprentice to old man Witzer. The only two younger people at the event that year were Lester II and me. Bildab's boy had been attending since he was ten, and some speculated that having witnessed the thing and been around the berries so long were what had turned him simple, but I knew young Lester in school before that and he was no ball of fire then either. Of the adults who participated, only eight actually partook of the Night Whiskey. Reed and Samantha Bocean took turns each year, one joining in the drinking while the other watched the bar, and seven others, picked by lottery, got to taste the sweetest thing on earth. Sheriff Jolle did the honors picking the names of the winners from a hat at the event and was barred from participating by a town ordinance that went way back. Those who didn't get to drink the Night Whiskey made do with conventional alcohol. Local musicians supplied the entertainment and there was dancing. From the snatches of conversation I'd caught over the years, I gathered it was a raucous time.

This native drink, black as a crow wing and slow to pour as cough syrup, had some strange properties. A year's batch was enough to fill only half of an old quart gin bottle that Samantha Bocean had tricked out with a handmade label showing a deer skull with berries for eyes, and so it was portioned out sparingly. Each participant got no more than about three quarters of a shot glass of it, but that was enough. Even with just these few sips it was wildly intoxicating, so that the drinkers became immediately drunk, their inebriation growing as the night went on although they'd finish off their allotted pittance within the first hour of the celebration. "Blind drunk" was the phrase used to describe how the drinkers of the Night Whiskey would end the night. Then came the weird part, for usually around two a.m. all eight of them, all at once, got to their feet, stumbled out the door, lurched down the front steps of the bar, and meandered off into the dark, groping and weaving like namesakes of the establishment they had just left. It was a peculiar phenomenon of the drink that it made those who imbibed it search for a resting place in the lower branches of a tree. Even though they were pie-eyed drunk, somehow, and no one knew why, they'd manage to shimmy up a trunk and settle themselves down across a few choice branches. It was a law in Gatchfield that if you tried to stop them or disturb them it would be cause for arrest. So when the drinkers of the Night Whiskey left the bar, no one followed. The next day, they'd be found fast asleep in midair, only a few precarious branches between them and gravity. That's where old man Witzer and I came in. At first light, we were to make our rounds in his truck with the poles bungeed on top, to perform what was known as the Drunk Harvest.

Dangerous? You bet, but there was a reason for it. I told you about the weird part, but even though this next part gives a justification of sorts, it's even weirder. When the natives gave the death-berry and the recipe for the Night Whiskey to our forefathers, they considered it a gift of a most divine nature, because after the dark drink was ingested and the drinker had climbed aloft, sleep would invariably bring him or her to some realm between that of dream and the sweet hereafter. In this limbo they'd come face-to-face with their relatives and loved ones who'd passed on. That's right. It never failed. As best as I can remember him having told it, here's my father's recollection of the experience from the year he won the lottery:

"I found myself out in the swamp at night with no memory of how I'd gotten there or what reason I had for being there. I tried to find a marker—a fallen tree or a certain turn in the path—by which to find my way back to town. The moon was bright, and as I stepped into a clearing, I saw a single figure standing there stark naked. I drew closer and said hello, even though I wanted to run. I saw it was an old fellow, and when he heard my greeting, he looked up and right then I knew it was my uncle Fic. 'What are you doing out here without your clothes?' I said to him as I approached. 'Don't you remember, Joe,' he said, smiling. 'I'm passed on.' And then it struck me and made my hair stand on end. But Uncle Fic, who'd died at the age of ninety-eight when I was only fourteen, told me not to be afraid. He told me a good many things, explained a good many things, told me not to fear death. I asked him about my ma and pa, and he said they were together as always and having a good time. I bid him to say hello to them for me, and he said he would. Then he turned and started to walk away but stepped on a twig, and that sound brought me awake, and I was lying in the back of Witzer's pickup, staring into the jowly, pitted face of Bo Elliott."

My father was no liar, and to prove to my mother and me that he was telling the truth, he told us that Uncle Fic had told him where to find a tiepin he'd been given as a commemoration of his twenty-fifth year at the feed store but had subsequently lost. He then walked right over to a teapot shaped like an orange that my mother kept on a shelf in our living room, opened it, reached in, and pulled out the pin. The only question my father was left with about the whole strange episode was "Out of all my dead relations, why Uncle Fic?"

Stories like the one my father told my mother and me abound. Early on, back in the 1700s, they were written down by those who could write. These rotting manuscripts were kept for a long time in the Gatchfield library—an old shoe repair store with book-shelves—in a glass case. Sometimes the dead who showed up in the Night Whiskey dreams offered premonitions, sometimes they fingered a thief when something had gone missing. And suppos-edly it was the way Jolle had solved the Latchey murder, on a tip given to Mrs. Windom by her great-aunt, dead ten years. Knowing that our ancestors were keeping an eye on things and didn't mind singing out about the untoward once a year usually convinced the citizens of Gatchfield to walk the straight and narrow. We kept it to ourselves, though, and never breathed a word of it to outsiders, as if their rightful skepticism would ruin the power of the ceremony. As for those who'd left town, it was never a worry that they'd tell anyone, because, seriously, who'd have believed them?

On a Wednesday evening, the second week in September, while sitting in the pickup truck, drinking a beer, old man Witzer said, "I think you got it, boy. No more practice now. Too much and we'll overdo it." I simply nodded, but in the following weeks leading up to the annual celebration, I was a wreck, envisioning the body of one of my friends or neighbors sprawled broken on the ground next to the bed of the truck. At night I'd have a recurring dream of prodding a body out of an oak, seeing it fall in slow motion, and then all would go black and I'd just hear this dull crack, what I assumed to be the drunk's head slamming the side of the pickup bed. I'd wake and sit up straight, shivering. Each time this happened, I tried to remember to see who it was in my dream, because it always seemed to be the same person. Two nights before the celebration, I saw a tattoo of a coiled cobra on the fellow's bicep as he fell and knew it was Henry Grass. I thought of telling Witzer, but I didn't want him to think I was just a scared kid.

The last Saturday in September finally came and after sundown my mother and father and I left the house and strolled down the street to the Blind Ghost. People were already starting to arrive and from inside I could hear the band tuning up fiddles and banjos. Samantha Bocean had decorated the place for the event—black crepe paper draped here and there and wrapped around the support beams. Hanging from the ceiling on various lengths of fishing line were the skulls of all manner of local animals: coyote, deer, beaver, squirrel, and a giant black bear skull suspended over the center table where the lottery winners were to sit and partake of their drink. I was standing on the threshold, taking all this in, feeling the same kind of enchantment as when I was a kid and Mrs. Musfin would hang lights and tinsel in the three classrooms of the schoolhouse for Christmas, when my father leaned over to me and whispered, "You're on your own tonight, Ernest. You want to drink, drink. You want to dance, dance." I looked at him and he smiled, nodded, and winked. I then looked at my mother and she merely shrugged, as if to say, "That's the nature of the beast."

Old man Witzer was sitting there at the bar, and he called me over and handed me a cold beer. Two other of the town's oldest men were with him, his chess-playing buddies, and he put his arm around my shoulders and introduced them to me. "This is a good boy," he said, patting my back. "He'll do Bo Elliott proud out there under the trees." His two friends nodded and smiled at me, the most notice I'd gotten from either of them my entire life. And then the band launched into a reel, and everyone turned to watch them play. Two choruses went by and I saw my mother and father and some of the other couples move out onto the small dance floor. I had another beer and looked around.

A few songs later, Sheriff Jolle appeared in the doorway to the bar and the music stopped mid-tune.

"Okay," he said, hitching his pants up over his gut and removing his black, wide-brimmed hat, "time to get the lottery started." He moved to the center of the bar, where the Night Whiskey drinker's table was set up, and took a seat. "Everybody drop your lottery tickets into the hat and make it snappy." I guessed that this year it was Samantha Bocean who was going to drink her own concoction since Reed stayed behind the bar and she moved over and took a seat across from Jolle. After the last of the tickets had been deposited into the hat, the sheriff pushed it away from him into the middle of the table. He called for a whiskey neat, and Reed was there with it in a flash. In one swift gulp, the sheriff drained the glass, banged it onto the tabletop, and said, "I'm ready." My girlfriend Darlene's stepmom came up from behind him with a black scarf and tied it around his eyes. Reaching into the hat, he ran his fingers through the lottery tickets, mixing them around, and then started drawing them out one by one and stacking them in a neat pile in front of him on the table. When he had all seven, he stopped and pulled off the blindfold. He then read the names in a loud voice and everyone kept quiet till he was finished—Becca Staney, Stan Joss, Pete Hesiant, Berta Hull, Moses T. Remarque, Ronald White, and Henry Grass. The room exploded with applause and screams. The winners smiled, dazed by having won, as their friends and family gathered round them and slapped them on the back, hugged them, shoved drinks into their hands. I was overwhelmed by the moment, caught up in it and grinning, until I looked over at Witzer and saw him jotting the names down in a little notebook he'd refer to tomorrow as we made our rounds. Only then did it come to me that one of the names was none other than *Henry Grass,* and I felt my stomach tighten in a knot.

Each of the winners eventually sat down at the center table. Jolle stood and gave his seat to Reed Bocean, who brought with him from behind the bar the bottle of Night Whiskey and a tray of eight shot glasses. Like the true barman he was, he poured all eight without lifting the bottle once, all to the exact same level. One by one they were handed around the table. When each of the winners had one before him or her, the barkeep smiled and said, "Drink up." Some went for it like it was a draft from the fountain of youth, some snuck up on it with trembling hands. Berta Hull, a middle-aged mother of five with horse teeth and short red hair, took a sip and declared, "Oh my, it's so lovely." Ronald White, the brother of one of the men I worked with at the gas station, grabbed his and dashed it off in one shot. He wiped his mouth on his sleeve and laughed like a maniac, drunk already. Reed returned to the bar. The band started up again and the celebration came back to life like a wild animal in too small a cage.

I wandered around the Blind Ghost, nodding to the folks I knew, half taken by my new celebrity as a participant in the Drunk Harvest and half preoccupied with watching Henry Grass still sitting at the table, his glass in front of him. He was a young guy, only twenty-five, with a crew cut and a square jaw, dressed in the camouflage sleeveless T-shirt he wore in my recurring dream. By the way he stared at the shot glass in front of him through his little circular glasses, you'd have thought he was staring into the eyes of a king cobra. He had a reputation as a gentle, studious soul, although he was most likely the strongest man in town—the rare instance of an outsider who'd made a place for himself in Gatchfield.

The books he read were all about UFOs and the Bermuda Triangle, the Chariots of the Gods; stuff my father proclaimed to be "dyed-in-the-wool-hooey." He worked with the horses over at the Haber family farm and lived in a trailer out by the old Civil War shot tower, across the meadow and through the woods. I stopped for a moment to talk to Lester II, who mumbled to me around the hard-boiled eggs he was shoving into his mouth one after another, and when I looked back at Henry, he'd finished off the shot glass and left the table.

I overheard snatches of conversation, and much of it was commentary on why it was a lucky thing that so-and-so had won the lottery this year. Someone mentioned the fact that poor Pete Hesiant's beautiful young wife, Lonette, had passed away from leukemia just a few months earlier, and another mentioned that Moses had always wanted a shot at the Night Whiskey but had never gotten the chance, and how he'd soon be too old to participate as his arthritis had recently given him the devil of a time. Everybody was pulling for Berta Hull, who was raising those five children on her own, and Becca was a favorite because she was the town midwife. Similar stuff was said about Ron White and Stan Joss and Henry.

I stood for a long time next to a table where Sheriff Jolle and my father and mother sat with Dr. Kvench, and listened to the doctor, a spry little man with a gray goatee, who was by then fairly well along in his cups, as were his listeners, myself included, spout his theory as to why the drinkers took to the trees. He explained it, amid a barrage of hiccups, as a product of evolution. His theory was that the deathberry plant had at one time grown everywhere on earth, and that early man partook of some form of the Night Whiskey at the dawn of time. Because the world was teeming with night predators then, and because early man was only recently descended from the treetops, those who became drunk automatically knew, as a means of self-preservation, to climb up into the trees to sleep so as not to become a repast for a saber-toothed tiger or some other onerous creature. Dr. Kvench, citing Carl Jung, believed that the imperative to get off the ground after drinking the Night Whiskey had remained in the collective unconscious and had been passed down through the ages. "Everybody in the world probably still has the unconscious command that would kick in if they were to drink the dark stuff, but since the berry doesn't grow anywhere but here now, we're the only ones who see this effect." The doctor nodded, hiccupped twice, and then got up to fetch a glass of water. When he left the table Jolle looked over at my mother, and she and he and my father broke up laughing. "I'm glad he's better at pushing pills than concocting theories," said the sheriff, drying his eyes with his thumbs.

At about midnight, I was reaching for yet another beer, which Reed had placed on the bar, when my grasp was interrupted by a viselike grip on my wrist. I looked up and saw that it was Witzer. He said nothing to me but simply shook his head, and I knew he was telling me to lay off so as to be fresh for the harvest in the morning. I nodded. He smiled, patted my shoulder, and turned away. Somewhere around two a.m., the lottery winners, so incredibly drunk that even in my intoxicated state it seemed impossible they could still walk, stopped dancing, drinking, whatever, and headed for the door. The music abruptly ceased. It suddenly became so silent we could hear the wind blowing out on the street. The sounds of them stumbling across the wooden porch of the bar and then the steps creaking, the screen door banging shut, filled me with a sense of awe and visions of them groping through the night. I tried to picture Berta Hull climbing a tree, but I just couldn't get there, and the doctor's theory started to make some sense to me.

I left before my parents did. Witzer drove me home and before I got out of the cab, he handed me a small bottle.

"Take three good chugs," he said.

"What is it?" I asked.

"An herbal tonic," he said. "It'll clear your head and have you ready for the morning."

I took the first sip of it and the taste was bitter as could be. "Good God," I said, grimacing.

Witzer wheezed. "Two more," he said.

I did as I was told, got out of the truck, and bid him good night. I didn't remember undressing or getting into bed, and luckily I was too drunk to dream. It seemed as if I'd just closed my eyes when my father's voice woke me, saying, "The old man's out in the truck, waiting on you." I leaped out of bed and dressed, and when I finally knew what was going on, I was surprised I felt as well and refreshed as I did. "Do good, Ernest," said my father from the kitchen. "Wait," my mother called. A moment later she came out of their bedroom, wrapping a robe around her. She gave me a hug and a kiss, and then said, "Hurry."

It was brisk outside, and the early-morning light gave proof that the day would be a clear one. The truck sat at the curb, the prods strapped to the top. Witzer sat in the cab, drinking coffee from a Styrofoam cup. When I got in beside him, he handed me a cup and an egg sandwich on a hard roll wrapped in white paper. "We're off," he said. I cleared the sleep out of my eyes as he pulled away from my house.

Our journey took us down the main street of town and then through the alley next to the sheriff's office. This gave way to another small tree-lined street, where we turned right. As we headed away from the center of town, we passed Darlene's house, and I wondered what she'd done the previous night while I'd been at the celebration. I thought of the last time we were together.

She was sitting naked against the wall of the abandoned barn by the edge of the swamp. Her blond hair and face were aglow, illuminated by a beam of light that shone through a hole in the roof.

She had the longest legs and her skin was pale and smooth. Taking a drag from her cigarette, she had said, "Ernest, we gotta get out of this town." She'd laid out for me her plan of escape, her desire to go to some city where civilization was in full swing. I just nodded, reluctant to be too enthusiastic. She was adventurous and I was a homebody, but I did care deeply for her. She tossed her cigarette, put out her arms, and opened her legs, and then Witzer said, "Keep your eyes peeled now, boy," and Darlene's image melted away.

We were moving slowly along a dirt road, both of us looking up at the lower branches of the trees. The old man saw the first one. I didn't see her till he applied the brakes. He took a little notebook and stub of a pencil out of his shirt pocket. "Samantha Bocean," he whispered and put a check next to her name. We got out of the cab, and I helped him unlatch the prods and lay them on the ground beside the truck. Samantha was resting across three branches of a magnolia tree, not too far from the ground. One arm and her long gray hair hung down, and she was turned so I could see her sleeping face.

"Get the ten," said Witzer, as he walked over to stand directly beneath her.

I did as I was told and then joined him.

"What d'ya say?" he asked. "Looks like this one's gonna be a peach."

"Well, I'm thinking if I get it on her left thigh and push her forward fast enough she'll flip as she falls and land perfectly."

Witzer said nothing but left me standing there and got back in the truck. He started it up and pulled it forward so that the bed was precisely where we hoped she would land. He put it in park but left the engine running, then got out and came and stood beside me. "Take a few deep breaths," he said. "Then let her fly."

I thought I'd be more nervous, but the training the old man had given me took hold and I knew exactly what to do. I aimed the prod and rested it gently on top of Samantha's leg. Just as he'd told me, a real body was going to offer a little more resistance than one of the dummies, and I was ready for that. I took three big breaths and then shoved. She rolled slightly, and then tumbled forward, ass over head, landing with a thump on the mattresses, facing the morning sky. Witzer wheezed to beat the band, and said, "That's a solid ten." I was ecstatic.

The old man broke a twig next to Samantha's left ear and instantly her eyelids fluttered. A few seconds later she opened her eyes and smiled.

"How was your visit?" asked Witzer.

"I'll never get tired of that," she said. "It was wonderful."

We chatted with her for a few minutes, filling her in on how the party had gone after she'd left the Blind Ghost. She didn't divulge to us what passed-on relative she'd met with, and we didn't ask. As my mentor had told me when I started, "There's a kind of etiquette to this. When in doubt, silence is your best friend."

Samantha started walking back toward town, and we loaded the prods onto the truck again. In no time, we were on our way, searching for the next sleeper. Luck was with us, for we found four in a row, fairly close by one another: Stan Joss, Moses T. Remarque, Berta Hull, and Becca Staney. All of them had chosen easy-to-get-to perches in the lower branches of ancient oaks, and we dropped them—one, two, three, four—easy as could be. I never had to reach for anything longer than the ten, and the old man proved a genius at placing the truck just so. When each came around at the insistence of the snapping twig, they were cordial and seemed pleased with their experiences. Moses even gave us a ten-dollar tip for dropping him into the truck. Becca told us that she'd spoken to her mother, whom she'd missed terribly since the woman's death two years earlier. Even though they'd been blind drunk the night before, amazingly none of them appeared to be hungover, and each walked away with a perceptible spring in his or her step, even Moses, though he was still slightly bent at the waist by the arthritis.

Witzer said, "Knock on wood, of course, but this is the easiest year I can remember. The year your daddy won, we had to ride around for four solid hours before we found him out by the swamp." We found Ron White only a short piece up the road from where we'd found the cluster of four, and he was an easy job, too. I didn't get him to land on his back, however. He fell face-first—not a desirable drop—but he came to none the worse for wear. After Ron, we had to search for quite a while, ultimately heading out toward the swamp. I knew the only two left were Pete Hesiant and Henry Grass, and the thought of Henry started to make me nervous again. I was reluctant to show my fear, not wanting the old man to lose faith in me, but as we drove slowly along, I finally told Witzer about my recurring dream.

When I was done recounting what I thought was a premonition, Witzer sat in silence for a few moments and then said, "I'm glad you told me."

"I'll bet it's really nothing," I said.

"Henry's a big fellow," he said. "Why should you have all the fun? I'll drop him." And with this, the matter was settled. I realized I should have told him weeks ago when I first started having the dreams.

"Easy, boy," said Witzer with a wheeze and waved his hand as if wiping away my cares. "You've got years of this to go. You can't manage everything on the first Harvest."

We searched everywhere for Pete and Henry—all along the road to the swamp, on the trails that ran through the woods, out along the meadow by the shot tower and Henry's own trailer. With the dilapidated wooden structure of the tower still in sight, we finally found Henry.

"Thar she blows," said Witzer, and he stopped the truck.

"Where?" I said, getting out of the truck, and the old man pointed straight up.

Over our heads, in a tall pine, Henry lay facedown, his arms and legs spread so that they kept him up while the rest of his body was suspended over nothing. His head hung down as if in shame or utter defeat. He looked, in a way, like he was crucified, and I didn't like the look of that at all.

"Get me the twenty," said Witzer, "and then pull the truck up."

I undid the prods from the roof, laid the other two on the ground by the side of the path, and ran the twenty over to the old man. By the time I got back to the truck, started it up, and turned it toward the drop spot, Witzer had the long pole in two hands and was sizing up the situation. As I pulled closer, he let the pole down and then waved me forward while eyeing, back and forth, Henry and the bed. He directed me to cut the wheel this way and that, reverse two feet, and then he gave me the thumbs-up. I turned off the truck and got out.

"Okay," he said. "This is gonna be a tricky one." He lifted the prod up and up and rested the soft end against Henry's chest. "You're gonna have to help me here. We're gonna push straight up on his chest so that his arms flop down and clear the branches, and then as we let him down we're gonna slide the pole, catch him at the belt buckle, and give him a good nudge there to flip him as he falls."

I looked up at where Henry was, and then I just stared at Witzer.

"Wake up, boy!" he shouted.

I came to and grabbed the prod where his hands weren't.

"On three," he said. He counted off and then we pushed. Henry was heavy as ten sacks of rocks. "We got him," cried Witzer, "now slide it." I did and only then did I look up. "Push," the old man said. We gave it one more shove and Henry went into a swan dive, flipping like an Olympic athlete off the high board. When I saw him in mid-fall, my knees went weak and the air left me. He landed on his back with a loud thud directly in the middle of the mattresses, dust from the old cushions roiling up around him.

We woke Henry easily enough, sent him on his way to town, and were soon back in the truck. For the first time that morning I breathed a sigh of relief. "Easiest Harvest I've ever been part of," said Witzer. We headed farther down the path toward the swamp, scanning the branches for Pete Hesiant. Sure enough, in the same right manner with which everything else had fallen into place we found him curled up on his side in the branches of an enormous maple tree. With the first cursory glance at him, the old man determined that Pete would require no more than a ten. After we got the prods off the truck and positioned it under our last drop, Witzer insisted that I take him down. "One more to keep your skill sharp through the rest of the year," he said.

It was a simple job. Pete had found a nice perch with three thick branches beneath him. As I said, he was curled up on his side, and I couldn't see him all too well, so I just nudged his upper back and he rolled over like a small boulder. The drop was precise, and he hit the center of the mattresses, but the instant he was in the bed of the pickup, I knew something was wrong. He'd fallen too quickly for me to register it sooner, but as he lay there, I now noticed that there was someone else with him. Witzer literally jumped to the side of the truck bed and stared in.

"What in fuck's name," said the old man. "Is that a kid he's got with him?"

I saw the other body, naked, in Pete's arms. It had long blond hair, that much was sure. It could have been a kid, but I thought I saw in the jumble a full-size female breast.

Witzer reached into the truck bed, grabbed Pete by the shoulder, and rolled him away from the other form. Then the two of us stood there in stunned silence. The thing that lay there wasn't a woman or a child but both and neither. The body was twisted and deformed, the size of an eight-year-old but with all the characteristics of maturity, if you know what I mean. And that face . . . lumpish and distorted, brow bulging, and from the left temple to the chin there erupted a range of discolored ridges.

"Is that Lonette?" I whispered, afraid the thing would awaken.

"She's dead, ain't she?" said Witzer in as low a voice, and his Adam's apple bobbed.

We both knew she was, but there she or some twisted copy of her lay. The old man took a handkerchief from his back pocket and brought it up to his mouth. He closed his eyes and leaned against the side of the truck. A bird flew by low overhead. The sun shone and leaves fell in the woods on both sides of the path.

Needless to say, when we moved again, we weren't breaking any twigs. Witzer told me to leave the prods and get in the truck. He started it up, and we drove slowly, about fifteen miles an hour, into the center of town. We drove in complete silence. The place was quiet as a ghost town—no doubt everyone was sleeping off the celebration—but we saw that Sheriff Jolle's cruiser was in front of the bunkerlike concrete building that was the police station. The old man parked and went in. As he and the sheriff appeared at the door, I got out of the truck cab and joined them.

"What are you talking about?" Jolle said as they passed me and headed for the truck bed. I followed behind them.

"Shhh," said Witzer. When they finally were looking down at the sleeping couple, Pete and whatever that Lonette thing was, he added, "That's what I'm fucking talking about." He pointed his crooked old finger and his hand was obviously trembling.

Jolle's jaw dropped open after the second or two it took to sink in. "I never . . . ," said the sheriff, and that's all he said for a long while.

Witzer whispered, "Pete brought her back with him."

"What kind of crazy shit is this?" asked Jolle, and he turned quickly and looked at me as if I had an answer. Then he looked back at Witzer. "What the hell happened? Did he dig her up?"

"She's alive," said the old man. "You can see her breathing, but she got bunched up or something in the transfer from there to here."

"Bunched up," said Jolle. "There to here? What in Christ's name . . ." He shook his head and removed his shades. Then he turned to me again and said, "Boy, go get Doc Kvench."

I ran to the doctor's house and pounded on the door. When he opened it, I didn't know what to tell him, so I just said there was an emergency over at the sheriff's office and that he was needed. I didn't stick around and wait for him, because I had to keep moving. To stop would mean I'd have to think too deeply about the return of Lonette Hesiant. By the time I got back to the truck, Henry Grass had also joined Jolle and Witzer, having walked into town to get something to eat after his dream ordeal of the night before. As I drew close to them, I heard Henry saying, "She's come from another dimension. I've read about things like this. And from what I experienced last night, talking to my dead brother, I can tell you that place seems real enough for this to happen."

Jolle looked away from Henry to me as I approached, and then his gaze shifted over my head and he must have caught sight of the doctor. "Good job," said the sheriff and put his hand on my shoulder as I leaned forward to catch my breath. "Hey, Doc," he said as Kvench drew close, "you got a theory about this?"

The doctor stepped up to the truck bed and looked down at where the sheriff was pointing. Doctor Kvench had seen it all in his years in Gatchfield—birth, death, blood, body rot, but the instant he laid his eyes on the new Lonette, the color drained out of him, and he grimaced like he'd just taken a big swig of Witzer's herbal tonic. The effect on him was dramatic, and Henry stepped up next to Kvench and held him up with one big tattooed arm across his back. Kvench brushed Henry off and turned away from the truck. I thought for a second that he was going to puke.

We waited for his diagnosis. Finally he turned back and said, "Where did it come from?"

"It fell out of the tree with Pete this morning," said Witzer.

"I signed the death certificate for that girl five months ago," said the doctor.

"She's come from another dimension . . . ," said Henry, launching into one of his Bermuda Triangle explanations, but Jolle held a hand up to silence him. Nobody spoke then and the sheriff started pacing back and forth, looking into the sky and then at the ground. It was obvious that he was having some kind of silent argument with himself, because every few seconds he'd either nod or shake his head. Finally, he put his open palms to his face for a moment, rubbed his forehead, and blinked his eyes. Then he turned to us.

"Look, here's what we're gonna do. I decided. We're going to get Pete out of that truck without waking him and put him on the cot in the station. Will he stay asleep if we move him?" he asked Witzer.

The old man nodded. "As long as you don't shout his name or break a twig near his ear, he should keep sleeping till we wake him."

"Okay," continued Jolle. "We get Pete out of the truck, and then we drive that thing out into the woods, we shoot it, and we bury it."

Everybody looked around at everybody else. The doctor said, "I don't know if I can be part of that."

"You're gonna be part of it," said Jolle, "or right this second you're taking full responsibility for its care. And I mean *full* responsibility."

"It's alive, though," said Kvench.

"But it's a mistake," said the sheriff. "Either of nature or God or whatever."

"Doc, I agree with Jolle," said Witzer. "I never seen anything that felt so wrong than what I'm looking at in the back of that truck."

"You want to nurse that thing until it dies on its own?" Jolle said to the doctor. "Think of what it'll do to Pete to have to deal with it."

Kvench looked down and shook his head. Eventually he whispered, "You're right."

"Boys?" Jolle said to me and Henry.

My mouth was dry and my head was swimming a little. I nodded. Henry did too.

"Good," said the sheriff. It was decided that we all would participate and share in the act of disposing of it. Henry and the sheriff gently lifted Pete out of the truck and took him into the station house. When they returned, Jolle told Witzer and me to drive out to the woods in the truck and that he and Henry and Kvench would follow in his cruiser.

For the first few minutes of the drive out, Witzer said nothing. We passed Pete Hesiant's small yellow house and upon seeing it I immediately started thinking about Lonette, and how beautiful she'd been. She and Pete had been only in their early thirties, a very handsome couple. He was thin and gangly and had been a star basketball player for Gatchfield, but never tall enough to turn his skill into a college scholarship. They'd been high school sweethearts. He finally found work as a municipal handyman, and had that good-natured youth-going-to-seed personality of the washed-up, once-lauded athlete.

Lonette had worked the cash register at the grocery. I remembered her passing by our front porch on the way to work the evening shift, and how one afternoon I overheard her telling my mother that she and Pete had decided to try to start a family. I'm sure I wasn't supposed to be privy to this conversation, but whenever she passed by our house, I tried to make it a point of being near a window. I heard every word through the screen. The very next week, though, I learned that she had some kind of disease. That was three years ago. Over time she slowly grew more haggard. Pete tried to take care of her on his own, but I don't think it had gone all too well. At her funeral, Henry had had to hold him back from climbing into the grave after her.

"Is this murder?" I asked Witzer after he'd turned onto the dirt path and headed out toward the woods.

He looked over at me and said nothing for a second. "I don't know, Ernest," he said. "Can you murder someone who's already dead? Can you murder a dream? What would you have us do?" He didn't ask the last question angrily but as if he were really looking for a plan other than Jolle's.

I shook my head.

"I'll never see things the same again," he said. "I keep thinking I'm gonna wake up any minute now."

We drove on for another half mile and then he pulled the truck off the path and under a cluster of oaks. As we got out of the cab, the sheriff pulled up next to us. Henry, the doctor, and Jolle got out of the cruiser, and all five of us gathered at the back of the pickup. It fell to Witzer and me to get her out of the truck and lay her on the ground some feet away. "Careful," whispered the old man, as he leaned over the wall of the bed and slipped his arms under her. I took the legs, and when I touched her skin a shiver went through me. Her body was heavier than I expected, and her sex was staring me right in the face, covered with short hair thick as twine. She was breathing lightly, obviously sleeping, and her eyes moved rapidly beneath her closed lids like she was dreaming. She had a powerful aroma, of flowers and candy, sweet to the point of sickening.

We got her on the ground without waking her, and the instant I let go of her legs, I stepped outside the circle of men. "Stand back," said Jolle. The others moved away. He pulled his gun out of its holster with his left hand and made the sign of the cross with his right. Leaning down, he put the gun near her left temple, and then cocked the hammer back. The hammer clicked into place with the sound of a breaking twig and right then her eyes shot open. Four grown men jumped backward in unison. "Good lord," said Witzer. "Do it," said Kvench. I looked to Jolle and he was staring down at her as if in a trance. Her eyes had no color. They were wide and shifting back and forth. She started taking deep raspy breaths and then sat straight up. A low mewing noise came from her chest, the sound of a cat or a scared child. Then she started talking backward talk, some foreign language never heard on earth before, babbling frantically and drooling.

Jolle fired. The bullet caught her in the side of the head and threw her onto her right shoulder. The left side of her face, including her ear, blew off, and this black stuff, not blood, splattered all over, flecks of it staining Jolle's pants and shirt and face. The side of her head was smoking. She lay there writhing in what looked like a pool of oil, and he shot her again and again, emptying the gun into her. The sight of it brought me to my knees, and I puked. When I looked up, she'd stopped moving. Tears were streaming down Witzer's face. Kvench was shaking. Henry looked as if he'd been turned to stone. Jolle's finger kept pulling the trigger, but there were no rounds left.

After Henry tamped down the last shovelful of dirt on her grave, Jolle made us swear never to say a word to anyone about what had happened. I pledged that oath as did the others. Witzer took me straight home, no doubt having silently decided I shouldn't be there when they woke Pete. When I got to the house, I went straight to bed and slept for an entire day, only getting up in time to get to the gas station for work the next morning. The only dream I had was an infuriating and frustrating one of Lester II, eating hard-boiled eggs and explaining it all to me but in backward talk and gibberish so I couldn't make out any of it. Carrying the memory of that Drunk Harvest miracle around with me was like constantly having a big black bubble of night afloat in the middle of my waking thoughts.

As autumn came on and passed and then winter bore down on Gatchfield, the insidious strength of it never diminished. It made me quiet and moody, and my relationship with Darlene suffered. I kept my distance from the other four conspirators. It went so far as we tried not to even recognize one another's presence when we passed on the street. Only Witzer still waved at me from his pickup when he'd drive by, and if I was the attendant when he came into the station for gas, he'd say, "How are you, boy?" I'd nod and that would be it. Around Christmastime I'd heard from my father that Pete Hesiant had lost his mind and was unable to work; he would break down crying at a moment's notice, couldn't sleep, and was being treated by Kvench with all manner of pills.

Things didn't get any better come spring. Pete shot the side of his head off with a pistol. Mrs. Marfish, who'd gone to bring him a pie she'd baked to cheer him up, discovered him lying dead in a pool of blood on the back porch of the little yellow house. Then Sheriff Jolle took ill and was so bad off with whatever he had, he couldn't get out of bed. He deputized Reed Bocean, the barkeep and the most sensible man in town, to look after Gatchfield in his absence. Reed did a good job as sheriff and Samantha doubletimed it at the Blind Ghost—both solid citizens.

In the early days of May, I burned my hand badly at work on a hot car engine and my boss drove me over to Kvench's office to get it looked after. While I was in his treatment room, and he was wrapping my hand in gauze, the doctor leaned close to me and whispered, "I think I know what happened." I didn't even make a face, but stared ahead at the eye chart on the wall, not really wanting to hear anything about the incident. "Gatchfield's so isolated that change couldn't get in from the outside, so Nature sent it from within," he said. "Mutation. From the dream." I looked at him. He was nodding, but I saw that his goatee had gone squirrelly, there was this overeager gleam in his eyes, and his breath smelled like medicine. I knew right then he'd been more than sampling his own pills. I couldn't get out of there fast enough.

June came, and it was a week away from the day that Witzer and I were to begin practicing for the Drunk Harvest again. I dreaded the thought of it to the point where I was having a hard time eating or sleeping. After work one evening, as I was walking home, the old man pulled up next to me in his pickup truck. He stopped and opened the window. I was going to keep walking, but he called, "Boy, get in. Take a ride with me." I made the mistake of looking over at him. "It's important," he said. I got in the cab and we drove off slowly down the street.

I blurted out that I didn't think I'd be able to manage the Harvest and how screwed up the thought of it was making me, but he held his hand up and said, "Shh, shh, I know." I quieted down and waited for him to talk. A few seconds passed and then he said, "I've been to see Jolle. You haven't seen him have you?"

I shook my head.

"He's a goner for sure. He's got some kind of belly rot, and, I swear to you he's got a deathberry bush growing out of his insides . . . while he's still alive, no less. Doc Kvench just keeps feeding him pills, but he'd be better off taking a hedge clipper to him."

"Are you serious?" I said.

"Boy, I'm dead serious." Before I could respond, he said, "Now look, when the time for the celebration comes around, we're all going to have to participate in it as if nothing had happened. We made our oath to the sheriff. That's bad enough, but what happens when somebody's dead relative tells them in a Night Whiskey dream what we did, what happened with Lonette?"

I was trembling and couldn't bring myself to speak.

"Tomorrow night—are you listening to me?—tomorrow night I'm leaving my truck unlocked with the keys in the ignition. You come to my place and take it and get the fuck out of Gatchfield."

I hadn't noticed but we were now parked in front of my house. He leaned across me and opened my door. "Get as far away as you can, boy," he said.

The next day, I called in sick to work, withdrew all my savings from the bank, and talked to Darlene. That night, good to his word, the keys were in the old pickup. I noticed there was another truck parked next to the old one on his lot to cover for the one we took. I left my parents a letter about how Darlene and I had decided to elope, and that they weren't to worry. I'd call them.

We fled to the biggest, brightest city we could find, and the rush and maddening business of the place, the distance from home, our combined struggle to survive at first, and then make our way, was a curative better than any pill Dr. Kvench could have prescribed. Every day there was change and progress and crazy news on the television, and these things served to shrink but never quite burst the black bubble in my thoughts. Still, to this day, though, so many years later, there's always an evening near the end of September when I sit down to a Night Whiskey, so to speak, and Gatchfield comes back to me in my dreams like some lost relative I'm both terrified to behold and want nothing more than to put my arms around and never let go.

A FEW THINGS
ABOUT ANTS

Tonight, on the drive home from work, it was raining like mad. Torrential rain, so that the wipers were on high and everything in the dark world beyond the windshield was severely warped. I'd hit these giant puddles I couldn't see on the side of my lane. They'd throw a momentary curtain of water up in front of me and push the car toward the oncoming traffic. Along Route 537, passing through farm country, I drove blindly into a puddle so huge I almost stalled. At the last second, I saw that there were two cars abandoned in it, and I performed a snaky maneuver of the wheel around them I'd never have been able to do if I'd had time to think about it. Somehow my car kept running, and as I climbed the hill beyond that sump, Elvis came on the radio, singing, "Love Me Tender." It was right at the top of that hill that I started thinking about ants. Why? I don't know. It started with a memory of the fat ants that climbed on the peach trees in the backyard of the house in which I grew up, and before I knew it there was an infestation of ants between my ears.

· · ·

My grandparents lived in the garage, which had been renovated into an apartment. Out back, next to the shed, my grandfather had this huge green barrel that was for testing boat motors. We didn't have any outboard motors, so the thing just sat there year in and year out, collecting rain water. My brother, Jim, discovered one summer morning that the water in the barrel was filled with what he called "skeleton fish." He showed me, and, yes, these tiny white creatures made all of white bones no thicker than thread with minuscule death's heads were swimming in the dark water of the barrel. "Watch this," he said. He walked over to the nearest peach tree and soon returned. Into the barrel, on the calm water, he placed a peach tree leaf, and then on top of that he put a big black ant. The ant, upon landing on the leaf, started scrabbling frantically all around the sides of it. While we watched, Jim sang, "Sailing, sailing, over the bounding main." Then the leaf started to take on water under the weight of the ant. A puddle formed in the middle of the shiny green boat and slowly grew. Eventually the leaf sank, and the ant was in the water, swimming like crazy with all its many legs, its antennae twitching this way and that. "Here they come," said Jim. The skeleton fish rose from the depths. In seconds, the ant was surrounded by them. They swarmed thickly, and then slowly, with the speed of a fat flat snowflake falling, they dragged the ant down and down, out of sight, where the rotted leaves of last summer lay. "Davy Jones's Locker," he said and was heading toward the tree for another when David Kelty came into the backyard and told us the bug spray guy was coming. We got on our bikes and followed the big yellow truck, traveling for blocks in the mysterious fog of its wake.

· · ·

Once I read a book about ants written by an ant expert. It had great photos of ants doing just about anything you could imagine—ants of all colors and sizes and constructions. It said that there are ants that are like farmers, planting and growing crops of fungus in underground fields. It said there are ants that make slaves of other ants. One type of ant herds smaller insects like cattle and keeps them penned up and fattened for the kill. Ants make war. Ants represent some outlandish percentage of the earth's biomass. It said their burrows are "marvels of engineering."

When my sons were younger, we used to take a walk to this place we called the Pit. It was a huge hole in the ground, in the woods, at the edge of town where the pine barrens started. How it got there, I don't know, but it looked like a meteor crater. It was the choice spot in the winter for sleigh riding—everybody launching off the sides and streaking down toward the center. There were plenty of collisions. Once I saw this woman from town, who eventually committed suicide, get struck by a kid on a speeding sleigh. Man, she flew up in the air just like in *The Little Rascals* episode where Spanky and Alfalfa and Darla and Buckwheat go sliding across a golf course on a door or something, hitting golfers. Before that I'd thought the way the golfers flew into the air was funny, overblown comedy, but when I saw it happen to this poor woman that old memory of humor returned mixed with nausea. Anyway, the Pit, yeah, it was remote. Lynn and I went for a walk there with the dog and we found a place where someone had built a fire, and in the charred remains were animal bones. I picked one up and Lynn looked at it and said it was probably the leg bone of a goat (she'd taken a lot of anatomy classes in school). "A fuckin' goat?" I said, all the time thinking, "Weird, suburban religious cult, practicing black magic." Another time I found a stone arrowhead there.

There was a spot at the rim of the Pit that jutted out over the downward slope. The kids and I would go there, and they would jump off the overhanging ledge of dirt and strike poses in the air before falling onto the slope, after which they'd roll down to the bottom. My job was to sit somewhere nearby, where I had a good view, and judge their jumps. It was nice work if you could get it, because when they were younger any chance to sit was a good thing. All I had to do was make sure that no matter what else happened, their scores added up to be exactly even at the end. The bonus was that all the running they did up to the top of the Pit for the next jump tired them out and they'd fall asleep pretty quickly on those evenings.

So one day, I was sitting there judging, and I looked down at the ground and saw a beautiful, completely clear stone, like a big round pebble made of water. I picked it up and inspected it. It was a perfect piece of quartz crystal—no apparent flaws. From then on, instead of going to the Pit to do the jumping game, we'd go treasure prospecting. In the following months, we found a lot of really nice specimens of clear quartz stones. I used to like to look at the sun through them. Then, on a hot summer afternoon, we were there, poking around in these mounds at the rim where the tree line started, and I noticed these really big ants crawling in and out of holes that had been burrowed in the hill. They were regular big black ants, but get this: on their back section, each had a patch of bright red—I mean like fire-truck red—hair. The color was striking, and when I got down right near them, I could make out the little individual strands of hair, and the patches looked like red crew cuts on their asses. I was amazed. I showed the kids. We went home and I tried to look it up on the Internet: "redihaired ants," "hairy ants," "hairy ass ants." No luck. I looked through my ant book. Nothing. I asked a guy at work who was a biology professor about them. He'd never heard of them. After a while, I just gave up and when I went back to the Pit I never saw them again. The Pit was filled in earlier this year. I really miss that hole in the ground.

For Christmas one year, when we were kids, my sister, Mary, got an ant farm. The box it came in had the coolest illustration on the cover, of ants in tunnels wearing miner's helmets and wielding pickaxes and shovels. One ant was in the foreground, winking out at you from the picture, and beneath him was a statement in red, block letters: SEE ANTS LIVE AND WORK. The ant farm was a clear plastic rectangle about three inches thick that sat on a stand and you had to fill it with dirt. Of course, it didn't come with ants. You had to send away to the company for them. So Mary set up the ant farm, filled it with dirt, and sent away for her ants. Well, a couple of months passed and the ants never showed up. The ant farm was relegated to the cellar, the place where all old, broken, and useless toys ended up—sort of a toy graveyard. We were playing down in the cellar one rainy day, and somehow the ant farm got smashed. Okay, nobody gave a damn. It was swept up and thrown out. About a year and a half went by when one day in the mail there came a little brown mailer envelope addressed to Mary, no return address. I was the only one home with her when it arrived. We were curious to see what was in it, because, back then, getting mail when you were a kid was exotic. Inside the envelope she found a plastic tube with a screw-off cap at one end. We had no idea what it was. She unscrewed the cap, tilted the tube, and out onto the marble-topped coffee table spilled about ninety-nine dead ants and one that was just barely alive. The living one turned in circles three times as if one of its back legs were nailed down and then it stopped moving. We sat there and just stared at the pile of dead ants. Then Mary said, with no emotion, "That present was worse than Sea-Monkeys." We'd thought that ant farm box's main ant's conspiratorial wink had meant, "Kids, you're in for something really special here," when all along, he was telling us, "Hey, you do know this ant farm thing's really just a stack of shit."

On Saturday nights, my brother and I used to stay up late and watch science-fiction and horror movies on the black-and-white TV. *Attack of the Mushroom People*, *Attack of the 50 Foot Woman*, *The Man with X-Ray Eyes* (Milland was the coolest), *The Giant Behemoth*. We'd eat cheap chocolate chip cookies, a quarter for a box, and drink store-brand root beer. It didn't get much better than that; we were farting in silk. One of our favorite movies was *Them*, a story about a giant ant with a bad attitude and an appetite for human flesh. It grew giant because it got too close to an atom bomb explosion. You could shoot this thing with a fucking bazooka and it didn't care. And back then, anything that could withstand the mighty blast of a bazooka was worthy of our admiration. The movie starred James Whitmore. You know who I mean? He's still around—the Miracle-Gro guy, whose eyebrows at some point got too close to an atom bomb explosion. You know the commercials I'm talking about, the ones where there's some goofy-looking woman standing in a garden and beneath her is the statement "World's Largest Tomato." Shatner made a giant-ant movie years after *Them*, but even though it's hard to beat Shatner's 100 percent cornpone emoting, *Them* is still our favorite. Whitmore plays a highway cop and his portrayal almost rivals the acting job the ant turns in. But there's one spot in the movie where Whitmore's deputy says something to him, as the ant is approaching, along the lines of "Where did it come from?" and Whitmore's response is "I don't care if it's from Upper Saddle River, New Jersey." Kind of a strange locale to refer to, no? Especially considering the film is set in the Southwest near where they'd test atom bombs in the fifties.

But more than a decade after those late nights watching *Them*, I would meet and marry a girl from Upper Saddle River, New Jersey. There are more things in heaven and earth . . . my friend.

At night, when he'd come in late from work, my father often brought me a carton, like the kind you get for Chinese takeout, filled with tapioca pudding. He told me it was frog eyes, and I was young enough to believe it. I'd sit with him at the dining room table while he ate his heated-up leftovers. We'd sit in the dark in the dining room, and he'd say nothing. I'd eat the pudding slowly because as soon as I was done I was supposed to go to bed. One night, after he finished eating, he pushed back his plate, lit a cigarette, and told me, "I heard a radio show on the way home from work about ants." I nodded. He said, "It was about these scientists who were studying a special kind of ant down in the Amazon jungle. They were interested in finding a queen ant to study, so they'd dig down into the ant burrows and find the queen's nest. The queen is bigger than all the other ants, so she was easy to find. They then took the queen from this one nest and put it in their field box to take back to the lab they'd set up, which was a half mile away. But when they got back to the lab, they found the ant was not in the box. It had vanished. This happened to them three days in a row and they couldn't figure out how the ant was escaping, since it was a plastic container with a snap-on lid that was always snapped shut when they'd go to open it. When they would go back to the ant hive the next day, they always found a new queen ant in the nest. Then one of the scientists got this crazy idea into his head that the queen ant they found every day was the same exact ant. Nobody believed him, so, when they collected the next queen, he marked it with a dot of blue dye. On the walk back to the lab, they checked the specimen box a couple times and the ant was in there, but when they reached the lab, they opened the box and it was gone. The next day, back at the nest, they found a queen ant and it was marked with the blue dye. The only explanation they could come up with was that it had somehow teleported itself out of the box, passing through the plastic and across space and time, and reappeared in the nest. Eventually the local natives corroborated the fact that the queen of this type of ant had the power to disappear and appear wherever and whenever it wanted to." My father looked at me and I nodded.

"What do you think of that?" he asked.

"How?" I asked.

"Well, the guy on the show said he thought it had developed this ability through evolution over millions of years as a defense mechanism."

"Oh," I said. I finished my pudding and went to bed.

This is a very vivid recollection for me, and in later years I wondered what the hell this radio show was he'd been listening to. I remember that one other time when he came home and I waited up for him, he told me about a show he'd listened to where they spoke about the fact that Catholicism was actually based on a mushroom cult and that all the stuff in the Bible was a secret code for information and stories about sacred mushrooms.

UNDER THE BOTTOM
OF THE LAKE

Under the bottom of the lake, in a grotto guarded by stalactites and stalagmites, like the half-open maw of a stone dragon, on a pedestal that's a tall white mushroom, there sits a bubble of rose-colored glass, within which swirls a secret story, told once but never heard. It's been there for so long that no one remembers its existence. I'm not even sure how I'm able to tell it, but then I'm not really remembering it, I'm making it up as I go, which allows me to know it all in the moment that it comes to me. Perhaps in the grotto of my imagination there was a glass bubble, containing a secret story, the story of, but not in, the bubble of rose-colored glass, and I have inadvertently knocked it over while groping blindly through my thoughts and now that story, the story about the grotto under the lake, has been released into my mind and I'm hearing the words of the tale now as I tell them. This tale can tell me nothing about the story contained within the rose-colored bubble but only about its existence and about the grotto that was like a dragon's mouth. Still, there are methods to get at the story in that bubble under the lake. What's called for is someone to discover it. For this, we'll need a character.

Here's one, easy as could be—she comes toward me out of the shadows of my mind, a young lady, perhaps fifteen, maybe sixteen. One moment, please. . . . Okay, her name is Emily, and she has long red hair, green eyes, and freckles across her nose. She's dressed in denim overalls, and beneath them she wears a T-shirt, yellow, with the word "AXIMESH" in black block letters, showing just above the top of the overall bib. On her feet, she wears cheap, coral-colored beach sandals. She's got long eyelashes, a hemp necklace with a yin/yang pendant, and, in her back left pocket, for good luck, there's a piece of red paper folded into the figure of an angel. When you pull on its feet the wings flap and the ring that's the halo above its head separates at the front and turns into two curved horns, sticking up.

I know she's walking along the sidewalk in her hometown, moving her lips, silently talking to herself, staring at the cracked concrete beneath her feet, but I don't yet know where she's going. Wait . . . she lifts her head. She hears someone calling her name. "Emily!" She turns around and sees a boy of about her age approaching from behind. I see him, and the instant I do, the dim nature of my imagination pushes back in a circle with these two as its center to reveal a perfect blue day in a small town. I see and hear them talking within that portal of brightness, and he's asking her where she's going. "To the cemetery," she tells him. He nods and obviously decides to follow her.

The boy has large ears, that much is clear. His hair is cut close to his scalp, and his face could either be construed as dim-witted or handsome, depending on how you construe. I'm no judge of looks. He's got a name that begins with a "V," but I'm not sure what it is. It's sort of exotic, but since I can't think of it, I'll call him Vincent just to have something to call him. I know he knows the girl and she knows him. They more than likely go to school together. I think they're in the same math class. She's good at math. He's not very good at it, and the teacher, an old woman the students call the Turkey, for the wattle beneath her chin, once gave him a zero for the day as a result of, as she said, his "gross ignorance." Emily felt bad for him, but she laughed along with the other students at the insult.

Emily's grandmother has recently passed away and Emily is telling Vincent that she's going to the cemetery to pay her respects. Vincent's wearing the same expression as when the Turkey calls him to the blackboard and sticks a piece of chalk in his hand and tells him to solve a fantastical division problem—one number as long as his arm going into another number as long as his leg. He wants to do something in both instances, say the right thing, do what's appropriate, but he's not sure how to so he just keeps walking beside Emily. When they stop at a corner to check both ways before crossing, he reaches into his pocket and pulls out a pack of licorice gum and asks if she wants some. She says okay and takes a piece.

As they cross the street, I start to lose sight of them, so I lean in close to the circle of light in which they are walking, and . . . aghhh, shit, I've knocked it onto the floor of my imagination and it's cracked. Their story is leaking out and I'm missing some and knowing the rest too fast. The light that had been in the bubble of their scene slowly dissolves. Hold on while I try to find them again. I can't see at all, but I know there are cars going by on the street every now and then. I hear a dog bark and someone's using a lawn mower. I smell crumb cake. There's just a flash of light and in that moment I see the sun in the leaves of an oak tree. But now, darkness . . .

Okay, they're now in the cemetery. They're walking among the gravestones and Vincent is telling Emily about how his father, whom he calls his "old man," is getting a divorce from his mother because he drinks too much. "My mom says he's screwed up because *his* old man was addicted to drugs from the war and was crazy, beating him and shit." Emily stops walking and looks at him. He's surprised that she's stopped and wonders why she did. "That's terrible," she says. "Which part?" he asks. "The whole thing," she says. He says, "Yeah," and then stares at a gravestone with the last name CAKE inscribed on it and eventually, after a long time, a tear appears in the corner of his right eye. Emily steps close to him and puts her arm around him. Vincent blows a big black bubble with his licorice gum, and when it pops it reveals this scene that had been swirling inside of it.

Emily kneels on the ground in front of a headstone with the name JUDITH SOCHELL carved into it. This is the gravesite of her grandmother on her mother's side. Vincent stands a few feet behind her and chews his gum. He's watching the trees blowing in the wind at the edge of the woods in the distance and wondering how long it will be before his parents discover he hasn't given them his most recent report card. Every now and then he turns back to see if Emily is crying. She isn't; instead she's remembering her grandmother in her final days—wasted, wrinkled beyond recognition, and always shivering and shaking as if naked in a blizzard. The old woman had lost her mind years earlier, had grown so feeble of intellect that at the time she died she could speak only one of four possible words: "eat," "no," "go," and "more." And the one she'd chosen for her final utterance, "more," was whispered to Emily as she stood holding her grandmother's bony hand. At the moment of the old woman's death, the girl remembered a story Grandma Judith had told her about a man who'd exchanged his soul with that of a mythical bird—a strange story that made no sense but was full of tragedy and sorrow—but Emily doesn't think about that now. As bad as she'd gotten, though, and up until the very end,

Grandma Judith was still capable, even with wildly shaking hands, to form the origami animals and figures she'd made from the time she was a little girl. During the wake, when she did remember the story, Emily put a specimen from her paper menagerie in the coffin with her grandmother, a piece of light blue paper folded into an amazing bird with wings that moved when its feet were pulled, a head that bobbed up and down, and a beak that opened and closed as if saying, "What a world. What a world."

Vincent's getting bored. "Come on, Em," he says.

"Shut up," she tells him.

He walks over to and looks more closely at an old, jagged-topped tree stump jutting four feet out of the ground. Only when he's upon it does he realize that the stump is made of stone and that there's a name chiseled into it. The moss that lightly covers it makes it look like the real thing, but in fact it's a marble grave marker.

It's later in the day now and Emily and Vincent are approaching a ruined mausoleum at the edge of the cemetery near the boundary of the woods. The columns of the marble structure, looking like the remains of a miniature savings and loan, are statues of women in togas, and their arms and faces, some with missing noses, are covered with green mold. Branching cracks run throughout the walls of the tomb, and pieces of it have crumbled off and fallen in chunks on the ground. The name above the portico where there's been a mishap of stone says AKE, but years ago it read CAKE. Don't ask me how, but I know this is the final resting place of Cassius Cake, a prominent member of the Cake family that still resides in Emily's town.

My imagination tells me that Cake made his fortune manufacturing medicines of an opiate nature, derived from giant mushrooms, to be used on battlefields, and that on his estate, which lay by the lake, on the other side of the woods, the boundary of which

his mausoleum now abuts, there was an aviary in which it was ru-
mored that he kept a single exotic bird, so beautiful the sight of it
could make you weep. The iron gate to his death chamber has long
since been rusted and chewed by Time, its lock broken.

Vincent takes Emily by the hand and they enter that dim place
of long-ago death turned to stone. The only light inside is offered by the setting sun seeping in through the diffuse colors of a
stained-glass window at the back—a scene of a brightly feathered
bird, rising from sharp-tipped, swirling flames. Once inside, the
boy and girl turn to face each other and kiss, and it breaks across
my consciousness like a wave that this is not their first kiss. I see
them in another place, a small cedar attic in one of their homes,
kissing. So they know each other better than I thought. At this
very moment, she's thinking of her grandmother's skull under the
ground, and he's thinking of his father's skull ablaze with liquid
fire, no bird rising from it. He's about to move his hand down her
back to rest it upon her rear end, but she turns away and points to
a perfectly round hole in the floor, directly between the sarcophagi
of Cassius Cake and his wife, Letti.

Emily gets down on all fours and peers into the hole in the marble floor. "There're steps," she says to Vincent.

"Okay," he says.

Then she stands up and pulls a pack of cigarettes out of the
bib pocket of her overalls. She takes a cigarette from the pack and
offers one to Vincent. He says no because he's a runner. He runs
the one hundred for the school track team. He's not the smartest
kid in school, but he might be the fastest, save for Jordan Squires,
who's the best at everything in school, even kissing, as Emily well
knows.

"Let's go down there," she says, pointing to the hole in the floor,
with the two fingers holding her cigarette.

"Why?" asks Vincent.

She doesn't have a ready answer, so I whisper to her just to coax things along, "There might be treasure." She ignores my suggestion and instead says, "I want to see what's there."

Vincent smells danger, but the scent of the smoke from the cigarette confuses the acrid aroma for him and he thinks he smells the possible deepening of his bond with Emily. In a way he's right, because Emily's testing him, seeing if he'll follow her anywhere, even underground in a cemetery. They descend into the dark through the circle of nothing that's the hole in the floor. At the bottom of the steps, they find a passageway, and the rock walls glow with phosphorescent lichen. They . . .

I've lost them again, and instead I have a very strong vision of a soldier lying wounded on a battlefield, being administered, by a medic, a small cup, like a shot glass, of orange liquid. Now I see the soldier's right leg is half of its former self, the bottom half blasted off and blood and bone showing through a shredded pant leg. The medic's shaking with fear and is barely able to get the medicine into his charge without spilling it. I see the man's face for an instant beneath his helmet with the red cross emblazoned on it and notice two weeks' growth of beard and dark circles around the eyes, but that's all I see, because just then a bullet pierces his back, rips through muscle and bone, and deflates his heart. He falls backward, out of sight. Shells burst overhead. Machine-gun fire and the screams of the dying echo across the misty marchland. The wounded soldier who's just been given the dose of Cake's Orixadoll thinks he's dying, but the feeling he has is just the hallucinogen kicking in. A feeling of warmth descends upon him. He no longer hears the sounds of war, but instead can make out, faintly, the voice of Judy Garland singing "Somewhere Over the Rainbow." When she sings the part about lemon drops melting, he realizes he feels no pain, and his vision sharpens into a circular field, a tunnel. He's flying through an underground tunnel, the walls of which are lit by phosphorescent lichen. Up ahead he sees a girl and boy in his path, and he blows around them, through them, lifting their hair and stealing their breath for a moment.

"What was that?" asks Emily.

"Underground winds blowing up from hell," says Vincent like he knows what he's talking about. Emily considers what he says, but then remembers that he's good only at kissing and running. They move on, and I'm stuck here watching them walk through a tunnel. I'm going to have a smoke while I wait for something to happen.

With my last drag I blow a smoke ring and inside it I see Vincent stop walking and say to Emily, "Let's go back."

"No," she says, "this tunnel leads somewhere. Somebody made this tunnel. Don't you want to know what's at the end?" At this point I'm pretty sure they've traveled under the woods and are down under the bottom of the lake.

Oh my God, a realization just exploded in my mind like one of those shells in the scene with the dying soldier. I get it now. I see Vincent's old man at the age Vincent is now, creeping through the woods at night. He comes clear of the trees and moves across a vast lawn in the moonlight. Ahead of him is a huge cage in the shape of a beehive where silvery beams from above glint off the thin brass bars. He approaches the cage, and inside he sees a beautiful bird with trailing plumage sitting on a perch. It has three long thin feathers, ending in pink pom-poms arcing off its forehead, and its beak is like that of a peacock. Even in the dark its colors are resilient—turquoise, orange, magenta, and a light, light blue like storybook oceans. But Vincent's old man as a young man has a bow slung over his shoulder and he's holding an arrow. He sets the arrow and aims through the bars. He releases, the arrow pierces the chest of the bird, it screams once, a shrill cry like the sound of a newborn baby, and then all its beautiful feathers burst into flame. Vincent's old man turns and runs across the moonlit lawn, Cake wakes in his canopied bed and clutches his chest, Emily calls over her shoulder, "Look at this," and points ahead to a grotto surrounded by stalactites and stalagmites; a dragon's mouth inviting entry.

I'm so close now, but instead of following Emily and Vincent to the white mushroom and the rose-colored glass bubble, I'm in Cake's bedroom, and he's fallen onto the floor and is flopping around in pain, clutching his chest. His wife rolls over to his side of the bed, and says, "Cassius, dear, you're making a racket. I was having a perfectly delightful dream."

"Letti," he croaks, "Letti, over in my dresser is a dose of Orixadoll. Get it. Hurry."

"Oh, you're in pain?" she says and smiles. Slowly she gets out of bed, slips on her slippers, and drapes her pink silk wrap around herself. Cake is still doing the landed bass, thumping the floor next to the bed, gurgling and grunting. Finally she returns. He reaches his hand up to her and into it she places, not the dose of his own medicine, but instead a tiny woman made of folded yellow paper. He holds it where he can see it. "Call *her*," says Letti, who then goes back to bed. A half hour later, after she's returned to her dream of a city with circular walls, he finally expires.

Back in the grotto there is an enormous white mushroom, perfectly formed, that serves as a pedestal for a rose-colored glass bubble, and Emily and Vincent approach it cautiously. This is something I hadn't been aware of before, because I was seeing the scene under the bottom of the lake from a distance, but the white mushroom gives off a kind of perfume—a sweet, tantalizing scent, like the aroma of orchids, but more substantial, more delicious, so to speak. That fungal reek, I'm just realizing, not smelling it but "understanding" the aroma they are smelling, also carries a soporific effect and Emily's long eyelashes are fluttering. Vincent

yawns and forgets all about his anxiety due to being underground
and in a mysterious grotto. Instead, he's hungry and finds himself
wanting to take a bite out of that big luscious white mushroom cap
that's grown as high as his chest. Emily's more interested in the
rose-colored bubble, and as she reaches for it, Vincent spits out his
licorice gum, leans over, and sinks his teeth into the marshmallow
meringue of the fungus.

"What are you doing?" says Emily and, even though she knows
what he's up to is dangerous, she finds it funny. Vincent reels backward, disoriented from the explosion of sweetness in his mouth.

"It's awesome," he says in between chewing. She doesn't notice
that he's now been brought to his knees by the overwhelming delight of the white morsel, because she's got the rose-colored bubble up to her eye and is staring inside, where she sees something
swirling.

What moves like a miniature twister within the see-through
boundary is the tale once told but never heard. She puts the bubble
to her ear but can hear nothing. She shakes it, taps it, and rolls it
from palm to palm. Then she simply drops it, and I watch as it
falls, slowly spinning in its descent. After an eternity, it explodes
against the rock floor and scatters a fiery revelation, like a bird of
flame careening off the walls within the grotto of my skull.

Once there was a yin/yang wizard who could perform great feats
of magic that drew power from the balanced forces of the universe.
Sometimes he worked for the sake of good, and when that enjoyed
too great an abundance he worked for the sake of evil. Swinging
like a pendulum between the two extreme states of human nature,
he spent his years conjuring and casting spells. His methods were
always the same. A pilgrim would travel into the desert and visit
his cave. That individual would ask him for assistance with some

life problem. If the wizard decided to help, he would turn to a great fire that roared at the back of his cave and call for his ghostly assistants to bring him his blowpipe. Turning whatever spell he was performing into a story, he'd speak it, so that none could hear it, into the glass blowing tube. In this way, when he was finished, the tale of his magic would be trapped within a rose-colored bubble. He didn't use ordinary glass, but instead his raw material was enchanted ice, crystal tears, and diamonds fallen from the moon. The pilgrim requesting the service would then have a spell cast in his or her behalf, which would invariably work, and would then be given the glass bubble containing the story of their spell, which they were expected to hide in a safe place. If anything happened to that globe, the spell would be broken. One thing remained: the pilgrim never knew if the spell cast by the wizard was one of a positive or a negative nature.

It was to this very wizard that Cassius Cake came in the twenty-third year of his life. He had traveled the world, searching for release from the pain of an unrequited love. From Paris to Istanbul to Peking, he wandered the globe trying to outrun his sorrow, searching for some method or elixir by which he might again be able to feel anything but heartache. Nothing was able to help him. It seems that he had fallen in love with a young woman, Judith Sochell, who worked in the kitchen on his father's estate. She was stunningly beautiful, and he greatly admired the delicate little creatures and people she was capable of creating from folded paper. Judith also had feelings for Cassius, but when Cake's mother noticed him spending an inordinate amount of time in the kitchen and eventually caught wind of the budding romance, she bribed the girl to tell her son she did not love him. Judith dared not lose her job as too many at home depended upon her salary, so she complied with the old woman's plot. On the very day she gave Cassius the brush-off, he fled home and booked passage on a steamship.

Two years of anguish had passed for Cake before he finally came to the cave in the desert. He begged for a cure, and the yin/yang wizard called for his blowpipe. The spell he cast upon Cake was one in which he took the young man's soul and placed it within a many-colored bird of beautiful plumage. Instantly Cake's heartache dissipated, and for the first time in years he had a clear thought. In fact, his thinking processes were many times clearer now, for with the relief of his anguish also had come the negation of his emotions. He left the cave with the remarkable bird in a cage and the rose-colored bubble in his pocket. On his travels back home, he encountered the world with an exponentially increased intellect, and it was then that he learned that war was coming and that drugs for use on the battlefield would be worth a fortune.

He invented Orixadoll, a mixture of the narcotics he himself had tried during the two-year-long international quest to ease his pain. His special elixir helped many soldiers to survive, even though they returned home horribly addicted. Black market sales of Orixadoll on the streets of his own country far outweighed what he made from sales to the military. He became wealthier than his father ever was. And, because it was a time period when the respectable needed to be married in order to move in certain circles of high society, he wed. Letti Mane had not always been a self-interested windbag, but after the ceremony it soon became clear to her that Cassius didn't love her; she was merely a decoration. He obviously cared more for the strange bird that was the sole inhabitant of an enormous aviary he'd had constructed on the grounds of his estate.

Cake was not happy, but happiness did not enter his mind. What filled his thoughts were new methods for increasing profit. This he did exceptionally well until one day when he found in the top drawer of an old dresser amid useless keys, stopped watches, and foreign coins a tiny, delicate woman made of yellow paper. The sight of this nudged his memory. It wasn't an emotion he felt, just a dull, distant pain, like the ghost of a toothache from a long-missing false tooth. Later that month, he tracked down Judith Sochell, who was by this time married with one child, Emily's mother. He sent her large sums of cash in exchange for origami. He would send a note as to what he wanted, she would create it, send it back, and he would forward her a stack of money.

Emily blinks and the bird of fire she momentarily believes she sees emanating from the broken glass bubble vanishes into mist. She rubs her eyes and takes a few deep breaths. Then she helps Vincent to his feet and leads him out of the dragon's mouth grotto and back into the tunnel. As she makes her way carefully up the dark passageway, with him stumbling behind, he tells her he's had a dream. "What was it?" she asks. "About my old man," he says. "In it we leave him and he goes away on a journey. He's gone a long time and he travels far until one day he comes to a cave in the desert where there's a man with a long mustache, smoking a cigarette, surrounded by ghosts. By the light of a huge fire that burns wildly at the back of the cave, this weird guy does magic on my father. With his bare hand he reaches through my old man's chest and removes a large turquoise feather from inside. 'Now there's room for your heart to grow back,' he says. My old man smiles and . . . that's all I remember."

At the end of the underground tunnel, they crawl back up into the mausoleum, and as they do, Emily notices that the marble lid to Cake's tomb has cracked and fallen in two large pieces onto the floor. The friends lean over and peer inside. Emily says, "Like your dream," and points into the remains at a feather, trapped by the rib cage where the heart is meant to be.

Vincent, who has begun to come around, nods and says, "Look

here," and reaches into the tomb to grab a skeletal wrist. As he lifts it, the bony fingers open, and a handful of creatures and figures made of folded paper fall out—a bird, a woman, a mushroom, a boy with a bow and arrow, a ship, and finally one of a yin/yang wizard, who spoke this story into glass.

PRESENT FROM THE PAST

After my mother finally quit drinking, she entered a brief epoch of peace in her life. Gone were the paranoia, the accusations, the belittlements, the bitter rage of judgment, the look of fear. For years, nearly every day a lost weekend, she had been possessed by the dark amber ghast of gag-sweet Taylor Cream Sherry. Living with her back then had been like living with a vampire whose bite drained but never conferred immortality. What eventually brought about her unexpected exorcism, I can now only guess, but when she resurfaced she was quiet and ready to laugh. She was watching and listening.

One day in the spring of her new self, she asked my father to go out and buy lumber for her. She told him that she wanted to do some woodcarving. My father purchased the planks she requested along with chisels, rasps, and other necessary tools. She set about her task, working on the picnic table beneath the cherry tree in the backyard, laying the boards flat and gouging away at them. She told me over the phone that her subject was the stations of the cross—Christ's fourteen-part journey to his own crucifixion. Each of the planks would bear a different tableau.

"When I'm done with the boards, I'm going to have your father make them into a bus shelter with a little bench attached inside," she said.

"Yeah, what are you going to do with it?" I asked.

"Sit in it and drink my coffee in the evening," she said.

A couple months later, Lynn and the boys and I drove to Long Island to visit my parents. From the kitchen window, I saw the bus shelter assembled beneath the giant oak at the back of their property. That evening, while Lynn took our two boys for a walk down to the school field, I sat with my mother inside her creation. We smoked and drank coffee, while my father sat facing us in a lawn chair.

The small structure had a slanted roof and its walls were painted the same redwood stain as the picnic table. The hand-carved figures that lined the inside were more crudely rendered than I had imagined they would be. They had no faces, just ovals, dug out and painted white. However, the folds of Christ's flowing garments were more detailed, as was the grain of the cross and the Roman soldiers' armor and helmets. In painting them, she'd used very bright colors—sunflower yellow, neon lime, sky blue, hot pink— that appeared resilient against the redwood stain. I had to duck slightly to fit inside and the bench held room for only two.

"You should have been here the day we finished putting that thing together," said my father. "A couple of weekends ago. It was a bright day but the wind was really blowing strong. Branches all over the streets. I finished nailing the roof and stood it upright in the middle of the yard. We stepped back to look at it, and then this enormous gust of wind came, got under it, and lifted it about ten feet in the air." My father's eyes were wide behind his glasses and he was looking up, his hands apart in front of him, one holding his coffee, one a cigarette. "Remarkable," he said.

My mother was staring off toward the clothesline, smiling. "It landed here," she said.

"Right on this spot," said my father, "so I anchored it down."

"That's some wind," I said.

"It was a strong wind," said my father. He took a drag of his cigarette. "This thing's nothing but a big wooden envelope and the wood is pretty thin. But it still surprised the shit out of me when it happened."

Throughout the remainder of that spring, my mother wrote a film script on the old manual typewriter in the room she called her office at the back of the house. In June she bought a used Super 8 camera and some film. By early July she had learned how to use it and began casting parts for her production.

"It's about a bullfighter," she said. She had called to see if I wanted a part. "It's got a Spanish theme."

I was unable to make the trip the Saturday of the filming, and didn't get to see the finished movie until September. We all sat in the dining room on the braided rug, facing a movie screen my father had found at the curb somewhere on trash day. Of course, since it was made with a Super 8 camera, the film was silent, but it was in color. For background music, my mother had taken the opening from the Motown hit, "I Heard It Through the Grapevine," and somehow created, on audio tape, an endless loop of just those jaunty, slightly sinister, first bars.

The film was shot right outside the back door of my parents' house on Pine Avenue, and nearly every family member had a part. Along the wall where the garage extends was hung a hand-painted backdrop of hundreds of faces in a stadium. Onto the screen walked Don Diego, portrayed by my portly brother, Jim, wearing a matador's costume and a penciled-in twirl of a mustache. Each of my two brothers-in-law played one end of the bull. After the great Don Diego slew the bull in the arena, he went to the fortuneteller—

my grandmother Nan—first glimpsed through a blazing fire. She wore a mantilla, a black shawl, and laughed wickedly. As she read the tarot deck for the bullfighter, she turned over the Death card. This caused Don Diego to lose all self-confidence, and a rival matador—my sister Dolores, dressed as a man—vied for the top spot in the arena and for the heart of Don Diego's mistress—my sister-in-law Patty—who clenched a long-stemmed red rose in her teeth. My brother's oldest boy, Jimmy, played a wooden religious statue that came to life; my father did a turn on the dance floor, wearing a gaucho hat with dingle balls; the bull returned from the dead for one last duel in the sun; and Don Diego regained his courage in the melodramatically protracted moment of his death just before the film ran out and slapped the projector.

That evening, on the very barbecue grill that had held the fortuneteller's veiling flame, my father created his meal of many meats—sausage, steak, chicken, hamburgers, and hot dogs. We all stood, sons and daughters, spouses and grandchildren, in the cool September twilight, holding grease-smeared paper plates, assiduously chewing. Nan sat in her lawn swing, smiling, a glass of wine tipped in her wobbly grip, threatening to spill. My mother played "Until the Real Thing Comes Along" on her guitar, and my father told stories about Kentucky, when he was stationed at Fort Knox, especially of the crumbling mansion that held a library.

"The place had four floors of bookshelves," he said. "And the librarians were these two ancient sisters, both blind, who knew where every book was."

One night after dinner, in November of the same year, my mother had a difficult time catching her breath. She admitted to my father that she had been experiencing this for a month or two but never quite as bad. He immediately called an ambulance. At the hospital, they found a tumor like a tree branch growing up out of her lungs and blocking her breathing passage. After the operation to remove the tumor, my mother began a series of chemotherapy and radiation treatments. The prognosis, however, was terminal. The initial treatments almost killed her, but she managed to survive them and fight back for almost two years.

Throughout this new struggle, I visited as often as I could, but I lived quite a distance away in South Jersey. Lynn and I both worked and we had the two young boys to look after. So I called my mother on the phone every day. Sometimes she didn't have much to say while other days we would talk for more than an hour. She often told me how tired she was and, occasionally, she told me her dreams, unsettling scenarios like the one in which she walked with the spirits up Pine Avenue in the rain. For a brief period of a couple months, she fumed with anger, trying to pick fights with me over everything from politics to parenting. I managed to "keep it light," as my father would say.

During one of her frequent stays in the hospital, well after it was obvious she wasn't going to make it, I went to visit her. It was the middle of the day, and the ward she was on was particularly quiet. She was sleeping when I arrived, so I sat down in the chair next to her bed. For a long time I stared out the window, watching the breeze in the leaves of the birches that lined the bay road. At the end of the road was a dock where I had once kept my clam boat years earlier before I had gone to college. I remembered the flats across the bay, the red-winged blackbirds, the cattails, and the sun on the water.

When I turned back toward her, she was awake and quietly watching me. She looked very frail. I took her hand, and she told me, "I'm not afraid of dying." We sat in silence for quite a while. Then I told her everything I could remember about my days clamming on the Great South Bay. She lay there smiling as I recounted those days, all of it except the one about the Trentino boy who had drowned scratch-raking in the flats. He had stepped in a sink hole, gotten stuck, and then the weather had turned bad, the tide had come up. My mother knew that story, though, and when I fell silent I wondered if, by my omission, I had caused her to remember it.

"You remind me of your father, right now," she said.

There were instances when I found myself detached from my emotions and could almost marvel at the complexity of her disease, as if the slow-motion process of her organic demise might offer some elusive truth. This variety of cancer, *oat cell* it was called, usually spreads from the lungs to the brain. The brain feels nothing, though. Once in the brain the cancer does its work painlessly, methodically shutting down the controls of the vital organs. What amazed me was that it was slow to scramble my mother's reasoning. She was conscious and could talk, with some effort, for quite a while.

My father brought her home and set up her hospital bed in the back room that had once been her office where she wrote her stories and painted. She was weak and slept much of the time, but when she was awake, propped up on pillows and accepting visitors, she exuded a strange contentment. She laughed a good deal and her silence drew honesty from those who came to see her. But the aperture of clarity through which she communicated closed a little more each week, until finally she could only take your hand and mumble a phrase that made no sense. One afternoon while I was there she told my sister, Mary, "You're bad at bad," and a while later told us both, "Chihuahua Mexicawa."

I saw much more of my brother and sisters during those months than I had in a long time. Jim was a year older than me, married, and had three boys. He lived only two towns away from my parents and was very close to my father, having followed in his footsteps and become a machinist. Our lives had gone in different directions, and we hadn't talked much in the intervening years since I had left home. While we conducted our deathwatch, he spoke a great deal, in a very self-assured manner. These utterances were more proclamations than any attempt to really communicate.

One evening, when we were all at the house during one of our weekend visits, I reached a point where the sight of my mother wasting away in that hospital bed, in that cramped room, became too much for me. I stepped away and went outside, around the corner of the house, to stand by the chimney where the irises always grew in spring. It was dark enough, so I took out a joint and lit up as surreptitiously as possible. Just as I was taking a big hit, Jim came around the corner. He saw me and stopped.

He shook his head and quietly laughed. "What the hell are you doing?"

"Catching a buzz."

Then he stepped up close to me, put his arm around my shoulders, and hugged me. It lasted only seconds, and I was startled.

"I'm going out for some beer," he said. "Let's sit at the picnic table tonight and have a few."

"Okay," I said, and we did. In the shadow of the cherry tree, moonlight slipping through, he interweaved tales of personal success at work with smatterings of his fundamentalist, Lutheran dogma. His church had him interpreting the Book of Nehemiah. I nodded and drank one beer after another.

My sister Mary was six years younger than me. She was also married and had two boys. They lived in Brooklyn. Mary could easily cry or laugh at any situation, and often did both within a matter of seconds of one another. Both she and her husband, Jerry, were artists. He was into realism, creating very fine line drawings, whereas Mary made huge abstract paintings, amalgamations of colors that had never before met each other on canvas. Later, Mary's creativity changed direction; the last time I visited their place, set all about the house were writhing amorphous lumps formed from chicken wire and papier-mâché.

My father was so dedicated to the care of our mother that he wouldn't eat properly. When we would take him out to the local diner to make him eat, Jerry'd stay at the house with the children— seven boys in all. They all usually played a game of Wiffle ball in the backyard. If the boys got too raucous, Jerry would threaten, "If you don't calm down, I'm going to have to have another beer." By the time we'd arrive home from dinner, Jerry would be crocked, passed out on the living room lounger, and the boys would be sitting quietly watching a video.

In the last days before my father was forced to return my mother to the hospital, a mouse was spotted in the house, and I had a dream that it was a projection of my mother's will, allowing her buried consciousness to dart around and overhear our conversations. One night I felt the little creature run the entire length of my body while I was sleeping on the couch. When I told Mary about my theory, she neither laughed nor cried, but merely nodded her head, and in earnest said, "Maybe."

Dolores, the youngest of us siblings, was only a few years out of college, but she faced this family challenge head-on, and, more than any of us save my father, actually took on the grim practical tasks. She dealt with the nurses who came to the house in the morning and at night, making sure they turned our mother often to prevent bedsores. When the nurses failed to show, Dolores took over their tasks. Perhaps it was Dolores's degree in philosophy that gave her the strength, though I doubt it. Her husband, Whitey, was an engineer, who I once watched sink 113 putts in a row on a roll-out green in his living room. He'd never before touched a golf club.

One night, after the boys were bedded down in their sleeping bags and most of the grown-ups had also retired, Dolores stood in the kitchen, hip propped against the drain board (my mother's drinking spot from the old days), and, leaning toward me across the narrow room, whispered: "This nurse down the hall with the white nail polish and frizzed hair"—pointing with her finger close to her body—"she's a trip. Real trailer trash, but a good nurse. She knows what she's doing." Dolores spoke so low then I had to turn my head to catch her words. "She told me she saw *the coffee*."

"She saw 'the coffee'?" I said.

"She told me that when people are very close to dying, they vomit up this brown grainy stuff that's known as *the coffee*. She said she saw the coffee."

"Man," I said and grimaced.

Dolores just shook her head, which then gave way to silent laughter. Her attempts to suppress her giddiness made me laugh too. When we regained control, she wiped her eyes and said, in a normal voice, "Could you possibly . . .?"—one of my mother's stock phrases from the days of wine and no roses.

Below the surface of this forced, seemingly amiable family reunion, there were secret tensions swirling. Mary's husband got fed up with my brother's decrees. When Jerry refused to carry out an order, Jim quietly offered to break his arm. Dolores was mad at Lynn, my wife, because, as a nurse, Lynn felt the care that my mother was receiving in the hometown hospital wasn't the best. But no one wanted to hear it, especially Dolores, who had been working hard with what she had been handed. There were recriminations, judgments, clashes of style that lived only until they were voiced to my father, who crushed them one by one, like ants in the kitchen, with a single word—"Bullshit." I, of course, laid low, my specialty perfected in childhood.

After she returned to the hospital for the last time, my mother soon fell into a coma that lasted for weeks. When I would think of her there, I always envisioned her room filled with bright sunlight and a view of the trees along the bay road. I never thought of her in the dark. To preserve this image, I never went to visit her during those final days. Dolores would call and complain to me that the nurses ignored our mother. "I'm afraid she'll die of thirst," she said. But I continued to make up excuses why I couldn't drive up to Long Island. No matter what I told him, my father always said, "Don't worry. I'll tell you if anything changes."

Then, in the middle of a particularly beautiful spring day, I took the boys out in the double stroller and we walked through the park and around the lakes. On our journey, passing through a small tract of woods, we came across a woman in a long raincoat and a man with a bow and a quiver of arrows strapped to his back. He looked a little like the actor Charles Bronson. A target with a bull's-eye was set up against a tree no more than four feet from where the guy stood. While the woman smoked a cigarette and watched, he shot arrows into the target. I said hello to them as we passed, and the man turned and made an angry face at us. The weirdness of the people and the presence of the bow frightened me, and I picked up the pace.

"What the hell was that all about?" I said, once we were out of the woods.

"Robin Hood," said Jack, the older of the two boys.

After we arrived back home and I was letting us into the house, the phone started ringing. It was Jim. "Mom's gone," he said, and in that instant, I pictured inside her mind, like a chamber in a deep cave, a candle going out.

On the afternoon of the wake, the immediate family was allowed a private viewing time before the other mourners arrived. My brother and sisters and I went with my father. We stepped into the parlor, made claustrophobic with floral wallpaper and dim light. I could look at my mother for only a second or two at a time. To me she was a frowning void in a turquoise dress. My father turned away and stepped to the back of the parlor. Facing the wall, he let out a sound I have never heard another person make. It was like the cry of an animal. Then his shoulders moved slightly and I could tell he was weeping. I wanted to approach him, but I could almost see an impenetrable aura around him that I knew I would never be able to pass through. A few minutes later, he dried his eyes and turned around to face the casket.

Through the entirety of my mother's illness, I had never seen my father show any emotion. Whatever needed to be done, he did. He always kept it light with my mother and never complained. Trying to continue at his job, taking care of her at home, the sleepless hours the nights the nurses failed to come, all had physically depleted him. He forgot to eat regularly and grew so thin we started referring to him as Gandhi. There were times when he was absolutely zombielike, stooped over, haggard, but somehow he continued to function.

When my brother and I were very young, our father took us out in the bay in an aluminum rowboat. He rowed way out by Captree Bridge. The water started to get choppy and the wavelets were slapping the prow, spraying water on us. Only minutes passed before the wind started to howl and the weather really got nasty. My father manned the oars—I can see the sleeves of his shirt rolled up over his biceps—and started rowing like a machine. There was never a look of concern on his face, even though we were heading against the wind. He held a lit cigarette in the corner of his mouth, and rowed steadily with great determination until we reached the shore three quarters of an hour later. When we landed, he said, "That was a little hairy." No matter how many short jabs to the head he had sustained through my mother's illness, no matter how many body shots or pummelings in the corner, I knew that relentless oarsman was at work inside him, pulling for shore.

One night back at the beginning of my mother's final decline, before any of us could know just how bad it was going to get, I found my father, at two in the morning, down in the basement—

his new smoking lounge. Sitting in his bathrobe on a folding chair, beneath a bare bulb, surrounded by the chaos of Christmas decorations, Mary's abstract paintings, mildewed books, and broken furniture, he pointed upstairs with the two fingers holding the burning cigarette and said to me, "I have to do this right."

Throughout the days of the wake, strange occurrences were reported in my parents' house. The television would turn itself on and off at will. This I personally witnessed, sitting in the living room at midnight drinking a beer. I was nowhere near the remote, and the television came on with a loud buzz to show a field of static snow. There were also strange knocking sounds in the walls, phone calls with only silence at the other end of the line, sudden cold breezes that blew down the hall, and photographs brushed off the wall.

These uncanny events brought to mind a student, an older Chinese woman, I had taught in a composition course a few years earlier, who had revealed to me her recipe for bird-spit soup. Mrs. Fan had written a paper about her husband's death, in which she told how it was important, each night for a month following the death of a loved one, to stand at the table when dinner was served and moan loudly for a few minutes. This kept the loved one's spirit centered, so as it waited for passage to the next world, it would not become confused and wander off on this earth to become a frustrated ghost.

The wake made me realize that it was so named because all one wanted to do was *wake* from it. Nothing I had ever experienced had been so much like a dream. Minutes became hours in the presence of the dead. In that flower-choked room, like a vault at the bottom of the ocean, people I had not seen or thought of in years approached me from every direction. I shook hands with guys I had lost track of in junior high school, relatives from Oklahoma I had met once when I was three. I could have sworn some of the older folks I chatted with had died years back. Mary and I called the two viewings each day the "matinee" and the "evening show."

The morning of the burial a small service was held at the funeral home before the casket was taken to the church for "a critical mass," as my father called it. At the gathering in the wake parlor, people were invited to share remembrances of my mother, read poems, and so on. My father had asked me to read a Tennyson poem he and my mother were fond of, "Crossing the Bar." I agreed even though it didn't seem like a very good choice to me. As I took the little red book in my hands and stepped up in front of the mourners, I was thinking instead of lines from Tennyson's "In Memoriam": "Time a maniac scattering dust, Life a fury slinging flame." I suddenly became aware that I was two lines into "Crossing the Bar." Something inside me gave way, like a flywheel snapping, and I put the book down on the table in front of me, excused myself, and left the room.

The next thing I knew I was outside the funeral home, and Lynn was standing in front of me. The day was cool and beautiful.

"I couldn't do it," I said.

"I know," she said. "That's okay. Do you feel all right?"

I lit a cigarette and shook my head. "Lame."

"Don't worry," she said, "your brother jumped up, grabbed the book, and finished the reading."

We both laughed, but I had a brief memory flash of being sick as a child, dizzy and weak, calling to my mother from the top of the stairs. I started to pass out, and the last thing I saw was Jim charging up the steps to catch me as I fell forward.

Lynn asked me if I wanted to go back inside.

I flicked the butt away. She took my hand and we returned to the parlor.

The church was a vaulted rib cage of wooden beams, frozen saints subtly winking in the stained-glass light of Christ's stations,

dolorous music, and incense-laden intonations mixed with muffled groans and sniffles. In all, a blur to me, save for the heft of the
casket on the way out to the hearse. It was only then, when we slid
my mother's shiny canoe into the back of the car, that my senses
returned.

Lynn and I and our two boys rode in a limo along with my
parents' neighbors from across the street, Dan and Rose Curd-
meyer. Old Dan was blotto, eyes red, hands quivering, reeking of
VO; when the car took a sharp turn, he'd lean way over. Each time,
Rose straightened him up nonchalantly, while recounting in her
brogue stories of her adventures with Nan and my mother. The
cemetery was some distance out on Long Island, the trip was slow,
and the car hot as hell. Without warning, my son Jack puked on
the black leather seat. Dan's eyes widened for a moment, he burped,
and Rose merely said, "The poor darlin'."

A high chain-link fence surrounded the cemetery. A few hundred
yards down the road from the entrance stood an abandoned strip
joint whose sign still clearly read INN OF A THOUSAND EYES. The
grounds of the cemetery were vast, green lawns rolling into the distance, here and there sprouting rows of gravestones. The procession
of cars wound through the grounds and then stopped a quarter of a
mile inside the gate at a spot where tree-lined roads intersected.

Cemetery employees—men and women dressed in black uni-
forms, like tuxedos—herded us about, and at one point had our
entire immediate family, and then the extended family, line up. A
woman carrying a huge armful of yellow roses walked down the
line and distributed a flower to each of us. When our turn came,
we were to walk forward and toss our flower onto the casket, which
hovered, as if by magic, over the open grave.

Jack, who was feeling better by then, held my hand as we moved
up in line. He pulled at my jacket and I looked down. He was pointing at my flower.

"Pink," he said.

I nodded to him. He moved his arm slowly so that it scanned the other mourners in our line. Then I realized what he was trying to tell me. The rose I had been given, from the dozens that had been distributed, was the sole pink one.

"We win," he whispered.

I put my finger to my lips and gave his hand a squeeze.

Following the funeral, there was a party back at the house on Pine Avenue. I spent the afternoon hanging out in the backyard, eating potato salad, drinking beer, and talking to cousins I hadn't seen in years. Charlie, who was studying Chinese herbal medicine, told me how to make a hallucinogen from crushing and boiling locust shells. Dylan described to me the plot of Whitley Strieber's alien abduction book, *Communion*. My uncle Darrel, who sold insurance and worked part-time as a Walt Whitman impersonator, raked his fingers through his great gray beard and lectured me about quitting smoking. Eventually, everybody but my sisters went home. My father had disappeared into his room and fallen asleep fully clothed on the bed. Dolores offered to wake him before Lynn and I and the kids left for South Jersey, but I told her not to.

Two days later, I called my father to see how he was getting along. He told me that the night of the funeral he woke up with a splitting headache, so he went down into the basement to have a cigarette.

"There's a good idea," I said.

"It didn't help. The pain was really bad, I could hardly see. I went upstairs, found the Tylenol and took about half a bottle of them."

"Jeez," I said.

"I know," he said. "It seemed like a good idea at the time. But it made me feel dizzy, so I decided to go out in my car and drive around with the window open."

"Hey, why not?" I said.

"I felt like I was going to pass out, so I pulled the car over and parked. *Then* I passed out."

"How long were you out for?" I asked.

"Not long, a couple of minutes maybe. I realized I hadn't eaten in about three days, so I drove to the all-night deli and bought a half pound of turkey breast."

"How was the driving?" I asked.

"A little wobbly."

"You're insane," I said.

"I ate that turkey like a sideshow geek," he said. "Right in front of the store."

"Did anybody see you?"

"Who gives a shit? I stumbled to the car, got back in, and drove home."

"What then?"

"I went to bed and woke up the next morning."

"You're lucky," I said.

"Yeah, sure, but wait a second . . . By morning I was feeling fine. I made a pot of coffee and took a cup outside and sat on the back stoop. It was a nice day. I was just sitting there, thinking, when suddenly I heard this loud cracking sound. I thought maybe the neighbor behind us was working on his house. A few minutes passed, and then I heard it again, only louder. I looked up and saw some twigs and crap fall out of the oak tree in the back. I looked closer and noticed it was swaying slightly. And then there came a sound of splintering wood and a crack so loud I jumped! I watched that giant oak tree break nine-tenths of the way to its base and just fall. It crushed the tool shed, blasted apart your mother's bus stop thing, and sheared off one side of the cherry tree."

"What do you think happened? That's a lot of tree."

"Must have died," he said.

"What, termites?" I asked.

"No," he said. "I'm sure it died of a broken heart."

A few days later Dolores phoned in her report.

"Did you hear about the tree?" she asked.

"Yeah," I said.

"Dad went out and bought this set of four gas-powered chain saws. One of them will even cut through metal. He said he could break out of a bank vault with it. He's busy taking the tree apart. That's all he does. He's cutting it up into these perfect little wheels, each about five inches in width and then cutting them each into four wedges."

"He told me it died of a broken heart," I told her.

"You should see the inside of it," she said. "I was there the other day. I'm telling you, it's riddled with the most amazing little tunnels. They run all throughout the tree. It's like lace inside. Like a work of art," she said.

"What's that all about?" I asked.

"How do I know? At least he's got something to keep himself busy."

I called my father every couple days for a while, and then he told me not to call him so often because he didn't have that much to say. He promised me that we would talk every Sunday morning. During our weekly conversation about two months after the tree came down, he told me he had finished cutting it up. All he needed to do now was pull the root out of the ground, and he wanted me to come to Long Island the next weekend and help him if I could.

"That root's probably huge," I said. "How are we going to get it out of there?"

"It's been dead for a while," he said. "We'll dig down around it and cut the roots with the saws. If I can get to the taproot, we can get it out. Your brother has a chain. Once the bole is free, we're going to hook it up to the back of his truck with the chain and pull it out."

"Sounds half-assed," I said. "I'm in."

When I arrived at his house early the next Saturday morning, I let myself in. He was sitting in the dining room with the lights out, drinking a cup of coffee and smoking a cigarette. All of the curtains and drapes were shut tight; the place needed to be vacuumed and dusted. The lawn mower was in pieces on the kitchen floor.

"Are you on the lam or something?" I asked him, opening the living room drapes.

He gave a brief snort. "Welcome to my world."

"Are you ready to give me a hernia?" I asked him.

"Jim's out there already, digging. Go ahead out, I'll be right there."

My brother showed me the stacked wedges of tree, the neatly bundled branches. "He puts only a few yards of it out a week, so the trash guy doesn't get pissed," he told me.

"How's the root?" I asked.

He shook his head and rolled his eyes. "A ball-buster," he said. "I told him we should just pour gasoline on the damn thing and burn it out. But no, we can't burn it."

My father came out and we set to work. I hadn't worked that hard since my days on the bay. It took all morning and well into the afternoon to move the huge tangled knot of wood enough to where my father could get under it with one of his saws. He climbed down into the trench we had dug around it, while Jim and I worked on the other side and pulled back on the loosened bole.

"Make sure you're cutting root and not leg," said Jim, just before my father got the saw going.

Through the saw's smoke and the flying wood chips, we saw my father's face. He had his teeth gritted and his eyes and hair were wild. It was like he was battling a monster. Jim and I looked at each other and started laughing so hard I could barely hold on.

The weight of the bole nearly pulled the bumper off my brother's truck, but we managed to get it out of the hole. It sat in the middle of the backyard like some weird brain sculpture, wooden tentacles twisting together and reaching out. As twilight started to come on, we pulled up lawn chairs around it. Jim went inside and brought out a twelve-pack of beer. We were all dirty and sweating. My father smoked. I tried to think of something to say but couldn't. We just sat there.

When it was barely light enough to see, my father leaned forward in his chair. "What's that?" he said, and pointed at the gnarled behemoth.

"Where?" I said.

He got up and walked over to it. "There's something in here," he said. Turning sideways, he stuck his arm into its tangled center. A few seconds passed while he worked to free whatever it was. Then he pulled out a small wrapped parcel. Walking back to where we sat, he handed it to Jim.

"What's that?" said my father.

Jim pulled away the outer layers of rotted string and tattered wax paper. When he had torn through to what lay beneath the wrappings, he said, "Holy shit, I think I know what this is." He sloughed off the brown dry husk and tossed the object to me. As it landed in my lap, I could see that it was an old black-and-white composition book, a little damp, slightly mildewed, but still intact. I opened the cover and a water bug rolled out onto the ground. The writing on the first page, in the errant script of a child, had been rendered in pencil.

While my father and brother set to making a fire in the barbecue, I sat in the gathering dusk, scanning my own forgotten words. Then night rose up around me, and with its first exhalation, the blue lines, the red margin, the backwards "b"s, the dotless "i"s, all vanished and that book became a clear window into the past. Staring hard through the thin, impenetrable boundary, I saw myself as a spindle-limbed, crew-cut boy in blue pajama bottoms, creeping quietly down the shadowed stairs after midnight. I passed my mother sleeping on the couch, passed the open, empty bottle on the kitchen counter, whose scent was ipecac and cotton candy, and let myself out the back door into the star-filled, cricket heat. Under my arm was a notebook, wrapped in wax paper and string, bound three times to protect the truth. I made my way over wet grass, beneath the lowering cherry tree, to the base of the oak where big roots erupted from underground and formed the opening of a small cave. There, I knelt, and thrust my words deep into the dark unknown.

THE
MANTICORE
SPELL

The first reports of the creature, mere sightings, were absurd—a confusion of parts; a loss of words to describe the smile. The color, they said, was like a flame, a hot coal, a flower, and each of the witnesses tried to mimic the thing's song but none could. My master, the wizard Watkin, bade me record in word and image everything each one said. We'd been put to it by the king, whose comment was "Give an ear to their drollery. Make them think you're thinking about it at my command. It's naught but bad air, my old friend." My master nodded and smiled, but after the king had left the room, the wizard turned to me and whispered, "Manticore."

We watched from the balcony in late afternoon as the king's hunters returned from the forest across the wide green lawn to the palace, the blood of the manticore's victims trailing bright red through the grass. "It's the last one, no doubt," said Watkin. "A very old one. You can tell by the fact that it devours the horses but the humans often return with a limb or two intact." He cast a spell of protection around the monster, threading the eye of a needle with a hummingbird feather.

"You want it to survive?" I asked.

"To live till it dies naturally" was his answer. "The king's hunters must not kill it."

Beneath the moon and stars at the edge of autumn, we sat with the rest of the court along the ramparts of the castle and listened for the creature's flutelike trill, descending and ascending the scale, moving through the distant darkness of the trees. Its sound set the crystal goblets to vibrating. The ladies played hearts by candlelight, their hair upswept and powdered. The gentlemen leaned back, smoking their pipes, discussing how they'd fell the beast if the job was theirs.

"Wizard," the king said. "I thought you'd taken measures."

"I did," said Watkin. "It's difficult, though. Magic against magic, and I'm an old man."

A few moments later, the king's engineer appeared at his side. The man carried a mechanical weapon that shot an arrow made of elephant ivory. "The tip is dipped in acid that will eat the creature's flesh," said the engineer. "Aim anywhere above the neck. Keep the gear work within the gun well-oiled." His highness smiled and nodded.

A week later, just prior to dinner, at the daily ritual in which the king assessed the state of his kingdom, it was reported that the creature had devoured two horses and a hunter, took the right leg of the engineer's assistant, and so twisted and crumpled the new weapon of the engineer that the poison arrow set to strike the beast turned round and stabbed its inventor in the ear, the lobe of which now looked like molten candle wax.

"We fear the thing may lay eggs," said the engineer. "I suggest we burn the forest."

"We're not burning down the forest," said the king. He turned and looked at the wizard. Watkin feigned sleep.

I helped the old man out of his chair and accompanied him down the stone steps to the corridor that led to our chambers. Before I let him go, he took me by the collar and whispered, "The spell's weakening, I can feel it in my gums." I nodded, and he brushed me aside, walking the rest of the way to his rooms unassisted. Following behind, I looked over my shoulder, almost positive the king was aware that his wizard's art had been turned against him.

I lay down in my small space off the western side of the workroom. I could see the inverted, hairless pink corpse of the hunch monkey swinging from the ceiling in the other room. The wizard had ordered it from Palgeria, or so said his records. When it finally arrived, I could see by his reaction that he could no longer remember what he'd meant to do with it. Eventually, he came to me and said, "See what you can make of this hunch monkey." I had no idea, so I hung the carcass in the workroom.

From the first day of my service to Watkin, five years earlier, he insisted that each morning I tell him my dreams of the previous night. "Dreams are the manner in which those who mean you harm infiltrate the defenses of your existence," he told me during a thunderstorm. It was mid-August, and we stood, dry, beneath the spreading branches of a hemlock one afternoon as the hard rain fell in curtains around us.

During the evening of the day the king's engineer encountered the manticore in the forest, I dreamed I followed a woman through a field of purple flowers that eventually sloped down to the edge of a cliff. Below, an enormous mound of black rock heaved as if it were breathing, and when it expanded I could see through cracks and fissures red and orange light radiating out from within. The dream woman looked over her shoulder and said, "Do you remember the day you came to serve the wizard?"

Then the light was in my eyes and I was surprised to find I was awake. Watkin, holding a lantern up to my face, said, "It's perished.

Come quickly." He spun away from the bed, casting me in shadow again. I trembled as I dressed. For some reason I recalled the time I'd seen the old man pull, with his teeth, the spirit of a spitting demon from the nostril of one of the ladies of court. Unfathomable. His flowered robe was a brilliant design of peonies in the snow, but I no longer trusted the sun.

I stepped into the workroom as Watkin was clearing things from the huge table at which he mixed his powders and dissected the reptiles whose small brains had a region that when mashed and dried quickened his potions. "Fetch your pen and paper," he said. "We will record everything." I did as I was told. At one point he tried to lift a large crystal globe of blue powder and his thin wrists shook with the exertion. I took it from him just as it slipped from his fingers.

Suddenly, everywhere, the scent of roses and cinnamon. The wizard sniffed the air and warned me that its arrival was imminent. Six hunters carried the corpse, draped across three battle stretchers, and covered by the frayed tapestry of the War of the Willows, which had hung in the corridor that ran directly from the Treasury to the Pity Fountain. Watkin and I stood back as the dark-bearded men grunted, gritted their teeth, and hoisted the stretchers onto the table. As they filed out of our chambers, my master handed each of them a small packet of powder tied up with a ribbon—an aphrodisiac, I suspected. Before collecting his reward and leaving, the last of the hunters took the edge of the tapestry and, lifting the corner high, walked swiftly around the table, unveiling the manticore.

I glanced for a mere second and instinctually looked away. While my eyes were averted, I heard the old man purr, squeal, chitter. The thick cloud of the creature's scent was a weight on my shoulders, and then I noticed the first buzz of the flies. The wizard slapped my face and forced me to look. His grip on the back of my neck could not be denied.

It was crimson and shades of crimson. And after I noted the color, I saw the teeth and looked at nothing else for a time. Both a wince and a smile. I saw the lion paws, the fur, the breasts, the long beautiful hair. The tail of shining segments led to a smooth, sharp stinger—a green bubble of venom at its tip. "Write this down," said Watkin. I fumbled for my pen. "*Female manticore,*" he said. I wrote at the top of the page.

The wizard took one step that seemed to last for minutes. Then he took another and another, until he was pacing slowly around the table, studying the creature from all sides. In his right hand he held the cane topped by a carved wizard's head. Its tip was not touching the floor. "Draw it," he commanded. I set to the task, but this was a skill I was deficient at. Still, I drew—the human head and torso, the powerful body of a lion, the tail of the scorpion. It turned out to be my best drawing, but it, too, was terrible.

"The first time I saw one of these," Watkin said, "I was a schoolboy. My class had gone on a walk to the lake, and we'd just passed through an orchard and into a large meadow with yellow flowers. My teacher, a woman named Levu, with a mole beside her lip, pointed into the distance, one hand on my shoulder, and whispered, 'A husband and wife manticore, look.' I saw them, blurs of crimson, grazing the low-hanging fruit by the edge of the meadow. On our way back to town that evening, we heard their distinctive trill and then were attacked by two of them. They each had three rows of teeth chewing perfectly in sync. I watched them devour the teacher as she frantically confessed to me. While I prayed for her, the monsters recited poems in an exotic tongue and licked the blood from their lips."

I wrote down all of what Watkin said, although I wasn't sure it was to the point. He never looked me in the eye, but moved slowly, slowly, around the thing, lightly prodding it with his cane, squinting with one eye into the darkness of its recesses. "Do you see the face?" he asked me. I told him I did. "But for that fiendish smile, she's beautiful," he said. I tried to see her without the smile and what I saw in my mind was the smile without her. Suffice it to say, her skin was crimson as was her fur, her eyes yellow diamonds. Her long hair had its own mind, deep red-violet whips at her command. And then that smile.

"When I was at the age between a man and a boy, there was a young woman who lived in the house next to ours. She had hair as long as this creature's but golden," Watkin said, pointing. "I, a little younger than you, she a little older. Only once we went out together into the desert and climbed down into the dunes. Underground there, in the ruins, we saw the stone-carved face of the hunch monkey. We lay down in front of it together, kissed, and went to sleep. Our parents and neighbors were looking for us. Late in the night while she slept, a wind blew through the pursed lips of the stone face, warning me of *treachery* and *time*. When she woke, she said in sleep she'd visited the ocean and gone fishing with a manticore. The next time we kissed was at our wedding."

"Draw that," he shouted. I did my best, but didn't know whether to depict the manticore or the wizard with her at the beach. "One more thing about the smile," he said. "It continually, perpetually grinds with the organic rotary mechanism of a well-lubricated jaw and three sets of teeth—even after death, in the grave, it masticates the pitch black."

"Should I draw that?" I asked.

He'd begun walking. A few moments later, he said, "No."

He laid down his cane on the edge of the table and took one of the paws in both his hands. "Look here at this claw," he said. "How many heads do you think it's taken off?"

"Ten," I said.

"Ten thousand," he said, dropping the paw and retrieving his cane. "How many will it take off now?" he asked. I didn't answer.

"The lion is fur, muscle, tendon, claw, and speed, five important ingredients of the unfathomable. Once a king of Dreesha captured and tamed a brood of manticore. He led them into battles on long, thousand-link, iron chains. They cut through the forward ranks of the charging Igridots with the artful tenacity his royal highness reserves for only the largest pastries."

"Take this down?" I asked.

"To the last dribbling vowel," he said, nodding and slowly moving. His cane finally tapped the floor. "Supposedly," he said, "there's another smaller organ floating within their single-chambered heart. At the center of this small organ is a smaller ball of gold—the purest gold imaginable. So pure it could be eaten. And if it were, I am told the result is one million beautiful dreams of flying.

"I had an a uncle," said the wizard, "who hunted the creature, bagged one, cut out its ball of gold, and proceeded to eat the entire thing in one swallow. After that, my uncle was sane only five times a day. Always, he had his hands up. His tongue was forever wagging, his eyes shivering. He walked away from home one night when no one was watching and wandered into the forest. There were reports for a while of a ragged holy man but then a visitor returned his ring and watch and told us they had been found next to his head. Once the head was safely under glass, I performed my first magic on it and had it tell me about its final appointment with a manticore.

"Take a lock of this hair, boy, when we're done," he said. "When you get old, tie it into a knot and wear it in your vest pocket. It will ward off danger . . . to an extent."

"How fast do they run?" I asked.

"How fast?" he said, and then he stopped walking. A breeze blew through the windows and porticos of the workroom. He turned quickly and looked over his shoulder out the window. Storm clouds, lush hedge, and a humidity of roses and cinnamon. The flies now swarmed. "That fast," he said. "Draw it."

"Notice," he said, "there is no wound. The hunters didn't kill it. It died of old age and they found it." He stood very silent, his hands behind his back. I wondered if he'd run out of things to say. Then he cleared his throat and said, "There's a point at which a wince and a smile share the same shape and intensity, almost but not quite the same meaning. It's at that point and that point alone that you can begin to understand the beast's scorpion tail. Sleek, black, poisonous, and needle-sharp, it moves like lightning, piercing flesh and bone, depositing a chemical that halts all memory. When stung you want to scream, to run, to aim your crossbow at its magenta heart, but alas . . . you forget."

"I'm drawing it," I said.

"Excellent," he said and ran his free hand over one of the smooth sections of the scorpion tail. "Don't forget to capture the forgetting." He laughed to himself. "The manticore venom was at one time used to cure certain cases of melancholia. There's very often some incident from the past at the heart of depression. The green poison, measured judiciously, and administered with a long syringe to the corner of the eye, will instantly paralyze memory, negating the cause of sorrow. There was one fellow, I'd heard, who took too much of it and forgot to forget—he remembered everything and could let nothing go. His head filled up with every second of every day and it finally exploded.

"The poison doesn't kill you, though. It only dazes you with the inability to remember, so those teeth can have their way. There are those few who'd been stung by the beast but not devoured. In every case, they described experiencing the same illusion—an eye-blink journey to an old summer home, with four floors of guest rooms, sunset, mosquitoes. For the duration of the poison's strength, around two days, the victim lives at this retreat . . . in the mind, of course. There are cool breezes as the dark comes on, moths against the screen, the sound of waves far off, and the victim comes to the conclusion that he or she is alone. I suppose to die while in the throes of the poison is to stay alone at that beautiful place by the sea for eternity."

I spoke without thinking, "Every aspect of the beast brings you to eternity—the smile, the purest gold, the sting."

"Write that down," said Watkin. "What else can you say of it?"

"I remember that day I came to serve you," I said, "and on the long stretch through the poplars, my carriage slowed for a dead body in the road. As the carriage passed, I peered out to see a bloody mess on the ground. You were one of the people in the crowd."

"You can't understand my invisible connection to these creatures—a certain symbiosis. I feel it in my lower back. Magic becomes a pinhole shrinking into the future," he said.

"Can you bring the monster back to life?" I asked him.

"No," he said. "It doesn't work that way. I have something else in mind." He stepped over to a work bench, laid his cane there, and lifted a hatchet. Returning to the body of the creature, he walked slowly around it to the tail. "That was my wife you saw in the road that day. Killed by a manticore—by this very manticore."

"I'm sorry," I said. "I'd think you'd have tried harder to kill it."

"Don't try to understand," he said. He lifted the hatchet high above his head, and then with one swift chop, severed the stinger from the tail of the creature. "Under the spell of the poison, I will go to the summer house and rescue her from eternity."

"I'll go with you," I said.

"You can't go. You could be stranded in eternity with my wife and me—think of that," said Watkin. "No, there's something else I need you to do for me while I'm under the effects of the venom. You must take the head of the manticore into the forest and bury it. Their heads turn into the roots of trees, the fruit of which are manticore pups. You'll carry the last seed." He used the hatchet to sever the creature's head while I dressed for the outdoors.

I'd learned to ride a horse before I went to serve the wizard, but the forest at night frightened me. I couldn't shake the image of Watkin's palm impaled on the tip of the black stinger and his rapidly accruing dullness, gagging, his eyes rolling back behind their lids. I carried the manticore head in a woolen sack tied to the saddle and trembled at the prospect that perhaps Watkin was wrong and the one sprawled on the worktable, headless and tail-less, was not the last. For my protection, he'd given me a spell to use if it became necessary—a fistful of yellow powder and a half dozen words I no longer remembered.

I rode through the dark for a few minutes and quickly had enough of it. I dismounted and thrust my torch into the soft earth of the path. It made a broad circle of light on the ground. I re-trieved the shovel I'd brought and the head. After nearly a half hour of digging, I began to hear a slight murmuring sound com-ing from somewhere nearby. I thought someone was spying from deeper in the forest, and then I realized it was coming from in-side the sack and was paralyzed by fear. When I looked, the smile was facing out. The manticore's eyes went wide, that chasm of a mouth opened, flashing three-way ivory, and she spoke in a foreign language.

I took her out of the sack, set her head in the center of the circle of torchlight, brushed back her hair, and listened to the beauti-ful singsongy language. Later, after waking from a kind of trance brought on by the flow of words, I remembered the spell Watkin had given me. Laying the powder out on the upturned palm of my hand, I aimed it carefully and blew it into the creature's face. She coughed. I'd forgotten the words, so said anything that I recalled them sounding like. Then she spoke to me, and I understood her.

"Eternity," she said and then repeated it, methodically, with the precise same intonation again and again and again. . . .

I grabbed the shovel and continued digging. By the time I had dug a deep enough hole, my nerves were frayed by her repetition. I threw the head into the hole and couldn't fill the dirt in fast enough. When the head was thoroughly buried, its endless phrase still sounding, muffled, beneath the ground, I tamped the soil down and then found an odd-looking green rock, like a fist, to mark the spot for future reference.

Watkin never returned from the place by the sea. After the venom wore off, his body was lifeless. I then became the wizard. No one seemed to care that I knew nothing about magic. "Make it up till you've got it," said the king. "Then spread it around." I thanked him for his insight, but was aware he'd eaten pure gold and now, when not soaring in his dreams, was rarely sane. The years came and went, and I did my best to learn the devices, potions, phenomena, that Watkin had bothered to record. I suppose there was something of magic in it, but it wasn't readily recognizable.

I was able to witness Watkin's fate by use of a magic looking glass I'd found in his bedroom and learned to command. In it I could see anywhere in existence with a simple command. I chose the quiet place by the sea, and there before me were the clean-swept pathways, the blossoming wisteria, the gray and splintering fence board. Darkness was coming on. The woman with golden hair sat on the screened porch in a wicker rocker, listening to the floor boards creak. The twilight breeze was cool against sunburn. The day seemed endless. As night came on, she rocked herself to sleep. I ordered the mirror to show me her dream.

She dreamed that she was at the beach. The surf rolled gently up across the sand. There was a manticore—her crimson resplendent against the clear blue day—fishing at the shoreline with a weighted net. Without fear, the woman with bright hair approached the creature. The manticore politely asked, with smile upon smile, if the woman would like to help hoist the net. She nodded. The net was flung far out and they waited. Finally there was a tug. The

woman with the golden hair and the manticore both pulled hard
to retrieve their catch. Eventually they dragged Watkin ashore,
tangled in the webbing, seaweed in his hair. She ran to him and
helped him out of the net. They put their arms around each other
and kissed.

Now I keep my ears pricked for descriptions of strange beasts in
the heart of the forest. If a horse or a human goes missing, I must
get to the bottom of it before I can rest. I try to speak to the hunters every day. Reports of the creature are vague but growing, and I
realize now I have some invisible connection to it, as if its muffled,
muted voice is enclosed within a chamber of my heart, relentlessly
whispering, "Eternity."

THE
FAT ONE

No shit, I really did quit smoking this time. Now, I know I've said before that I was in the midst of quitting smoking, but, at most, the whole affair never lasted longer than a couple of weeks. At one point I wrote down the dreams I had when I'd leave the nicotine patch on all night—crazy, vivid-as-life CIA conspiracy scenarios with a blue rhinoceros, entire nights crawling along towering roller-coaster tracks, conversations with a bushman of the Kalahari while he mixed, in a cauldron, various liquids from different colored cut-glass bottles, a perfume called Tears of Carthage. Once I even dreamed I stuck my finger in a wall socket and my insides lit up to show I was the devil. But all that foolishness is in the past, because I've been off the butts for a good long time now.

I used the patches again, but this time I didn't leave them on overnight and make a game of it. I played it for real and dutifully stuck with the program. It was rough, but I managed. It's been more than six months now. Not bad, right? The downside was that I just didn't write anything during that time. Nothing. I tried. I sat in my office and stared at the screen, and the more I sat in my office, smelling ghost smoke from the cigs of Christmas Past, the crazier it would make me. I could just about feel that harsh smog hitting the back of my throat. I used pretzel sticks, but they don't light well. So, no writing, just sitting and staring and grinding my teeth. The other problem, and health-wise this was even a bigger issue, I just started eating like mad. I wasn't exactly thin before my ordeal started, but the jinni was out of the bottle, the gloves had come off, and it was mindless munching from sunup to sundown. My plan was to stay off the butts at all costs, and I figured I could deal with the extra weight afterward. But, man. . . .

My food group of choice quickly established itself—the hot dog. Don't bother, I've already contemplated six ways to Sunday the Freudian nature of it. Yes, what Ralph Nader referred to as "America's Most Dangerous Missile." What they make out of the lips, toes, beaks, and whatever else is swept up off the slaughterhouse floor. I'd like to say I ate only the kosher ones, but that would have meant that I'd have had to cook them myself. I had no time to cook, because I had to sit in front of the computer and stare at the screen. So here's how it went down. . . .

I'd get Jack, my older son, who now drives, to go to the store for me and buy me two hot dogs and a bottle of water. We have this kind of convenience store near us, Wawa. If you live in Jersey, you know Wawa. At Wawa the regular hot dogs are pretty lame, more bun than actual dog. But they have a variety and if you're solvent you can up the ante and get something a little more worthwhile. They have these hot sausages, too, but I can't eat them because they're gray verging on yellow—I know, it makes no sense, but take my word for it. They're also spicy, which I'm not crazy about, and the deal breaker was that once I ate one and chewed on what was either a piece of fingernail or a little tooth. So the hot sausage, although more substantial, was out.

My choice of dog was the quarter pounder. That's right, the *Hindenburg* of Wawa processed meat products. Two of those and you were doing a half pound of sodium nitrates (is that the stuff they use for explosives?) and animal by-products with a little food coloring added. This stuff can't be good for you. Even while I was biting into these things, I was picturing a third eye growing in my asshole. It was Russian roulette and I was putting the barrel to my head at least twice a day. I'd become addicted to hot dogs while on the rebound from cigarettes.

Then one day I made a big mistake. Sometimes when I'd send Jack on a trip to the Wawa, he'd get something for himself. He'd often come back with a tall, black can of this stuff called Rockstar. Who knows what that piss is. If I catch a whiff of it the hair on the back of my neck stands up straight. It's supposed to give you energy and has ginseng and something called "guarano" in it (isn't that bat shit?). Anyway, I busted his balls about drinking the Rockstar and told him it was bad for his health. He broke into a smile and shook his head. "Look at you," he said, "the health expert. Gimme a fuckin' break. Maybe I should eat four fatties a day instead." Thus was born the term "fatties" for my quarter pounders.

The next day, I sent Jack on a run for two fatties, and I insisted he put the mustard on this time, since he always forgot in the past. A little while later, he came back and had my two, each in its own little plastic fatty coffin. "Did you get the mustard?" I asked him. "Yes, oh, Prince of Whales," he said. When I opened the first fatty box, that boiled pink reek wafted up and I beheld the quarter pound. The mustard had been applied, so I slipped Jack a couple bucks for a successful run. Then he said, "Read it."

"Read what?" I asked, removing the object of my affection from the container.

"The mustard," he said.

I looked more closely, and there in bright yellow, looping script were the words "Douche Bag."

As time went on, he got better and better with the script. At first it was a steady barrage of profanity. We laughed like hell. Soon enough the curses got tiresome, though, and he started coming up with titles for me—*King ¼ Pound*, *Master of Fat*, *F Is for Fatty*. When he was able to cram neatly onto one dog *High Imam of Immobility*, I knew we were dealing with some kind of real talent.

While my own writing lay fallow, his abilities blossomed. It was somewhere in the middle of my second month off the butts that he did his first mustard drawing—a landscape of a cabin by a lake. From the very beginning his golden art was exceptional. I almost couldn't bring myself to eat it it was so beautiful. He'd gained such dexterity with the mustard bottle, it was amazing. Granted, there were days when he was in a hurry and he'd just scribble, "You Suck!," but a lot of times there were pictures. God, I remember a portrait he did of my wife. If I could have found a frame that size and shape, it'd be hanging on the wall right now. Jack told me that he'd become something of a celebrity down at the Wawa, and that people would gather around him now when he did one of his mustard jobs. He was really into it, taking it to new heights. There was a Jackson Pollock splatter deal that was sheer genius.

I downed those fatties like a fatty eating machine that needed fatty energy on which to run in order to eat more fatties. Even though he could have really gone somewhere with his mustard art, Jack told me one day, "Dude, you're a pile. You gotta stop eating fatties and get some exercise." I blew him off, but after that every fatty that he delivered was inscribed in stark block letters with the phrase EAT YOUR DEATH! I was slow to get on board with what he was saying. I was smoke-free, but my brain was three-fifths pig hoof and jowl by then. He finally told me he wouldn't get me another fatty. I made a deal with him—just one more. One more fat one and then I'd quit and start exercising and walking. He agreed. When he got back from that final Wawa run, he said to me, "Check this out. You hit the jackpot." Then he unveiled it from the bag, cracked open an extra-long plastic coffin, and revealed what was obviously the next step in fatty evolution—what Wawa called the De Lux Dog. As he passed it over to me he said, "Suck on that bad boy." It had to be a foot long and it had melted cheese on it and two long strips of bacon. Written in the clearest, spicy brown script, from north to south, was the word "Nirvana." After I ate it, I was dizzy for half an hour and had a pain in my left kidney.

I walk now every day, long meandering journeys around town, and the open air and the slow rhythm of my zombie steps takes my mind off the butts and the hot dogs and the writing. Every once in a while a car will pull up next to me, the passenger window will slide down, and I'll realize it's Jack. "Keep moving," he yells. "You're almost there." Then the tires screech and he's gone.

THE DISMANTLED INVENTION OF FATE

The ancient astronaut John Gaghn lived atop a mountain, Gebila, on the southern shore of the Isle of Bistasi. His home was a sprawling, one-story house with whitewashed walls, long empty corridors, and sudden courtyards open to the sky. The windows held no glass and late in the afternoon the ocean breezes rushed up the slopes and flowed through the place like water through a mermaid's villa. Around the island, the sea was the color of grape jam due to a tiny red organism that, in summer, swarmed across its surface. Exotic birds stopped there on migration, and their high trilled calls mixed with the eternal pounding of the surf were a persistent music heard even in sleep.

Few ever visited the old man, for the mountain trails were, in certain spots, treacherously steep and haunted by predators. Through the years, more than one reporter or historian of space travel had attempted to scale the heights, grown dizzy in the hot island sun, and turned back. Others simply disappeared along the route, never to be heard from again. He'd seen them coming through his antique telescope, laboring in the ascent, appearing no bigger than ants, and smiled ruefully, knowing just by viewing them at a distance which ones would fail and which determined few would make the cool shade and sweet aroma of the lemon groves of the upper slopes. There the white blossoms would surround them like clouds and they might briefly believe that they were climbing into the sky.

On this day, though, Gaghn peered through his telescope and knew the dark figure he saw climbing Gebila would most definitely make the peak by twilight and the rising of the ringed planet in the east. He wanted no visitors, but he didn't care if they came. He had little to say to anyone, for he knew that Time, which he'd spent a life abusing on deep space voyages sunk in cryogenic sleep and hurtling across galaxies at near the speed of light, would very soon catch up and deliver him to oblivion. If this visitor wanted to know the history of his voyages, he felt he could sum it all up in one sentence and then send the stranger packing. "I've traveled so far and yet never arrived," he would say.

After his usual breakfast of a cup of hot water with the juice of a whole lemon squeezed into it, a bowl of tendrils from the telmis bush, and the still-warm heart of a prowling valru, he tottered off, with the help of a cane, into the lemon grove to sit on his observation deck. He settled his frail body gently into a bentwood rocker and placed upon the table in front of him a little blue box, perfectly square on all sides, with one red dot in the center of the face-up side. His left hand, holding in two fingers a crystal the shape of a large diamond, shook slightly as he reached forward and positioned the point of the clear stone directly above the red dot.

When he drew back his hand, the crystal remained, hovering a hairbreadth above the box. He cleared his throat and spoke a word—"Zadiiz"—and the many-faceted stone began to spin like a top. He leaned back in the rocker, turning his face—a web of wrinkles bearing a grin, a wide nose, and a pair of small round spectacles with pink glass lenses—to the sun. As the chair began to move, a peaceful music of flutes and strings seeped out of the blue box and spiraled around him.

He dozed off and dreamed of the planets he'd visited, their landscapes so impossibly varied, the long cold centuries of frozen slumber on deep space journeys filled with entire dream lives burdened by the unquenchable longing to awake, the wonderful rocket ships he'd piloted, the strange and beautiful aliens he'd befriended, bartered with, eluded, and killed, the suit that preserved his life in hostile atmospheres with its bubble helmet and jetpack for leaping craters. Then he woke for a moment only to doze again, this time to dream of Zadiiz.

He'd come upon her in his youth, on one of the plateaus amid the sea of three-hundred-foot-high red grass covering the southern continent on the planet Yarmit-Sobit. He'd often wondered if it was random chance or destiny that he'd chosen that place at that time of all the places and times in the universe to set down his shuttle and explore. The village he came upon, comprised of huts woven from the red grass, lying next to a green lake, was idyllic in its serenity.

The people of the village, sleek and supple, the color of an Earth sky, were near-human in form, save for a ridged fin that ran the length of the spine, ending in a short tail. They had orange eyes without irises and sharp-edged fingers perfectly suited for cutting grass. In their sensibility, they were more than human, for they were supremely empathetic, even with other species like his, valued friendships, and had no word for "cruelty." He stayed among them, fished with them off the platforms that jutted out over the deep sea of grass for the wide-winged leviathans they called hurrurati, and joined in their ceremonies of smoke and calculation. Zadiiz was one of them.

From the instant he first saw her, flying one of the orange kites crafted from the inflated bladder of a hurrurati on the open plateau, he had a desire to know her better. He challenged her to a foot race, and she beat him. He challenged her to a wrestling match, and she beat him. He challenged her to a game of tic-tac-toe he taught her using a stick and drawing in the dirt. This, he finally won, and it drew a laugh from her—the sound of her joy the most vibrant thing he'd encountered in all his travels. As the days went on, she taught him her language, showed him how to find roots in the rich loam of the plateau and how to wrangle and ride the giant, single-horned porcine creatures called sheefen, and explained how the universe was made by the melting of an ice giant. In return, he told her about the millions of worlds beyond the red star that was her sun.

Eventually the mother of the village came to him and asked if he would take the challenge of commitment in order to be bonded to Zadiiz for life. He agreed and was lowered by a long rope off the side of the plateau into the depths of the sea of red grass. In among the enormous blades, he discovered schools of birds that swam like fish through the hidden world and froglike creatures that braved the heights, leaping from one thick strand of red to another. Even deeper down, as he finally touched the ground where almost no sunlight fell, he encountered large white insects with antennae and six arms each that went about on two legs. He'd hidden his ray gun in his boot, and thus had the means to survive for the duration of his stay below the surface.

Upon witnessing the power of his weapon against a carnivorous leething, the white insects befriended him, communicating through unspoken thoughts they fired into his head from their antennae. They showed him the sights of their secret world, cautioned him to always be wary of snakes (which they called weeha) and took him to stay overnight in the skeletal remains of a giant hurrurati where they fed him a meal of red grass sugar and revealed their incomprehensible philosophy of the sufficient. When he left, they gave him an object they'd found in the belly of the dead hurrurati for which they had no name, although he knew it to be some kind of metal gear. Two days later, the rope was again lowered and he was retrieved back to the plateau. Zadiiz could hardly believe how well he'd survived and was proud of him. During their bonding ceremony, Gaghn placed the curio of the gear, strung on a lanyard, around her neck.

It wasn't long before the astronaut's restlessness, which had flogged him on across the universe, finally returned to displace the tranquillity of life on the plateau. He needed to leave, and he asked Zadiiz to go with him. She courageously agreed, even though it was the belief of her people that the dark ocean beyond the sky was a sea of death. The entire village gathered around and watched as the shuttle carried them up and away. Legends would be told of the departure for centuries to come.

Gaghn docked the shuttle in the hold of his space vessel, the *Empress,* and when Zadiiz stepped out into the metal, enclosed world of the ship, she trembled. They spent some time merely orbiting her planet, so that she might grow accustomed to the conditions and layout of her new home. Then, one day, when he could withstand the impulse to travel no longer, he led her to the cryo-cradle and helped her to lie down inside. He tried to explain that she would experience long, intricate dreams that would seem utterly real, and that some could be quite horrendous, but to remember they were only dreams. She nodded. They kissed by fluttering their eyelashes together, and he pushed the button that made the top of her berth slide down over her. In the seconds before the gas did its work, he heard her scream and pound upon the lid. Then came only silence, and with a troubled conscience, he set the coordinates for a distant constellation and went, himself, to sleep.

Upon waking, light-years away from Yarmit-Sobit, he opened

her cradle and discovered her lifeless. He surmised that a nightmare that attended the frozen sleep had frightened the life out of her. Her eyes were wide, her mouth agape, her fists clenched against some terror that had stalked her imagination. He took her body down to Eljesh, the planet the *Empress* now orbited, to the lace forest at the bottom of an ancient crater where giant, pure white trees, their branches like the entwining arms of so many cosmic snowflakes, reached up into an ashen sky. He'd intended the beauty of this place to be a surprise for her. Unable to contemplate burying her beneath the soil, he laid her on a flat rock next to a milk-white pool, closed her eyes, brushed the hair away from her face, and took with him, as a keepsake, the gear he'd given her.

When he fled Eljesh, it wasn't simply the wanderlust drawing him onward; now he was also pursued with equal ferocity by her memory. He always wondered why he couldn't have simply stayed on the plateau, and that question became his new traveling companion through intergalactic wars, explorations to the fiery hearts of planets, pirate operations, missions of good will, and all the way to the invisible wall at the end of the universe, after which there was no more, and back again.

He knew many, and many millions more knew of him, but he'd never told a soul of any species what he'd done until one night, high in the frozen mountains, near the pole of the Idiot Planet (so named for its harsh conditions and a judgment upon any who would dare to travel there). Somehow he'd wound up in a cave, weathering a blizzard, with a wise old Ketuban, universally considered to be the holiest and most mystical cosmic citizens in existence. This fat old fellow, eyeless but powerfully psychic, looked like a pile of mud with a gaping mouth, four tentacles, and eight tiny legs. He spoke in whispered bursts of air, but spoke the truth.

"Gaghn," said the Ketuban, "you have sorrow."

John understood the language and moved in close to the lumpish fellow so he could hear over the howling of the wind. Once he understood the statement, the sheer simplicity of it, the heartfelt tone of it, despite the rude sound that delivered it, he told the story of Zadiiz.

When he was finished, the Ketuban said, "You believe you killed her?"

Gaghn said nothing but nodded.

"Some would call it a sin."

"I call it a sin," said the astronaut.

The storm outside grew more fierce, and the roar of the gale hypnotized Gaghn, making him drowsy. As he drifted toward sleep, his memory awash with images of Zadiiz, teaching him to fish with spear and rope and tackle, sitting beside him on the plateau beneath the stars, moving around the dwelling they'd shared on a bright warm morning in spring, singing the high-pitched bird songs of her people. Just before he fell into sleep, he heard his cave mate's voice mix with the constant rush of the wind. "Rest easy. I will arrange things."

When Gaghn awoke, the storm had abated and the Ketuban had vanished, leaving behind, on the floor of the cave, a crude winged figurine formed from the creature's mud. He also realized the Ketuban had taken the gear he'd worn around his neck since leaving Zadiiz on Eljesh. As the astronaut made his way cautiously over ice fields fissured with yawning crevices back to his shuttle, he remembered the mystic alien's promise. In the years that followed, though, he found no rest from his compulsion to journey ever farther, nor from the memories that tormented him, and he realized that this must be the fate that was arranged—no peace for him as punishment for his sin.

More memories of his travels ensued as the ancient astronaut woke and slept, the music from the blue box washing over him, the scent of the lemon blossoms and the heat of the sun, his weak heart and failing will to live, mixing together into their own narcotic that kept him drowsy. One last image came: his visit to the laboratory of the great inventor, Onsing, inside the hollow planet, Simmesia. The aged scientist, whose mind was once ablaze with what many considered the galaxy's greatest imagination, was laid low by the infirmity of age, on the verge of death. The sight of this had frightened John, and he'd thought if he went far enough, fast enough, he'd escape the fate the dying inventor assured him in labored whispers came to all.

Then Gaghn woke to the late afternoon wind of the island, saw the ringed planet had risen in the east, and in the failing light, noticed a tall dark figure standing before him.

"I've traveled far and yet never arrived," he said.

The visitor, nearly eight feet tall, as broad as three men, and covered in a long black cloak, the hem of which brushed against the stone of the deck, stepped forward, and the old man saw its face. Not human, but some kind of vague imitation of a human face, like a mask of varnished shell with two dark holes for eyes, a subtle ridge for a nose, and another smaller hole that was the mouth. Atop the smooth head was a pair of horns whose sharp points curved toward each other.

"You may leave now," said the old man.

The tall fellow, his complexion indigo, took two graceful steps forward, stopping next to Gaghn's rocker. The astronaut focused on the empty holes that served as eyes and tried to see if some sign of a personality lurked anywhere inside them. The stranger leaned over and, quicker than a heartbeat, a long tapered nozzle, sharp as the tips of the horns, sprang out of the mouth hole, passed through Gaghn's forehead with the sound of an egg cracking, and stabbed deep into the center of his brain. The astronaut gave a sudden sigh. Then the nozzle retracted as quickly as it had sprung forth. The old man fell forward, dead, across the table, his right arm hitting the blue box sideways, sending the crystal plinking onto the stone floor of the deck.

The indigo figure stepped away from the body and sloughed its long cloak. Once free of the garment, the two wings that had been folded against its back lifted and opened wide. They were sleek, half the creature's height, pointed at the lower tips and ribbed with delicate bone work beneath the slick flesh. Its entire manlike form suggested equal parts reptile and mineral. From down the mountain came the death cry of some creature, from off in the grove came the sorrowful call of the pale night bird, and beneath them both could be heard, in the distance, the persistent pounding of the sea. The visitor crouched, and with great power, leaped into the air. The wings spread out, caught the island wind, and carried him, with powerful thrusts, into the night sky. He flew, silhouetted before the bright presence of the ringed planet from pole to pole, higher and higher, as the figure of John Gaghn receded to a pinpoint, became part of the island, then the ocean, then the night. Hours later, the winged visitor pierced the outer membrane of the planet's atmosphere and was born into space.

The Aieu, people of the jump-bone animal, blended flawlessly with the white trees in the lace forest. A dozen of them—hairless, perfectly pale, crouching still as stone gargoyles among the branches—silently watched the movements of the dark giant. Its wings, its horns, told them it would be a formidable opponent, and they wondered how their enemies had created it. After it had passed beneath them, the elder of their party motioned for the swiftest of them to go quickly and warn the queen of an assassin's approach. The small fellow nodded, and then, on clawed feet, took off, running through the branches, leaping soundlessly from tree to tree, in the direction of the hive. Those who remained behind spread out and followed the intruder, their leader all the while plotting a strategy of offense for the time his force would be at full strength.

Zadiiz, the powder-blue queen, sat in her throne at the center of the hive, the children of the Aieu gathered around her feet. Nearly too feeble with age to walk, let alone run and climb, she could no longer lead the war parties or the hunt as she once had. She was not required to do anything at all as her subjects owed their very existence to her, but she wanted to remain useful for as long as she could, both to pass the time and to set an example. She instructed the young ones on everything from the proper way to employ the deadly jump-bone against a foe to the nature of existence itself, as she saw it. On this day, it was the latter. In her weak voice, quivering with age, she explained:

"Look around you, my dears. All of you, everything you see, the white forest, the gray sky, your distant past, and whatever future we have left, everything is a dream I am dreaming. As I speak to you, I am really asleep in a great vessel, in the clutch of a cradle that freezes the body but not the dream, flying through the darkness above, amid the stars, to a far place where I will eventually awake to be with my life companion, John Gaghn."

The children looked into her orange eyes and nodded, although they could hardly understand. One of the brighter ones spoke up: "And what will become of us when you awaken?"

Zadiiz could only speak the truth. "I'm not sure," she said, "but I'll do everything I can to keep you safe inside my memory. You'll know if I've done this when, if I appear to die, you are still alive." Upon the mention of her own death, the children gasped, but she went on to allay their fears. "I won't have really died, I'll merely have emerged into another dream, or I'll truly have awakened, the vessel having reached its destination." She could see she had confused them and frightened them a little. "Go and think on this for now, and we'll discuss it more tomorrow." The small, dazed faces, which, at one time, back on the plateau of the red grass lands of her own planet, she might have considered ugly, now were precious to her. The children came forward and lightly touched her arms, her legs, her face, before leaving the hive. She watched them scamper out and take to the branches that surrounded her palace in the treetops, and then sat back and tried to understand, for herself, what she had said.

John had warned her that the dreams would come and they would be deep and sometimes terrible, and there were parts of this one she believed herself presently imprisoned in that were, but there was also beauty and the reciprocal love between the Aieu and herself. How many more dream lives would she need to experience, she wondered, before waking? This one began with her opening her eyes, staring up into the pale faces of a hunting party of the people of the jump-bone animal. Later, when she'd come to learn their language, they told her that even though many of them thought her dead when they'd found her lying on the flat stone next to the pool, their herb witch listened closely, placing her ear to the blue queen's ear and could hear, though very weak, the faint murmur of thoughts still alive in her head. Then, slowly, by employing a treatment of their most powerful natural drugs and constantly moving her limbs, they'd brought her around to consciousness.

Zadiiz was roused from her reverie by the approach of one of her subjects. He was agitated and began spouting in the Aieu gibberish before he'd even reached her side. "An intruder, an assassin," he was shouting, waving his needle-sharp jump-bone in the air. She shook her head and put both hands up, palms facing outward to indicate he should slow down. He took a deep breath and bowed, placing his weapon on the floor at her feet. "What is this intruder?" she asked, feeling so weary she could hardly concentrate on his description.

He put the two longest fingers of each of his three-fingered hands, pointing atop his wrinkled forehead. She understood and nodded. He then made as blank an expression as he could with his face, closing his eyes, turning his mouth into a perfect "O." She nodded. When he saw she was following him, he held his right hand up as high as he could and then leaped up to show the stranger's height. Last, he said, "Thula," which meant "deadly." In response, she made a fist, and he responded by lifting his weapon and exiting out upon the treetops to summon the forces of the Aieu.

As old and tired as she was, there still burned within her a spark of envy for those who now swarmed away from the hive to meet the threat of this new enemy. She lit her pipe, ran her hand across the old crone stubble on her chin, and, with a vague smile, found in her memory an image of herself when she could still run and climb and fight. It hadn't taken her long, once the Aieu had brought her around, before she was back on her feet and practicing competing with the best hunters and wrestlers her rescuers had among them. She'd taken to the treetops as though she'd been born in the lace forest, and a few days after they'd demonstrated for her the jump-bone-throwing technique, she was more accurate and deadly with it than those who were still young before the jump-bone animal had been hunted to extinction.

But it was in the war against the Fire Hand that she'd proven herself a general of keen strategic insight and unfailing courage. Utilizing the advantage of the treetops, and employing stealth and speed to defeat an enemy of greater number, she'd helped the Aieu turn back the bloodthirsty hordes that had spilled down over the high lip of the crater and flooded the forest. It was this victory that had elevated her to the status of royalty among them. She drew on her pipe, savoring the rush of imagery from the past. As the smoke twined up toward the center of the hive, a distant battle cry sounded from the forest, and in the confusion of her advanced age, she believed it to be her own.

The victory shouts of the Aieu warriors woke her as they led their prisoner into the hive. The giant indigo creature, wings bound with woven white vine around its chest, hands tied together at the wrists in front, a choker around its muscular neck, strode compliantly forward, surrounded by its captors, who brandished jump-bones above their heads.

"Bring him into the light," commanded Zadiiz, and they prodded the thing forward to stand in the glow of the two torches that flanked her throne. When she beheld the huge indigo form, she marveled at the effectiveness of her battle training on the Aieu, for it didn't seem possible that even all who lived in the treetop complex surrounding the hive could together subdue such a monster. "Good work," she said to her people. Then her gaze came to rest on the emotionless, shell mask of a face with its simple holes for eyes and mouth, and the sight of it startled her. It shared, in its blank expression, the look of another face she could not help but remember.

It was in the dream that had preceded her waking into the lace forest and the people of the jump-bone animal, the first of her sleeping lives that John Gaghn had promised after he'd closed her in the cradle. In this one, she'd lived alone in a cave on a barren piece of rock, floating through deep space. She spent her time watching the stars, noting, here and there, at great distances, the slow explosions of galaxies, like the blossoming of flowers, and listening to endlessly varied music made by light piercing the darkness. A very long time passed, and she remembered the weight of her loneliness. Then one day, a figure appeared in the distance, heading for her, and slowly it revealed itself to be a large silver globe. Smoke issued from its back and it buzzed horribly, interfering with the natural song of the universe.

The vessel rolled down onto the deep sand beside the entrance to her cave. Moments later, a door opened in the side of it and out stepped a man made of metal. The starlight reflected on his shiny surface and he gave off a faint glow. At first she was frightened to behold something so peculiar, but the metal man, whose immobile face was cast in an expression of infinite patience, spoke to her in a friendly voice. He told her his name was 49 and asked if he could stay with her until he managed to fix his craft. Zadiiz was delighted to have the company, and assured him he could.

She offered him some of the spotted mushrooms that grew on the inner walls of the cave, her only sustenance. They tasted to her like the flesh of the hurrurati. 49 refused, explaining that he was a machine and did not eat. Zadiiz didn't understand the idea of a robot, and so he explained that he had been made by a great scientist named Onsing, and that all of his parts were metal. He told her, "I have intelligence, I even have emotion, but I was made to fulfill the need of my inventor, whereas beings like you were made to fulfill your own desires."

"What is your master's need?" asked Zadiiz.

"Onsing has passed on into death," said 49, "but some time ago, while he still lived, he discovered through intensive calculation, using a mathematical system of his own devising and entering those results into a computer that not only rendered answers as to what was possible but also what could, given an infinite amount of time, be probable, that his sworn enemies, the Ketubans, would some day create a mischievous creature that could very likely manipulate the fate of the universe."

Zadiiz simply stared at 49 for a very long time. "Explain 'infinite' and 'probable,'" she finally said.

The robot explained.

"Explain 'fate,'" she said.

"Fate," said 49, and a whirring sound could be heard issuing from his head as he stared at the ground. Sparks shot from his ears. "Well, it is the series of events beginning at the beginning of everything that will eventually dictate what must be. And all you would need to do to change the universe would be to undo one thing that must be and everything would change."

"Why must it be?" she asked.

"Because it must," said the robot. "So, to prevent this, Onsing created a machine of one thousand parts that could, once its start button was pressed, send out, in all directions, a wave across the universe that would eventually find this creature and melt it. When he had finished the machine, he hoped to always keep it running so that it could forever prevent the Ketubans from undermining fate."

"And did he?" asked Zadiiz.

"Poor Onsing never had a chance to start his machine, because it was destroyed by the evil Ketubans, loathsome creatures, like steaming piles of organic waste with tentacles and too many legs. They used their psychic power to automatically disassemble the machine, and all of its individual parts flew away in as many different directions as there were pieces. Onsing, too determined to give up, but knowing he would not live long enough to rebuild the machine or find all of the parts scattered across the universe, created one thousand robots like me to go out into space and fetch them back. Nine hundred and ninety-nine of the robots have found their parts, and they have assembled all of the machine but for one tiny gear that is still missing. That is my part to find, and they wait for my success. Once I find it, I will return with it. It will be fitted into the machine. The robot that has been designed to press the start button on the machine will fulfill its task and the fate of the universe will be protected."

"How long have you searched?" asked Zadiiz.

"Too long," said 49.

Eventually, Zadiiz grew weary, as she always did when eating the mushrooms, and fell asleep. When she awoke, she found that

49 was gone from the cave. She ran outside only to discover that his sphere of a vessel was also gone. Some time later, she realized that the metal gear that had hung around her neck was missing, and the thought of having to live the rest of that lonely dream life without even the amulet's small connection to John Gaghn sent her into shock. Her mind closed in on itself, shut down, went blank. When she awoke, she was surrounded by the pale faces of the people of the jump-bone animal.

She surfaced from her memory, again surrounded by the Aieus' pale faces; this time in the hot and crowded hive. They'd been waiting in expectant silence for her to pronounce the fate of the assassin they'd brought before her. Zadiiz realized she'd had a lapse of awareness, and now tried to focus on the situation before her. She looked the horned figure up and down, avoiding another glimpse at the face. She wondered who could have sent this thing. Because of its unknown nature, its obvious power and size, she could not allow it to live. She was about to order that the creature be drowned in the white pool when she noticed the fingers on its left hand open slightly. Something fell from between them but did not continue on to the floor. It was caught and suspended by a lanyard looped through one of its small openings.

Upon seeing the gear, she gasped and struggled to her feet. The fact that she'd just been thinking of it made her dizzy with its implications. "Where did you get that?" she asked. The implacable face remained silent, but her obvious reaction to the sight of the curio sent a murmur through those assembled. "Who sent you?" she asked. Its eye holes seemed to be staring directly at her. She started down the two steps from her throne, and her people came up on either side to help her approach the creature. As she drew near, she felt a flutter of nervousness in her chest. "Did John send you from his own dream?" she said.

When she was less than a step away from the prisoner, she

reached out for the amulet, and that is when the indigo creature inhaled so mightily the ropes binding its wings snapped. In one fluid motion, it ripped its wrists free of their bonds, the vines snapping away as if they were strands of hair, and took Zadiiz by the shoulders. She was too slow to scream, for he had already leaned forward and the pointed nozzle had shot forth from its mouth. There was the sound of an egg cracking. The Aieu did not recover from their shock until the nozzle had retracted, and by then the creature had torn the lead from its neck and leaped into the air. At the same moment, Zadiiz fell backward into her subjects' waiting arms. Jump-bones were thrown, but the assassin flew swiftly up and out of the opening at the top of the hive.

The indigo creature flew on and on for light-years through space, past planets and suns, quasars and nebulae, black holes and wormholes, resting momentarily now and then upon an asteroid or swimming down through the atmosphere of a planet to live upon its surface for a year or two, and no matter the incredible sights it witnessed in the centuries it traveled its expression never once changed. Finally, in a cave whose walls were covered with spotted mushrooms, on an asteroid orbiting a blue-white star, it found what it had been searching for—a large metallic globe and, sitting next to it upon a rock, a robot, long seized with inaction due to the frustration of its inability to accomplish the task its master had set for it.

Dangling the gear upon its lanyard in front of the eye sensors of the robot, the indigo creature brought the man of metal to awareness. Robot 49 reached up for the gear, and the creature placed it easily into his ball-jointed fingers. The two expressionless faces stared at each other for a moment and then each turned away, knowing what needed to be done. The robot moved to his globe of a space vessel, and the indigo creature sprinted from the cave and spread its wings. Even before the sputtering metal ball had exited the cave and set a course for the hollow world, the indigo creature had disappeared into the vast darkness of space.

On an undiscovered world where a vast ocean of three-hundred-foot-tall red grass lapped the base of a small mountain, the creature landed and set to work. Time, which had passed in long lazy skeins to this point, now was of the essence, and there could be no rest. At the peak of the mountain, the winged being cleared away a tangled forest of vines, telmis, and wild lemon tress, uprooting trunks with its bare hands and knocking down larger ones with its horns. Once the land was cleared, it set about mining blocks of white marble from a site lower down the slope, precisely cutting the hard stone with the nail of its left index finger. These blocks were flown to the peak and arranged to build a sprawling, one-story dwelling, with long empty corridors and sudden courtyards open to the sky.

When all was completed upon the mountain peak, the creature entered the white dwelling, passed down the long empty corridors to the bedroom, and sat down upon the edge of a soft mattress of prowling valru hide stuffed with lemon blossoms. It could see through the window opening the ringed planet begin its ascent as the day waned. Twilight breezes scudding off the sea of red grass rushed up the slopes and swamped the house. The indigo creature folded its wings back and stretched its arms once before lying back upon the wide, comfortable bed it had made.

As the horned head rested upon a pillow, many light-years away, at the center of the hollow planet, robot 49 fitted the small gear into place within Onsing's remarkable machine. Cheers went up from the 999 metallic brethren gathered behind him. And the 1,001st robot, designed solely to press the start button on the machine, finally fulfilled its task. A lurching, creaking, clanging of parts moving emanated from the strange device. Then invisible waves that gave off the sound of a bird's call issued forth, instantly disabling all of the robots, traveling right through the hollow planet and outward, in all directions across the universe.

The indigo creature heard what it at first believed to be the call of the pale night bird, but soon realized it was mistaken. It then made the only sound it would ever make in its long life, a brief sigh of recognition, before it began to melt. Thick droplets of indigo ran from its face and arms and chest, evaporating into night before staining the mattress. Its horns dripped away like melting candle wax, and its wings shrank until they had both run off into puddles of nothing. As the huge dark figure disintegrated, from within its bulk emerged a pair of forms, arms clasped around each other. With the evaporation of the last drip of indigo, John and Zadiiz, again young as the moment they first met, rolled away from each other, dreaming.

In the morning they were awakened by the light of the sun streaming in the window without glass and the sounds of the migrating birds. They discovered each other and themselves, but had no memory, save their own names, of their pasts or how they came to be on the mountain peak. All they remembered was their bond, and although this was an invisible thing, they both felt it strongly.

They lived together for many years in tranquillity on the undiscovered planet, and in their fifth year had a child. The little girl had her mother's orange eyes and her father's desire to know what lay out beyond the sky. She was a swift runner and climbed about in the lemon trees like a monkey. The child had a powerful imagination and concocted stories for her parents about men made of metal and dark-winged creatures, of incredible machines and vessels that flew to the stars. At her birth, not knowing exactly why, John Gaghn and Zadiiz settled upon the name of Onsing for her and wondered how that name might direct her fate.

WHAT'S SURE
TO COME

· ONE ·

Outside on the cracked concrete sidewalk stood a wooden Indian with headdress and hatchet, which my grandfather had christened Tecumseh. Inside, the place smelled like a chocolate egg cream laced with cigar smoke and filtered through the hole of a stale doughnut. From beneath a pervasive layer of dust, one could dig out *Green Lantern* comics and *Daredevil: The Man Without Fear*. In the back, next to the phone booth with flypaper glass, were wooden shelves holding plastic models of planes, monsters, and the awe-inspiring car designs of Big Daddy Roth. There were spinning racks of paperback books, rows of greeting cards, crinkly bags of plastic soldiers, paper and pens and crayons. At the soda fountain, they made cherry Cokes, black-and-whites, and malteds that were hooked up to a green machine and cycloned into existence. My father bought his Lucky Strikes there. My grandfather bought his horse paper there. My mother would go in once a year, stir the dust, and come out with a notebook to keep her thoughts in.

The owners, Leo and Phil, carried on a subdued argument day

in, day out, which occasionally erupted into shouts of "Shmuck" and "Stick your ass in a meat grinder." Leo was tall with glasses and a bald head. He always wore a green T-shirt and a graying apron with which he would swipe your glass before setting it under the soda jet. The brown, smoldering length of stiff rope he smoked throughout the day made him talk out of the side of his mouth in a voice like a ventriloquist's dummy. "Put 'em back in your head," he would bark from behind the counter when he'd see my gaze drift up over the comics to where the *Playboy*s were kept. He worked the register, but the register never worked. So when you brought your purchase to him, he'd blow smoke in your face and add the prices out loud: "Eh, let's see here, fifty-four, twenty-eight, seventy-five, ahhhh . . . a buck ninety."

Leo's brother-in-law, Phil, was short, with a broken nose and one walleye always looking to the left. Mrs. Millman said the bad eye was a result of all of those years of spying on Leo at the cash register. Phil was crankier than his partner and would scurry around with a dirty rag, dusting. Many of his days were spent in the center aisle, trying to remove a giant wad of gum that had been flattened into the linoleum and blackened by a million footfalls. "It's a sin, watching him go at it," my mother said. Once he brought in a buffing machine with the idea of whisking that sin away, but when he turned it on the thing went out of control, knocking fat Mrs. Ryan on her rear end and denting a shelf. The presence of children made Phil nervous and he gave us names—Cocker, Fuck Knuckle, Putzy Boy, and something that sounded like Schvazoozle.

In the back of the store, through a small doorway you could only get to from behind the fountain counter, was a cramped stockroom. Old centerfolds were the wallpaper, and chaos reigned among the shelves. At the center of that room, beneath a single bare bulb, sat a card table and four chairs. On Thursday nights after closing, those chairs were occupied by Leo, Phil, Dr. Geller, and my grandfather. They played a two-card game of their own invention called Fizzle—quarter ante, deuces high, fold on any pair, ace of spades takes all. They moved like reptiles in the cold, eyeing their cards, drinking whiskey, cigar smoke swirling with nowhere to go.

One Thursday night when my grandmother had taken sick after dinner and my father was not home from work yet with the car, my mother sent me to fetch my grandfather from the store. I wasn't usually allowed out that late, but my grandmother needed the milk of magnesia and my grandfather had put it somewhere and never told her where it was. It was a week before Halloween and the night was cold and windy. The trip down the back road spooked me as barren branches clicked together and dead leaves scraped the pavement. When the Beware of Dog lunged out of the shadows, barking behind its chain-link fence, I jumped and ran the rest of the way, thinking about a boy who had lived on that block and had been hit by a car and killed over the summer.

When I made it to the store, I opened the door and went inside. The lights were out and the place was still. I walked quietly up the aisle, noticing how all of the toys and books appeared different at night, as if when no one was looking they might come to life. A muffled voice drifted up from the back of the store, and I followed its trail behind the soda fountain to the door of the stock room. They all saw me standing there, but no one acknowledged my presence because the doctor was talking. I stood still and listened, trying not to seem too interested in the ladies on the walls.

Dr. Geller was a short, heavyset man with wavy black hair and a face nearly as wide as the seat of a fountain stool. I never saw him that he wasn't yawning or rubbing his eyes. When he'd come to the house on visits to tend to my brother and me, he would finish his examinations and then sit down in my mother's rocker where he'd fall asleep, smoking a cigar. In his vest pocket he had a silver watch on a chain he would let us see if we did not flinch at the bite of the needle.

His voice came out cracked and weary amid sighs of defeat as he told about how Joe, the barber, had a heart attack and was lying on the floor of his shop facedown among the curls of hair. "Five minutes after I checked his vital signs and pronounced him dead," said Geller, "Joe stood up, took the little whisk broom from his back pocket, cleaned the chair he was closest to, and then spun it around for the next customer. His eyes were rolled back in his head and blood was leaking from his nose, but he spoke to me. 'Trim and a shave?' he asked. And I said, 'Nothing today, Joe.' After that he fell back onto the floor and died for good." The doctor drew on his big cigar, and my grandfather called me over and put me on his lap.

· TWO ·

My grandfather was a powerful man even in old age. He had been a boxer, a merchant marine, a deep-sea diver. There was a tattoo on his left bicep that when looked at straight on was a heart with an arrow through it, filigree work around the borders. Across the center of the heart, written in vein blue, was my grandmother's name, Maisie. When you looked at the same design over his shoulder, as he had my brother and me do sometimes, standing on the dining room table, the image became a naked woman bending over, waving to you from between her legs.

"Don't tell your mother," he'd say and laugh like a bronchial wolf.

He was well respected among the card players, because he had

an inside line at the track. He worked in the boiler room at Aque-
duct Raceway—the Big A. Over the years he had struck up as many
friendships as he could with the jockeys, the paddock boys, the
ticket punchers. Whatever the word was on a given horse, he made
it his business to know before it was led into the starting gate. In
addition, he studied the *Telegraph*, which he called the horse paper,
as if it were a sacred text, working the odds, comparing the results
of stakes races, jotting down times and blood lines in the mar-
gins. He knew a lot about Thoroughbreds and won a considerable
amount of the time, but, still, he was not the best handicapper
in the house. A constant point of aggravation for him was not so
much that when my grandmother bet she would invariably win
but that her method lacked any logical cogitation.

Her winners came from her dreams. "Last night, I saw yards
and yards of burgundy silk," she said at breakfast one morning,
and later that day she put two dollars to win on a horse, Rip's Burgundy, running in the eighth. My grandfather scowled and rolled
his eyes. "Bullshit," he said, but when the race was over, a horse he
had considered a total pig had come out of nowhere on the back
turn and scorched the field.

Whenever she was about to go to the track she had these
dreams. Sometimes she saw numbers, sometimes it was just a
fleeting glimpse of something that had to do with a horse's name
she'd find in the morning line. No matter how sure she was of her
bets, though, she would never play more than two dollars. Because
of this, her winnings never seemed as spectacular as my grandfather's.

Her other talent was for reading futures from an ordinary deck
of playing cards. About once every two months, she and my mother
would have a little get-together of the neighborhood ladies. They'd
drink sherry from teacups, eat thin sandwiches with the crusts cut
off, and gossip. After everyone was a little tipsy, the women would

beg my grandmother to take out the cards and read their fortunes. Everyone pretended it was just for fun, but even from the back room, where I'd be perusing the latest *Green Lantern*, I knew when it was happening because of the sudden silence. Then I'd drop my comic and hurry out to see.

She'd be sitting at the dining room table across from Mrs. Sutton or Mrs. Kelty, her pupils obscured by the rims of her glasses, her lips pursed and moving, staring at the white tablecloth where she was about to place the cards. She would then say, "You must cross my palm with silver." A quarter was the going rate. The blue curtains behind her were always filled with a breeze when the cards hit the table. "To your self, to your heart, to your home, to what you least expect and what's sure to come." She'd lay the cards faceup in groups of five. This was followed by a period of silence in which the ladies smiled at one another. Her first line was always, "You are about to meet a man," and broken clues to this liaison would, thereafter, pepper the reading.

The only vacations my grandparents ever took were to racetracks. The autumn following the summer of the death of Joe, the barber, they took a trip up to Rockingham Park in New Hampshire. The first night at the hotel, my grandmother ate oysters and had a dream about violet smoke. She told my grandfather at breakfast and he said, "Jeez, here we go," and checked the morning line to see if there were any horses names that had anything to do with violet smoke. She made him slowly read off the names and finally decided on a horse in the fifth race called Quiet Pleas.

"What's that got to do with smoke?" asked my grandfather.

"It's kind of wifty like it," she said.

"You're wifty," he said and shook his head, but later, at the ticket window, he had a feeling and also put fifty dollars on Quiet Pleas to win. When the horse paid enough for them to ride home in a new car, he began to see the beauty of it.

• THREE •

One Thursday night, instead of meeting in the stockroom of the store, the card players came to the house. My grandfather answered the door and greeted them. Leo came in first, took his cigar briefly out of his mouth, and shook hands with my mother and father and grandmother. Phil entered behind him, gave a wave to the grown-ups, and then pointed at my brother and me and said, "How's the ball choppers?" Dr. Geller arrived a few minutes later, looking like he hadn't slept in a week. My mother served deviled eggs and everyone drank whiskey and beer, cigar and cigarette smoke dimming the room. After some slow conversation, Leo said, "Let's do this before we get three sheets to the wind." Everyone agreed and they moved into the dining room, my grandmother taking up her place at the table.

It had been decided that Leo would be the one to represent the group, so he sat closest to my grandmother and took from his pocket a silver dollar to lay in her outstretched palm. Although the old men were all gravely quiet, I could see my mother and father standing in the kitchen silently laughing. I sat on my grandfather's lap and watched closely as the blue curtain lifted and the cards hit the table. "To your self, to your heart, to your home, to what you least expect and what's sure to come."

"Maisie," said my grandfather, "remember, he just wants a lucky number."

She stared hard at my grandfather for the interruption.

"Don't give me that crap," he said.

"All right," she said. "A lucky number," and lifted the pile of cards that had fallen under "what's sure to come."

Leo bit down hard on his cigar as she shuffled the cards out in front of her. Phil watched the proceedings with his bad eye while at the same time staring down my brother, straight on, who was fidgeting in the chair across from him. The doctor leaned over to me and said, "And me, a man of science." My grandfather overheard him and laughed low in his chest. Then my grandmother held out the facedown cards to Leo and said, "Pick one." Leo reached in, grabbed the card at the exact center of the spread, and turned it over, placing it faceup on the table.

The ace of spades was always frightening to me back then, because any time it came up, my grandmother would slip it off the table and give a forced laugh.

"Doesn't that mean death?" Mrs. Crudyer asked her once at a luncheon.

"Well," she answered, "it means a lot of things, but . . . here, I see a man with flowers for you. A dozen yellow roses."

It was less than four months later that Marion Crudyer's liver gave out and she passed. That dark ace had come up in a reading my grandmother had done once for me, and afterward my brother told me to make out a will and leave everything I owned to him. I walked around for two weeks awaiting sudden death. My mother dissipated my fears by telling me it was "no more than a fart in a windstorm."

I went to my grandmother and asked her how she had learned the cards. She told me that Mrs. Harris, one-time mistress of the tea leaves, who had lived in her apartment building in Jamaica, Queens, had taught her. On the night old Mrs. Harris died, my grandmother and her sister, Gertrude, saw a banshee floating outside the third-story landing window, combing its blue hair and moaning.

"Number one is the number," she now told Leo. "I see one."

"Fizzle," said Dr. Geller, and the card players all smiled.

After the reading we moved back into the living room and my

grandfather brought out his mandolin. In between barrages of conversation, someone would say, "Mac, can you do, 'Goodnight, Irene'?" and he would play it, double stringing and singing the words in his wolf voice. "September Song," "Apple Blossom Time," "Till the Real Thing Comes Along"—even my father sang, and my grandmother drank beer.

The doctor told about a child he had recently treated who was haunted by an evil spirit that broke dishes and furniture and left bite marks. The final diagnosis was too much television and sugar. Phil explained how he was considering using hydrochloric acid to eat away the gum wad at the store. Through snatches of stories and one-word comments, they compiled verbal obituaries for the town's recently dead. Then they talked nothing but horses as I slowly drifted off to sleep in the corner of the couch.

Saturday afternoon, my father, my grandfather, and I sat in the car in the parking lot behind the five-and-ten in Babylon. They were up front talking, and I was in the back, watching the rain make rivulets on the window.

"Listen, Jim," my grandfather said to my father, "this morning Maisie got up and told me that she had a dream last night about an Indian and a shooting star. I forgot about it until I was having my coffee and looking over the *Telegraph*. In the eighth race, where we're putting all our money to win on number one, there's a horse at the five spot—Tecumseh."

There was a rain-filled pause. "Well?" my father asked and waited.

"I don't know," said my grandfather, shaking his head. He reached into his pocket, pulled out a huge roll of bills, and looked at it.

"I'll take a piece," said my father and handed over some money.

My grandfather laughed and added it to the wager.

"An arrangement made in hell," said my father before lighting a cigarette.

My grandfather sat for a few moments in silence with his eyes closed, then he opened the door and got out of the car.

Through the rain-streaked windshield, we watched him walk across the parking lot and along the front row of cars to stop beneath a streetlamp beside a chain-link fence enmeshed in dead honeysuckle vines.

"Here he comes," said my father as I climbed over into the front seat and kneeled next to him. When I looked again, I saw a thin man dressed in a black topcoat and hat, talking to my grandfather.

"Watch him pass the money with the handshake," said my father.

I waited and the handshake came. It lasted only a second but I didn't see the money. The thin man looked up suddenly and then turned and ran, down through a row of cars and into the back entrance of the five-and-ten. When my father sat upright in his seat and threw his cigarette out the window, I knew something was wrong. The cop cars the bookie had seen entering the parking lot now came into view.

"It's a bust," said my father.

My grandfather didn't move as the police jumped out of their cars and walked quickly toward him. As they approached him from the front, my grandfather had his hand behind his back and he was waving for us to take off. My father grabbed me and we ducked down beneath the dashboard. Seeing my worried look, he put his finger to his lips and smiled. We hid for ten minutes. When we finally looked again, the cop cars were gone and so was my grandfather.

· F O U R ·

Dr. Geller showed up at our door with his black bag, a stethoscope around his neck and blood on his shirt. My mother got up and let him sit in her rocker. We were gathered around the television, drinking whiskey sours my father had created in the blender with Four Roses, Mi-Lem, crushed ice, and cherries. My father gave my brother and me each a sour and we stole handfuls of cherries. There was onion dip and potato chips, sardines and pepperoni. We each bet a quarter on the seventh race, and the doctor won with a horse named Hi Side. He kept one of the quarters for himself and then split the rest of his winnings between my brother and me. My father filled the doctor in on what had happened with the bookie.

"Did Mac have time to get the bet in?" he asked.

"I think so," said my father.

My grandmother shushed them, because the horses for the eighth race were on the track.

The number one horse, Rim Groper, pranced and skittered sideways past the camera as it was introduced. It was white and its mane was in curls. The announcer told us that its colors were magenta and black and that its grandfather had been the amazing Greenbacks.

"Looks like it's got some life in it," said my mother.

"Seems crazy," said the doctor and lit a cigar.

My grandmother watched the horses parading toward the starting gate and laughed. The two, the three, and the four horses went by, each looking much like the other—sleek and shiny, leg muscles bulging. Number five, Tecumseh, passed the camera, swaybacked and lethargic.

"There's a wooden Indian," said my father, laughing at his own joke.

Before we knew it, they were in the starting gate and ready to go. The rain fell in black and white on a black-and-white track that was pure mud.

My grandmother had her fists clenched and her eyes closed. The doctor leaned forward in the rocker. My father put his drink to his mouth and kept drinking until the announcer yelled, "And they're off." Coming out of the gate first, Rim Groper bucked, but Pedro Avarez held on and moved into a clear lead. The next horse, Cavalcade, was two lengths back, and the rest of the pack was a length behind him with Tecumseh bringing up the rear. My mother said, "Come on, come on," through clenched teeth. My grandmother tightened her fists, and the thick blue veins of her wrists became visible. My father shoved a cracker with three sardines on it into his mouth.

On the back turn, Rim Groper bucked again, and this time Avarez flew off, hitting the mud with a splash. He was trampled by the pack, rolled and kicked like a log. The camera stayed on the horses as they rounded the turn and moved into the home stretch. Rim Groper, now free of his mount, flew ahead of the other horses. Tecumseh made a startling move on the outside and gained on Cavalcade. The jock on Cavalcade used the whip to force a burst of speed. Tecumseh kept closing. Rim Groper crossed the finish line four lengths in front of the competition. When the real leaders crossed the line, they were nose hair for nose hair and a photo finish was called.

While we waited for the results, the announcer told us that Pedro Avarez had broken his left leg but that he was conscious. "A true competitor," said the announcer.

"A true bum," said the doctor.

"The number one horse did finish first," said my father.

My grandmother shook her head sadly. "I saw the one," she said. My mother reached over and patted her knee.

"What a tangled web we weave," said the doctor.

My father made another round of sours. Just after the doctor left, they announced that Tecumseh had edged out Cavalcade, paying thirty to one. Then it was time for my father and me to go pick up my grandfather at the police station.

On the way home, my grandfather told us that later on that afternoon the police had brought in the bookie and busted the whole operation.

"They said they'd let me off if I fingered the guy in the parking lot," he said. "I saw him there in the lineup, but I'm not that stupid. They tried to sweat me, but eventually I told them they had nothing on me and they had to agree."

"Did you make the bet?" my father asked.

"Nah," he said. "I told the guy I couldn't make the wager and since I do so much business with him he accepted my apology this time."

"I saw the handshake, though," said my father.

"Just a handshake," said my grandfather as he leaned over and reached for something beneath the seat of the car. "I had my own dream that the whole thing was bullshit." He held the roll of cash up for us to see.

My father laughed so hard, he nearly drove off the road.

"I'm going to let them stew over it a little and then give back their cash on Thursday."

"What was your dream?" asked my father.

"Some crazy twaddle," he said. "Maisie was in it."

· FIVE ·

As it turned out, my grandfather never got the chance to give the others their money back, because on the following Wednesday afternoon, Leo was in a head-on collision on Sunrise Highway and was launched, bald dome first, through the car windshield. My father told me that at the wake Phil put a box of Leo's special cigars in the coffin with him. The card players never met on Thursday nights again.

Following Leo's funeral, the store was closed for quite a few weeks, and when Phil returned, he seemed to have lost all of his frantic energy. The first thing he did was bolt a sign onto the soda fountain that announced that it was permanently closed. He no longer bothered with the black spot in the center aisle and it began to slowly grow. Finally the stress of the loss of his partner caused Phil's right eye to also turn outward. Thinking of what Mrs. Millman had said was the cause of his left eye going bad, I wondered what he was now watching for.

The day he had Tecumseh carted away, Phil stood with his hands in his pockets, leaning against the entrance to the store, unable to focus on us kids to call us by the names he had concocted. I heard from my mother that he moved to Florida to live with his son, whose wife despised him. The store was sold to a young couple, who cleaned it up so that it was shining white inside. They had no names for us, no *Playboy*s over the comics, no dust to make each purchase a discovery.

On Christmas Eve of that same year, the doctor was called out on an emergency. Mrs. Ryan wasn't well. When he arrived at her house sometime after midnight, he found her passed out on the floor next to her bed. More than likely, he determined she had had a stroke, and then, attempting to lift her, he had one himself and keeled over. It was the news of this incident that infused the dark ace with all its old terror for me again. I went to his wake and funeral as did the rest of the town. When he was laid out in his coffin, I was glad to see that he no longer looked tired. I thought about one time when I was younger and he had come through a blizzard to treat a fever I had. When the fever broke, and I woke from a maddening dream of moonlight and banshees on the baseball diamond, he was sleeping in the rocking chair next to the couch where I lay, his pocket watch in his right hand.

Not too long after the doctor's death, my grandfather had a heart attack while cursing out Dick Van Dyke, whom he hated more than any man alive, and whose show my grandmother insisted on watching every week. The episode didn't kill him, but it paralyzed his left side and made him very weak. After a long stay in the hospital, they sent him home to live out the few weeks he had left.

One afternoon when I was given the task of watching him, he woke up after a long deathlike sleep and told to me to go and fetch my father. When my father got to his bedside, my grandfather used whispers and grunts to instruct him to open the top drawer of the dresser and reach in the back.

"There's a black silk sock back there with something in it," he managed to get out through the corner of his mouth.

My father reached in, felt around, and pulled out the sock. He turned it over, gave it a shake by the toe, and out fell the wad of money, still rolled and held fast by a green rubber band.

"Play the six in the eighth this Saturday," he told my father.

My grandfather slipped away three days later. The day of the wake, my father sat my brother and me down on the love seat in the living room and told us, "Mac lived a life. . . ." He told us stories about the old days till he cried, and then he told us to go outside and play. My mother stared horribly through the whole thing, and my grandmother moaned at night. On Saturday, the day of the funeral, after the guests had left the house, my father and I watched the eighth race. The number six horse, Tea Leaf, went off at twelve-to-one and finished second to last.

I was there on Sunday morning in my grandmother's room when my father gave her the money. She sat in the recliner, looking particularly frail and wrinkled and ancient.

"Mac told me to give this to you for the funeral," said my father.

Closing her eyes, she took the money and held it above her heart. Then she turned to me and pointed, her hand shaking. "Never forget what you least expect," she said.

THE WAY
HE DOES IT

You've got to see the way he does it. It's pretty remarkable for a man his age. He does it with a cigarette jutting from the corner of his mouth and a look in his eye like there's nothing finer in all creation than doing it that way. There's a certain grace to his movements, a certain cosmic aplomb in his manner. Occasionally he'll grunt, and some observers claim to have heard him call for his mother when he's almost finished. His eyes get really wide, his lip curls back, and you can see the sweat form on his brow. He probably uses more muscle groups while doing it than he would if he were swimming the butterfly. On special occasions he will do it by candlelight with soft music playing in the background, but it's more expensive to see him do it that way.

There was a time when he didn't charge for the sight of it, but that was before when he was still perfecting his method. Back then, when he'd do it, he'd get red in the face and would often wet himself with the exertion, but he seemed to do it more out of obsession than any sense of advancing his craftsmanship. A fellow by the

name of Roger Brown, one of his former neighbors from that earlier time, has said, "When he would do it in those days, he wasn't
nearly as refined, but, my God, the energy with which he did it.
You'd think he was going to go right through the back wall of the
house."

There are many theories as to how he came up with it. Of course,
as with anything this remarkable, there is plenty of sensational-
ist speculation. One such item of foolishness is that it had been
taught to him by extraterrestrials who'd contacted him by way of
an AM radio channel, and another is that when he does it, he is
possessed by the Holy Ghost. The most bizarre conjecture has to
be that it had been a common practice among the populace of the
lost civilization of Atlantis and that he dreamed the ancient technique through his collective unconscious. In a 1989 interview, he
himself attested, "I just got down on the floor one day and started
doing it. As I was doing it, I asked myself the question, 'How can I
do it better?'"

Others have tried it, both male and female, attempting to copy
his methods. Two prominent examples are Nettie Stuart and
Branch Berkley. Stuart got farther along with the process than
Berkley, but in the end they both killed themselves attempting it.
Berkley inadvertently set himself on fire, and Nettie Stuart broke
a rib, which in turn impaled her heart. Their families got together
and started a fund, the proceeds of which would be used to try
to bribe people away from trying it. Few took the money; of the
rest, the ones who did not perish in their bid for glory you can see
today, hobbling down the street or talking to themselves outside
convenience stores. We tend to treat these failures with equal parts
of tenderest pity and sharpest derision.

He swore he would never fully disclose his secrets, but back
in the seventies, before his fame became manifest, he did release
an audio tape in which he described each step of the act while he

was doing it. Although he narrates as if you are there in the room watching him and, therefore, is never quite specific enough for the listener to visualize what exactly he is doing, it is said that from his voice alone a certain mystical energy can be garnered by the listener. The following is an excerpt from a crucial part of that recording:

. . . so when you utilize the tongue and eye in unison, man, it feels good. Then you take this and put it around behind, like that. When you've got that where you want it, then you've got to quickly grab this and tense up like it's all there is in the universe. You'll start to notice a little swelling and that's when it gets creative. If you feel like screaming here, go ahead and scream. Be my guest. At the last second, just let it all go and snap your head back. This will lead you to do it the way it was meant to be done.

Once, when he was asked by the press what his wife thought of it, he quickly replied, "Oh, she loves it. The kids love it too," but by then everyone knew that his wife had left him because of it. To this day, she is still bitter over the memory of it and told me, "He'd do it right there in the living room with the kids running around him. Call me old-fashioned, but how many times was I supposed to be witness to that? The day he did it in front of my parents, I gathered up the kids and went home with them. In the months that followed, he would call me late at night and tell me he was going to do it to me. I didn't see how that was possible, but still I went out and bought a gun."

It wasn't until the early eighties that he came to the conclusion that his abilities were a proverbial gold mine. He started doing it in public after he lost his regular job as a night watchman at a chemical factory. One lonely morning when his refrigerator held nothing but half a beer and a head of cabbage, he went down to the corner of Eighth and Dupin and just started doing it, right there on the sidewalk. In no time a crowd had gathered, and within minutes bystanders were tossing handfuls of change, one- and even five-dollar bills. One old gentleman threw Burger King coupons.

It was only six months after the historic Eighth and Dupin performance that he got his first gig in a cocktail lounge. He was the scourge of many a torch singer and hypnotist. Who could top him? And he always demanded to go on first. He would take half the door money and a quarter of the liquor profits of a given night. His public loved to drink while they watched him, and he requested that they drink Pink Ladies. This alone was the reason for that drink's great surge in popularity in the mid-eighties. The T-shirts he sold at his shows, bearing a photograph of him in the midst of his passion, were the creamy color of Pink Ladies.

An anecdote that is often recounted about these nightclub years concerns his preoccupation with handsome women. One of the acts that he worked with at the Republic, a seedy place down on the waterfront, was billed as "Prince Mishby and His Virgin Bride." Mishby, a lanky young man wearing a high-collared shirt and a bow tie, with arms as thin as pipe cleaners and a high reedy voice, tap danced while his beautiful wife sang arias. The couple would then break into a patter wherein Mishby would speak to his bride in lascivious double entendres and this would send the crowd of sailors and waterfront toughs into paroxysms of laughter. On their third night of sharing the same bill, Mishby caught our subject besmirching the Virgin Bride in her dressing room.

What followed was, to some, unpardonable. To others it was as inevitable as big fish eating little fish. Not only did he have his way with Mishby's wife, but afterward, when the tap dancer lunged at him with a pen knife, he did it so brutally to the lanky young man that from that day forward Mishby had to get about on a board with wheels. "He did it to me without remorse," Mishby now attests, "and no one came to my rescue. In fact, they cheered him on as I screamed in agony. I guess when you can do it the way he does it, no rules apply."

He continued to work for a few years at places like the Republic, Sweet Regrets, A Slice of Green Moon, which was, in those days, located between Front and Chase in the diamond district. Then, one night after his act, he was approached by a heavy, well-dressed man sporting a cane.

"When I see you do it, I am humbled," said the man.

"Naturally," he said.

"My name is Arthur Silven, and I would like to represent you. Here's my card. I believe the scope of your talent deserves a more fitting venue."

"You're a fat pig" was his response.

"But I'm a pig with a bite," said Silven.

They shook hands, and for the next five years he did it under the auspices of Silven Entertainment.

He did it in sold-out concert halls and stadiums so large that people in the back rows and top bleachers looked on with binoculars. He did it before royalty and heads of state, and dignitaries of foreign powers courted his friendship. The money poured in, and he and Silven became wealthy beyond measure. By the end of five years, though, he had done it so much, so well, and for so long, that he felt he might like to *not* do it for a while. Silven would hear none of it and threatened a breach of contract suit. So, one foggy night, he broke into the agent's house and did it to Silven so completely they had to clean up what was left of the agent with a shovel.

Of course, he had a rock-solid alibi of having been at a magic show all that evening. There were numerous people at the event who swore they saw him there, and it was recounted that the magician, an acquaintance of his from the old days at the Republic, even

called him up onstage at one point, had him get into a box with a
sliding curtain, and made him disappear for a solid half hour.

He never served any time for the death of Silven, although the
D.A. did fleetingly consider prosecution on circumstantial evi-
dence. As it turned out, the case was determined to be too weak.
When the photographs of Silven's mangled form hit the tabloids
and television, though, the general public was not convinced of his
innocence and was put off by the viciousness the attack displayed.
As one elderly woman described her reaction to the incident and
attendant photos, "It gave me a feeling like when I see a piece of
meat at a barbecue that has cooked too long and the flies are risk-
ing their lives to get to it, kids have dropped marshmallows onto
the hot coals, and there's grease burning too." The international
press started referring to him as "The Savage American." The
noted ethical philosopher, Trenton Du Block, came out against
him, as did Mothers Against Drunk Driving.

He walked away from it all and built himself a mansion in the
swamps of Louisiana. There, amid the forbidding black waters and
moss-strewn cypresses, he shrouded himself from the world. It is
said that he raised llamas and peacocks behind the high walls of
his estate. The only person from the outside world who still had
access to him was his valet, Ruben Charles. Charles has claimed
that even he very rarely got to see his employer during these years.
"I usually took my orders from a voice that issued from a darkened
room," he's said.

"At night," Charles wrote in his memoirs, "I would hear him rum-
maging around the mansion. Then I would hear him in the backyard, doing it to one of the peacocks. The screams were ungodly, and
I would cower beneath my covers. When I slept it was always with
one eye open. Make no mistake, the day finally came when he did
it to me. It was in the trophy room. He charged out from behind a
stuffed bear and did it to me like there was no tomorrow."

Charles could not honestly say whether his boss had been doing it on a daily basis during their years in the swamp. All the valet could testify to was that the day after a bad storm, when the brick wall was knocked down in one spot by a falling tree and dozens of alligators had invaded the sanctuary, slaughtering and devouring all of the livestock, his employer did it on the veranda, overlooking the carnage, with magnificent precision and beauty.

In September of that year, he let Charles go and sold the mansion to the alleged head of a drug cartel. After this, he disappeared for a time. Scattered sightings of him were sporadically reported over a period of the next few years. Individuals told of encounters with him in far-flung locations around the globe. It's since been discovered that certain tribes in the interior of New Guinea carve figures that seem to bear a perfect likeness to him in the act of doing it.

Some believe that he lived a mundane existence with a woman in an apartment in a small town on the Canadian border. Supposedly he'd gone back to working as a night watchman. Judith Nelson, the woman with whom he'd purportedly been living publicly, denies ever having met him, but her family and friends say that she had, for this time period, often been seen in the presence of a strange man who fits his description. One of Nelson's subsequent lovers claims that her body still bore the marks of it having been done to her repeatedly.

When he definitively surfaced again on a street corner in the small town of Fortescue in southern New Jersey, he looked much older. His thinning hair was long and he wore it in a ponytail. A gray beard and the crow's-feet around his eyes made him appear far less fierce than he had in his youth. It was noted that he'd switched to a filtered cigarette. Still, his body was in near-perfect condition, and one could tell from watching him do it that he'd been practicing all along.

The small-town audiences he performs for these days, traveling in his van from street corner to street corner, say that to see him do it now is no longer the sublime terror, the agonizing beauty, it once was. The effect, as I have experienced it myself, has become one of precision and clarity, an exquisite longing for a paradise lost, an empathetic magnet for petty paranoia.

When I went to interview him for the first time on Money Island at the southernmost tip of Jersey, I told him how closely I'd followed his career and that I was thinking about writing a magazine article based on his life. He told me I was in luck, because at his first show that evening on the library field, he was going to do it to the town's mayor. "I thought you didn't do it like that anymore," I said to him. He looked into my eyes and waved his hand in disgust. "Hey, do it to yourself," he said and walked away.

That evening in the summer heat, beneath a huge oak tree on the library field, the people of Money Island gathered to watch him do it to the mayor. He did it so gently, and with such care, a young man in front of me broke into tears. The mayor gasped with delight as if before her eyes she was witnessing a passing parade of priceless treasures, and when he was done with her, she seemed to glow. The mayor declared a town holiday in honor of his art and later, on the high school football field, I watched in awe as he did it again, this time alone, beneath a sky ablaze with fireworks.

THE
SCRIBBLE
MIND

When I was in graduate school, during the mid-eighties, I'd meet Esme pretty much every Sunday morning for breakfast at the Palace A down on Hepson Street. The runny eggs, the fried corn muffins, the coffee, and our meandering conversations carried all of the ritual of a Sunday mass minus the otherwise grim undertones. There was a calm languor to these late-morning meals and something that had to do with the feeling of home.

We'd gone to the same high school, grown up in the same town, and vaguely knew each other back then—friends of friends—but we'd moved in distinctly different social orbits; hers somewhat closer to the sun. Six years had passed since we'd graduated—I hadn't had a single thought about her—and then one day, late in the summer, just before my first semester at the university was about to start, I'd left my flop loft in the seedy First Ward and ventured out for some groceries. I was walking down Klepp Street, and I noticed this good-looking girl about my age walking toward me, talking to herself. She was tall and thin, with a lot of black curly hair, and dressed in an orange T-shirt, jeans, and cheap, plastic beach sandals on her feet. She was smoking a cigarette and mildly gesticulating with her free hand. The fact that she was talking to herself made me think she might be crazy enough to talk to me, so I frantically ran through a few icebreaker lines in my head, searching for one to snag her interest. I immediately got confused, though, because the T-shirt she was wearing bore the name of my high school along with the distinctive rendering of a goofy-looking lion. As we drew closer, I saw her face more clearly and knew that I knew her from somewhere. All I could muster when the moment came was "Hi." She stopped, looked up to take me in, and said, without the least shock of recognition, "Hey, Pat, how are you?" like I'd seen her the day before. Then I realized who she was and said, "Esme, what are you doing here?"

She invited me to come along with her to the Palace A to get a cup of coffee. I'd been pretty lonely since arriving in town, what with classes not having started yet and knowing no one. I couldn't have ordered up a better scenario than running into her. We spent an hour at the diner, catching up, filling in the blanks of all the years and miles we'd traveled. She'd been at the university a semester already, but whereas I was there for a master's degree, she'd already gotten one in mathematics at a different school, producing a thesis on fractals and chaos theory, and now was going for a second one in art. Coincidentally, art was my major also, and I admitted, with a whisper and a tinge of embarrassment in my voice, that I was a painter. This admission on my part deanimated her for a moment. She cocked her head to the side and stared at me, took a drag of her cigarette, pursed her lips, and then eventually nodded as if she could almost believe it. Paint, of course, wasn't her thing—all of her work was done on the computer, plotting points and manifesting the rules and accidents of the universe in shape and color. This stuff was new back then and I had no way to conceive of what she was talking about, but the casually brilliant way in which she discussed Mandelbrot sets and strange attractors interested me almost as much as her hair and her smile. When I told her I liked the paintings of Redon and Guston, she laughed out loud, and although I knew she was disparaging my chosen influences, I was enchanted by the sound of it, like a ten-year-old's giggle.

We parted that first day after making plans to meet for breakfast on Sunday. Even then, although I knew we might become good friends, I suspected things would never go further than that. As fascinating as she was, she had a distinct aloofness about her even when she was staring me straight in the eye and relating the details of her mother's recent death. It was as if a scrupulously calculated percentage of her interest was held constantly in abeyance, busy working the solution to some equation. In addition, I had, at the time, an irrational, Luddite inclination that there was something morally bankrupt about making art with a computer.

The semester began, and I soon discovered that abstract painting was still the order of the day at the university. Most of the professors had come of age in their own work during the late fifties and sixties and were still channeling the depleted spirit of Jackson Pollock; second- and third-rate abstract expressionists tutoring young painters in the importance of ignoring the figure. The canvases were vast, the paint applied liberally, and the bigger the mess the more praise the piece garnered. From the start, I was somewhat of an outcast among the students with my crudely rendered cartoon figures frozen in drab scenes that bespoke a kind of world weariness; a mask to hide the fact that I felt too much about everything. I was barely tolerated as a kind of retarded mascot whose work had a certain throwback charm to it. Esme, for her part, was on similar footing. No one understood, save the people in the computer science division, how she made her glorious paisley whirls, infinite in their complexity, or what they represented. The art crowd feared this technological know-how.

I'd done all of my excessive drinking, drug taking, and skirt chasing as an undergraduate, and now I threw myself into the work with a commitment that was something new for me. When I think back to that place I had on Clinton Street, I remember the pervasive reek of turpentine, the beat-up mattress someone had put by the curb that became my bed, the dangerous mechanical heater with its twisting Looney Tunes funnel going up through the ceiling that portioned out warmth by whim, and the bullet hole in the front window I'd covered with duct tape. I worked late into the nights when the neighborhood crystal meth dealer met his clients under the lamppost across the street in front of the furniture warehouse and after the other tenants of my building had turned off the flames under their relentlessly simmering cabbage pots and fallen from minimum wage exhaustion into their beds. Then I'd make some coffee, put Blossom Dearie low on the old tape machine, and start mixing oils. Each brushstroke carried a charge of excitement. The professors who dismissed my work still had valuable secrets to impart about color and craft and materials, and I brought all of these lessons to bear on my canvases.

The months rolled on and in the midst of my education, I also gleaned a few insights into Esme. Outside of our booth at the Palace A, where the conversation orbited pretty strictly around a nucleus of topics—her diatribes promoting an electronic medium and mine concerning the inadequacies of abstraction; a few catty comments about our fellow students' work; the lameness of the professors—she proved to be something of a sphinx. With the exception of her telling me about her mother's bout with cancer that first day, she never mentioned her private life or her family. Anything I learned on that score came through sheer happenstance.

After class one day, I was talking to this guy, Farno, another painter in the graduate program, in the hallway outside a studio and Esme walked by. I interrupted my conversation and said hi to her, and she said, "I'll see you Sunday." When I turned back to the guy, he was shaking his head, and when she was well out of earshot, he said, "You know her?"

"Yeah, we went to high school together."

"So you must have fucked her," he said.

I took a step back, surprised at his comment, and said, "What are you talking about? We're just friends."

"I don't think she has any friends," he said.

My sudden anger made me silent.

"Listen, don't get upset," he said. "I'm just trying to warn you. It happened to me just like all the others. She'll come on to you. You go to dinner or a movie, things wind up back at her place. I mean, she's charming as hell, brilliant. You think to yourself, 'Wow, she's great.' You can't help but fall for her. Eventually, it's off to the bedroom. She's aggressive, like she's trying to fuck the life out of you, like she wants to eat your soul. Then, either the next morning or occasionally even late at night, you'll wake up and she'll be crying and then yell at you like a kid pitching a tantrum to get the hell out. I've talked to some of the others about her, both guys and girls, even some of the professors. She's whacked."

"Well, we're friends," I said in her defense and walked away.

Later that week, on Sunday, when we went to breakfast, that guy's story was circling in my head like a twister, but I kept my mouth shut about it. Since I'd never gone down that road with Esme, instead of thinking her crazy because of what I'd been told, I just felt, whether I should have or not, kind of bad for her. While all this was going through my head, she was giving me some rap about how chaos theory showed that the universe was both ordered and chaotic at the same time. I could barely concentrate on what she was saying, my mind filled with images of her fucking different people in the art department like some insatiable demon. Finally, she ended her explanation, making a face rife with dissatisfaction for the indecisive nature of creation, and asked me to pass the sugar.

In the next couple of weeks, the indecisive universe dropped two more revelations about her into my lap. I was in the university library one night, looking for a book of Reginald Marsh's Coney Island paintings, when I found myself upstairs near the study carrels. My department didn't think enough of me to grant me one of these. Department heads doled them out—like popes might grant indulgences—to their favorite students. I knew Esme had one, though, courtesy of the computer science people, and I knew she used it from time to time. I walked along the narrow corridor, peering in the little windows on the doors. Most of them were dark and empty. Eventually I found hers and she was in there, sitting at the desk.

In front of her was a computer with a screen full of numbers. To her right, on the desk, was an open book, and, with her right hand, she was intermittently flipping through the pages and working the computer mouse, her attention shifting rapidly back and forth from the page to the screen. At the same time, on the left-hand side of the desk was a notebook in which she was scribbling with a pencil to beat the band, not even glancing at what she was writing down. While all this was going on, she was also wearing earphones that were plugged into a boom box sitting on the floor. When she turned her attention to the book, I caught a glimpse of her eyes. The only way I can describe her look, and this isn't a word I'd normally think to use, is *avaricious*. I was going to knock, but to tell you the truth, in that moment I found her a little frightening.

The second piece of the puzzle that was Esme came to me from, of all people, my mother. I'd called home and was chatting with her about how my studies were going and what was up with the rest of the family. True to her mother-self, she asked me if I'd made any friends. I said I had, and then remembering that Esme had come from our town, I mentioned her. When I said her name, my mother went uncharacteristically silent.

"What?" I asked.

"Her family . . . sheesh."

"Do you remember them?"

"Oh, yeah, I remember her mother from the PTA meetings and such. A block of ice. You didn't want to get near her for fear of frostbite. And the father, who was much more pleasant, he was some kind of pill addict. At least they had a lot of money."

"She's okay," I said.

"Well, you know best," she said, obviously implying that I didn't.

Esme's *condition,* or whatever you want to call it, haunted me. I don't know why I cared so much. To me she was just a breakfast date once a week—or was she? She was fun to talk to and I enjoyed meeting her at the Palace A for our rendezvous, but when I started to find myself thinking about her instead of thinking about painting, I made a determined effort to ignore those thoughts and dive back into my work.

One Sunday afternoon in my second semester, somewhere right at the cusp between winter and spring, we were sitting in the diner celebrating with the steak-and-egg special a positive review of my recent work by my committee. I held forth for Esme on the encouraging comments made by each of the professors. When I was done, she smiled and said, "Pat, that's terrific, but think how much weight you put behind what they say now. I remember a few months ago when by your own estimation they were fools." That took a little of the wind out of my sails. Still, I could undeniably feel that my paintings were finally coming together and the creativity just seemed to flow down my arm and through the brush onto the canvas. I knew I was on to something good, and nothing Esme said could completely dampen my spirits. Instead, I laughed at her comment.

She got up to go to the bathroom, and I sat paging through the catalog of a spring show that was to hang in the university gallery and would include some graduate student pieces and some by well-established professionals. I'd been asked to put a piece in that show, and I was ecstatic. When she returned, I was looking at a page with a reproduction of a painting by the artist Thomas Dorphin, the best known of the artists who would be at the opening.

"What's that you're looking at?" she asked as she slid into the booth.

"A piece by that guy Dorphin. Do you know his stuff?"

She shook her head.

"It's kind of like that Cy Twombly crap, only it looks three-dimensional, sort of like a mix between him and Lichtenstein." Twombly had done a series of pieces that were scribbles, like a toddler loose with a crayon, on canvas and the art world was still agog over them. The painting by Dorphin was also a scribble, only the line was rendered with a brush and the illusion of three-dimensionality; instead of obviously being a line from a crayon, it appeared to be a piece of thick twine. The technique was pretty impressive, but it left me cold.

"Let me see," she said.

I turned the catalog around to her and she drew it closer.

She looked at it for about two seconds, and I noticed a nearly undetectable tremor of surprise. Then her complexion went slightly pale.

"What's wrong?" I said.

Still clutching the catalog, she slid out of the booth and stood up. She reached into the pocket of her jeans and pulled out a wad of bills, too much for what we'd both had, and threw it on the table.

"I want you to come with me to my place," she said, looking a little frantic.

Immediately, I thought that my time had come to be fucked like she was eating my soul. I got nervous and stammered about having to get back to work, but she interrupted me and said, "Please, Pat, you have to come. It won't take long. I have to show you something."

I was leery, but she seemed so desperate, I couldn't refuse her. I nodded, got up, and followed. I'd never been to her apartment before; it was only two blocks from the diner in a renovated warehouse on Hallart Street. She walked in front of me, keeping a quick pace and every now and then looked over her shoulder to make sure that I was still behind her. When she glanced back at me, I smiled, but she made no expression in return. At the rate we were walking, it took only minutes to get to the front door. She retrieved her keys and let us in. We took an old freight elevator to get to her place on the fifth floor. As we ascended, I said to her, "What's all this about?"

"You won't believe it," she said and then flipped open the catalog to the page with the Dorphin on it for another look. She stared at it till the elevator reached the fifth floor.

If order and chaos existed simultaneously in the universe, her apartment was one of the places where order hid out. It was a nice space, with a huge window providing a view of the river in the distance. There was a big Persian carpet on the floor with a floral mandala design. The walls were painted a soothing sea green and hung with framed pieces of her fractal art. However it was done, the lighting made the room seem like a cozy cave. After being there for no more than a minute, I felt the tension just sort of slough off me like some useless outer skin. On the desk, next to a computer, was a row of sharpened pencils lined up from left to right in descending order of length. I had a sudden flashback to the crusted dishes piled in the sink back at my place.

"Beautiful," I said to her as she hung up her jacket.

"It's okay," she said absentmindedly. "Stay here for a minute, I have to look for something in the bedroom."

In her absence, I went to the nearest bookcase and scanned the titles. My gaze came to rest not on one of the many volumes of art books, but upon a photograph on the top shelf. It was in a simple silver frame—the image of a severe-looking middle-aged woman with a short, tight permanent and her arms folded across her chest. She was sitting at a table in front of a birthday cake, its candles trailing smoke as if just having been extinguished. The woman's jaw and cheekbones were no more than cruel, angular cuts, as if her face had been hacked from granite with a blunt pick, and her eyes stared directly through mine and out the back of my head. I surmised she was the Snow Queen of the PTA my mother had told me about.

When Esme emerged from the other room, she called me over to a card table near the back of the apartment in front of the window. The sun was bright that day, and I remember squinting out at the view of the light glinting in diamonds off the river just before taking a seat across from her. In addition to the catalog, her cigarettes, an ashtray, and a lighter, she laid on the tabletop what appeared to be a plastic Mylar bag, the kind that comic book collectors keep their treasures in. From where I sat, it looked as if it held only a sheet of white 8½ x 11 paper.

She lit a cigarette, and while clamping it in the corner of her mouth as she returned her lighter to the table, began speaking. "Remember the 7-Eleven back in Preston?" she asked.

I nodded. "Yeah, it was the only place in town that would sell us beer."

"I think I remember seeing you in there," she said. "Well, if you made a right at that corner and headed down toward the municipal garage, do you recall that little day-care center on the left side of the road?"

I couldn't really picture it, but I nodded anyway.

"I worked in that center the summer after senior year. It was one of those places where parents drop their kids off when they go to work. Mostly toddlers, some a little older. I liked the kids but there were too many of them and not enough of us."

"Never work with animals or children," I said.

"Not if you mind wiping noses and asses all day," she said. "It was a good introduction to chaos theory, though." She paused, took a drag of her cigarette, and shook her head as if remembering. "Anyway, one day near the end of the summer, about an hour before the parents came to pick the kids up, I was sitting on a tiny kid's chair, completely exhausted. I was so motionless for so long, I think the kids kind of forgot that I was there. They had the dress-up trunk out, and hats and masks and old costume stuff was flying all over the place.

"There was this one strange little kid who was there every day. He was really young, but he had an amazing sense of presence, like he was a little old man. The other kids all loved being around him, and sometimes they just stared for the longest time into his eyes, which were like turquoise-colored crystal. His name was Jonathan. So this other kid, a little bit older, walks up to Jonathan, and I'm sitting there quietly, watching this go down. The other kid seems sad or tired. Keeping his voice a little low, he says, 'Tell me what it was like inside your mommy, I'm starting to forget.'"

"What?" I said.

"Yeah," said Esme, and she nodded, smiling.

"That's wild."

"Right after the kid said this to Jonathan, another little girl, who'd dressed up in a fairy princess outfit—she had a little tiara on her head and was carrying a wand—walked between them, turned to the kid who had asked the question, waved the wand, and said in a soft chant, "Go away. Go away. Go away.""

"Did he?"

"Yeah. I swear I thought he was going to start crying. Then, for a little while, I guess my mind was preoccupied, trying to think back and see if I remembered my earliest memory. If I could recall being in the womb. Nothing. All I got was a big, frustrating blank. When I looked up I noticed Jonathan and the kid had met up again off in the corner of the room. The kid was leaning down and Jonathan, hand cupped around his mouth and the kid's ear, was whispering something to him. The kid was smiling."

"What do you think he was telling him?"

"I don't know," she said, "but just then my boss came in and saw that the other kids were getting wild. She had me calm them down and hand out paper for them to draw on until it was time to leave. She always liked them quiet for when the parents came to get them. Time was finally up and the parents showed and when the last of the little crumb snatchers was gone, I started cleaning up. Most of them had left their drawings behind on the tabletops. I went around and collected them. I always got a charge out of seeing their artwork—there's just always a sense of rightness about the pictures from kids who haven't gone to school yet—fresh and powerful and so beautifully simple.

"When I got to the place where the kid who wanted to remember his mother's womb had sat, I found that he'd left this big scribble on his paper. I can't really describe it, but it was like a big circular scribble, overlapping lines, like a cloud of chaos, in black crayon. I thought to myself that that wasn't such a good sign after what I'd witnessed. But check this out," she said and drew the Mylar bag next to her closer and opened the zip top. "When I got to Jonathan's picture, it lay facedown on the desk. I turned it over, and . . ." Here she reached into the bag and pulled out two sheets of drawing paper. As she laid them down in front of me I saw there was black crayon on both. "The same exact scribble. Absolutely, exactly the same."

"Nah," I said, and looked down at the two pages.

"You show me where they differ," she said.

My glance darted back and forth from one to the other, checking each loop and intersection. Individually, they appeared to have been dashed off in a manner of seconds. There was no sense that the creators were even paying attention to the page when they did them. Eventually, I laughed and shook my head. "I give up," I said. "Are you pulling my leg? Did you do these on the computer?"

"No," she said, "but even if I had, now check this out." Here she opened the catalog to the page with the reproduction of the Dorphin painting. "It's rendered as if three-dimensional, but look closely. It's the same damn scribble made to look like a jumble of twine."

I looked and she was right. Reaching across the table, I took one of her cigarettes and lit it. I sat and smoked for a minute, trying to get my mind around her story and the pictures before me. For some reason, right then, I couldn't look into her eyes. "So what are you trying to tell me?" I finally said.

"I'm not *trying* to tell you anything," she said. "But I've seen it in other places. Once when I was in New York City, I was on the subway. It was crowded and I took a seat next to a guy who had a drawing pad with him. I looked over and he was sketching some of the other passengers, but down in the corner of the page was that same scribble. I pointed to it and said to him, 'That's an interesting design.' He looked at me and asked, 'Do you remember?' I didn't answer, but I was taken aback by his question. He must have seen the surprise in my eyes. Without another word, he closed the book, put it in his knapsack, stood up, and brushed past me. He moved through the crowd and went to stand by the door. At the next stop, he got off."

"Get out," I said. "That really happened?"

"You'll see it," she said. "If you don't know what to look for, you'd never notice it. It just looks like a scribble, like somebody just absentmindedly messing around with a crayon or pen. But you'll see it now."

"Where am I going to see it?" I asked.

"Hey, don't believe me, just call me when you do and tell me I was right."

"Wait a second. . . . So you think it has to do with . . . what?" I asked, not wanting to say what I was thinking.

"I think it's some kind of sign or symbol made by people who remember all the way back to the womb," she said.

"Is that even possible?" I asked, stubbing out my cigarette in the ashtray.

She shrugged. "I don't know. What do *you* make of it?"

I didn't answer. We sat there for quite a while, both looking at the two drawings and Dorphin's painting.

"You kept these drawing all these years?" I said, breaking the silence.

"Of course, in case I wanted to tell someone. Otherwise they wouldn't believe me."

"I still don't believe you," I said.

"You will," said Esme.

During the walk back to my apartment and all afternoon, I thought about the drawings and their implications. What Esme'd really been hinting at, but didn't come out and say, was that there was afoot in the world a conspiracy of in-utero-remembering scribblers. Was there some secret knowledge they were protecting, did they have powers far beyond those of mortal men, were they up to no good? The concept was so bizarre, so out of left field, my paranoia got the better of me and I had to wonder whether Esme had concocted the whole thing, having first seen the Dorphin painting and knowing I'd eventually show her the catalog or we'd come across it at the university. If that was true, then it represented an outlandish effort to dupe me, but for what? A momentary recollection of her in the library carrel gave me a shiver.

That night, I found I couldn't paint. The great ease of conception and movement of the brush I'd felt in recent weeks was blocked by the chaotic scribble of my thoughts. I lay on the mattress, staring at the ceiling, trying to think back to my own beginning. The earliest experience I could recall was being in a big snowsuit out in our backyard, sitting atop a snow drift, staring at a red, setting sun and my mother calling from the back door for me to come in. When my thoughts hit the wall of that memory, they spun off in all directions, considering what exactly it might be that the scribblers were remembering. A state of mind? A previous life? Heaven? Or just the underwater darkness and muffled sounds of the world within the belly?

By Wednesday, I'd seen that damn scribble three times. The first was in the men's room of the Marble Grill, a bar down the street from my apartment where I ate dinner every once in a while. The place was a dive, and the bathroom walls were brimming with all kinds of graffiti. I'd gone in there to take a piss, and while I was doing my thing, I looked up, and there, just above the urinal, staring me right in the face, was a miniature version of that tumbleweed of mystery. Recognizing it gave me a jolt, and I almost peed on my sneaker. I realized that in the dozen or so other times I'd stood there, looking directly at it, it might as well have been invisible.

I saw it again, later that very night, on the inside back cover of a used paperback copy of this science-fiction novel, *Mindswap*, I'd bought a few weeks earlier at a street sale. The book was pretty dog-eared, and I don't know what made me pick it up that night out of all the others I had lying around. After finding the scribble in the back, I turned the book over. On the inside front cover, written in pencil, in a neat script, was the name *Derek Drymon*, who I surmised was the original owner. Whoever this guy was, wherever he was, I wondered if he was *remembering* as I lay there on my mattress wishing I could simply forget.

The last instance, which happened two days later, the one that drove me back to Esme's apartment, was finding a rendition of the scribble on a dollar bill I whipped out at the university cafeteria to pay for a cup of coffee. The girl behind the cash register reached toward me, closed her fingers on the note, and at that moment I saw the design. She tugged, but I couldn't let go. My gaze remained locked on it until she said, "You paying for this, or what?" Then I released my hold, and it was gone.

Later that afternoon, I found myself on Hallart Street, standing on the steps of Esme's building, waiting for her to buzz me in. In the elevator, I prepared myself to eat crow. When the elevator opened at the fifth floor, she was standing there waiting for me in the doorway to her apartment. She had a smile on her face and the first thing she said was "Go ahead."

"What do you mean?" I asked.

"An apology, perhaps? Esme, how could I have doubted you?" she suggested.

"Fuckin' scribble," I muttered.

She laughed and stepped back to let me in. As I passed, she patted me on the back and said, "Maddening, isn't it?"

"Well," I said, "you're right, but where does that get us? It's got me so I can't paint."

"Now that we both know, and I know I'm not crazy," she said, "we're going to have to figure out what it's all about."

"Why?" I asked.

"Because the fact that you don't know will always be with you. Don't you want to know what you're missing?"

"Not really," I said. "I just want to get past it."

She took a step closer to me and put her palms on my shoulders.

"Pat, I need you to help me with this. I can't do it by myself. Someone has to corroborate everything."

I shook my head, but she pulled me over to her desk. "Before you say anything, check this out." She sat down in the chair, facing the computer. With a click of the mouse, the machine came to life.

"Okay, now," she said, spinning on the seat so she could look up at me. She took my left hand in both of hers, more than likely so that I couldn't escape. "After you were here last Sunday, and I had the pictures out, I studied them closely for the first time in a long while. I can't believe I didn't think of this before, but in concentrating on the intersections of the lines, I wondered what these points would reveal if they were plotted on a graph. So I scanned the drawing into the computer and erased the lines, leaving only the points of intersection."

She clicked the mouse once and an image of the scribble appeared on the screen. After letting that sit for a few seconds, she clicked again and revealed only the points, like a cloud of gnats.

"I set them on a graph," she said. Another click and the entire swarm was trapped in a web. "Then for a long time, I looked for sequences, some kind of underlying order to them. It wasn't long before I saw this." She gave another click, and there appeared a line, emanating from a point close to the center of the cluster and looping outward in a regular spiral, like the cross-section of a nautilus shell.

"Interesting," I said, "but it only utilizes some of the dots. You could easily make just as many irregular designs if you linked other dots."

"Yes," she said. "But do you know what that shape represents?" she asked.

"It's the Golden Section," I said. "We studied it earlier in the year when we were covering Leonardo. You can find it in all of his paintings, from *St. Jerome in the Wilderness* to the *Mona Lisa*. A lot of painters swore by it—Jacopo, Seurat . . ."

Tracing the spiral on the screen with her index finger, she said, "You're good. It's a Fibonacci series. Consciously used in art and architecture but also found occurring spontaneously everywhere in nature. To the ancients the existence of this phenomenon was proof of a deity's design inherent in the universe. It's holy. It's magic."

"Back up, though," I said. "It doesn't utilize all of the dots, and there's so many dots there that connected in the right way you could come up with a shitload of different designs as well."

"True," she said, "but look. . . ." She clicked the mouse again. "At any one time, depending on what you choose as your starting point, you can plot five Golden Sections within the scribble, the five using all of the dots except one. Order in chaos, and the one representing the potential of the chaotic amid order."

The picture on the screen proved her point with lines that I could easily follow curling out from central points. She clicked the screen again.

"Change the originating points and you can make five different golden spirals," she said.

Just as I was able to take in the next pattern, she clicked the mouse again, waited a second, and then clicked it again. She clicked through twelve different possible designs of spiral groups before stopping. Turning on the seat, she looked up at me.

"That's all I had time for," she said.

"You're industrious as hell," I told her and took a step backward.

She stood up and came toward me. "I have a plan," she said.

By the time I left Esme's place, it was dark. "Who do we know for sure remembers?" she'd asked, and I'd told her, "No one." But as she'd revealed, that wasn't true. "Dorphin," she said, and then told me how she was going to take one of the scribble drawings she had to the opening at the university gallery and try to convince him she'd done it and was one of *them* in an attempt to get him to talk. I'd told her I wanted nothing to do with bothering Dorphin. After long arguments both reasonable and passionate, when I'd still refused, she'd kicked me out. As I walked along the night streets back to my apartment, though, it wasn't her scheme I thought about. What I couldn't help remembering was that brief period before she turned on the computer when she'd held my hand.

That Sunday, when I got to the Palace A, she wasn't there, and I knew immediately she wouldn't be coming. I took a seat anyway and waited for an hour, picking at a corn muffin and forcing down a cup of coffee. Her absence was palpable, and I realized in that time how much I needed to see her. She was my strange attractor. I finally left and went by her apartment. Standing on the steps, I rang the buzzer at least six times, all the while picturing her at her computer, tracing spirals through clouds of dots. No answer. When I got back to my place, I tried to call her, but she didn't pick up.

There were many instances in the following week when I considered writing her a note and leaving it in her mailbox, telling her I was sorry and that I would gladly join her in her plan to flush out Dorphin, but each time I stopped myself at the last second, not wanting to be merely a means to an end, another Fibonacci series used to plumb the design of the ineffable. Ultimately, what exactly I wanted, I wasn't sure, but I knew I definitely wanted to see her. I hung around campus all week, waiting for her outside the classes I knew she had, but she never showed herself.

Saturday night came, the night of the opening, and I should have been excited with the prospect of so many people seeing my painting hanging in the university gallery alongside those of well-known artists, but I was preoccupied with whether or not she would be there. Still, I had the presence of mind to clean myself up, shave, and throw on my only jacket and tie. The exhibit was packed, wine was flowing, and quite a few people approached me to tell me how much they admired my piece. Dorphin was there, and the neo-cubist, Uttmeyer, and Miranda Blench. Groups of art students and faculty clustered around these stars. Just when I'd had a few glasses of wine and was letting myself forget Esme and enjoy the event a little, she walked in. She wore a simple, low-cut black dress and a jeweled choker. I'd never seen her in anything besides jeans and a T-shirt. Her hair glistened under the track lighting. She walked toward me, and when she drew near, I said, "Where were you on Sunday?" Without so much as a blink, she moved past me, heading for Dorphin, and I could feel something tear inside me.

Moving out of the crowd, I took up a position next to the wine and cheese table, where I could keep a surreptitious eye on her. She bided her time, slowly circling like a wily predator on the outskirts of Dorphin's crowd of admirers, waiting for just the right moment. I noticed that she carried a large manila envelope big enough to hold one of the drawings. The artist, a youthful-looking middle-aged guy with sandy hair, seemed shy but affable, taking time to answer questions and smiling through the inquisition. Now that Esme was on his trail, I was disappointed that he didn't come off as a self-centered schmuck. Behind him hung his painting, and from where I stood, his slightly bowed head appeared directly at the center of the scribble, which formed an aura, a veritable halo of confusion.

A half hour passed in which other students stopped to say hello and congratulate me on my painting being accepted for the show, and each time I tried to dispatch them as quickly as possible and get back to spying on Esme. It was right after one of these little visits that I turned back to my focal point and saw that in the few minutes I was chatting, she'd made her move. The first thing I noticed was a change in Dorphin's look. His face was bright now, and he no longer slouched. He was interested in her—who could blame him?

They were already deep into some conversation. She was smiling, he was smiling, she nodded, he nodded, and then I saw her open the manila envelope. Pulling out a sheet of white paper, no doubt one of the drawings, she offered it to him. He turned it around, took a quick look at the picture and then over each shoulder to see if anyone else was near. He spoke some short phrase to her, and she hesitated for only an instant before nodding.

One of my professors walked over to me then and I had to turn away. What started as a friendly conversation soon turned into a gas-bag disquisition on his part, and he was one of those talkers who takes a breath at odd times so you can't follow the rhythm and intuit the free moment when you can get a word in and escape. I managed to remain in the realm of polite respect and still steal a few glances into the crowd. On my first, I noticed that Esme and Dorphin had moved off into a corner and were talking in what seemed to me to be conspiratorial whispers. The next time I looked, he had his hand on her shoulder. And when my professor had spent his brilliance on me and gone in search of another victim, I looked to that corner again and they were gone.

I stepped into the crowd and spun around, trying to locate them. Two rotations and it appeared they were no longer in the gallery. I walked the perimeter once to make sure I hadn't missed them in my survey while a growing sense of desperation blossomed in my gut. I went out in the hallway and checked up and down, but they weren't there either. At that moment, I couldn't have put into words what I was feeling. I was certain I'd lost Esme, not that I had ever really had her. The realization made me stagger over to a bench and sit down. What came to mind were all of those Sunday mornings at the Palace A, and as each memory appeared it evaporated just as suddenly, gone as if it had never happened.

"Where is she?" I heard a voice pierce through my reverie. I looked up to see a tall, thin guy with blond hair standing over me.

"Who?" I asked, only then realizing it was Farno.

"Did Esme leave with Dorphin?" he asked.

"Why?" I asked.

"Yes or no?" he said, seeming agitated.

"I think she did, what of it?"

He leaned down and whispered to me, "She's in danger. Dorphin's an imposter."

"What do you mean?" I said.

Instead of answering, he pulled a pen out of his pocket, moved over to the wall where a flyer hung, and, in a second, had made a mark on the paper. I stood and walked up behind him. He pointed to what he'd drawn. It was a miniature facsimile of the scribble. I'd seen the design enough times to know his was authentic.

"Look, I'm sure she told you about the scribble," he said. "Dorphin is passing himself off as someone who remembers as a way of drawing us out. He's working for someone else. I can't explain now. You've got to trust me. I'm telling you, she's in serious trouble."

I stood there stunned. "Okay" was all I could say.

"I have a car," said Farno. "He's from out of town but close enough that I doubt he's booked a room. Where would she take him?"

"Her place," I said.

He was already running down the hallway toward the exit. "Come on," he yelled over his shoulder.

Running to Farno's car in the parking lot, I don't remember what, if anything, I was thinking at the time. The entire affair had become just too bizarre. Once we were in the old four-door Chevy, he turned to me and said, "She still lives on Hallart, right? That renovated warehouse building?"

I nodded.

"They're only a few minutes ahead of us," he said. By now we were on our way. He was driving within the speed limit, but I could see his anxiety in the way he hunched up over the dashboard and nervously tapped the steering wheel at the first red light we stopped at.

"What exactly is going on?" I finally asked. "Dorphin is dangerous?"

"I shouldn't be telling you any of this, but I might need your help," he said, "so try to keep it to yourself, okay?"

"I can do that," I said.

"I can remember," he said. "You know what that means."

I nodded.

"That time I told you about, when Esme brought me to her place, she revealed the drawings to me and her theory. So I was aware she'd stumbled onto the scribble, something she wasn't supposed to know about. She's not the first, but for the most part it's gone unrecognized for centuries. When I saw you two hanging out together, I tried to make you think she was crazy so that if she told you about it, you'd dismiss it as just one of her delusions."

"You mean all that stuff you told me about her fucking all those people wasn't real?" I asked.

"No," he said. "That part's true, but I thought if I told you, you'd be more circumspect about her theory."

"Jeez," I said. "What about Dorphin? Where does he come in?"

"Like I said, some people have gotten hip to the scribble over time. You can't keep something like this a complete secret for eternity. In the past, even if people were suspicious, they just wrote it off to mere coincidence or some innocuous aberration of reality. But somewhere in the late 1960s, somebody put things together and decided that the ability to remember and all that went with it was something that was either dangerous to the rest of the populace or could be mined for economic benefit. We don't really know what their motivations are, but there is a group, as secretive as we are, who want to get to the bottom of the phenomenon."

"Dorphin's been a painter for years," I said.

"He's been co-opted by this group. A lot of people with the scribble mind turn out to be artists—painters, musicians, writers—but not all of them. So they either paid Dorphin a huge sum of money or blackmailed him or something to work for them. They gave him the design, no doubt, which it's obvious they now know, and he produced this painting and took it on the road to try to flush us out. Believe me, no one who remembers would go that public with the *Vundesh*. I knew it was a ploy when I saw the catalog and that painting, and I knew Esme would see it too."

"The *Vundesh*?"

"That's the name of the scribble design."

"This is completely insane," I said. "What will they do to Esme?"

"Well, if Dorphin believes she really remembers, she could disappear for good," he said. "It all depends on if he has the device with him or not."

"What device?" I asked, but I felt the car stopping. I looked and saw that Farno had pulled up to the curb in front of Esme's building. Another car was parked a few yards in front of the Chevy.

We jumped out and ran up the steps. The moment we were at the door, I reached up and hit the buzzer for her apartment. We waited but there was no answer. I hit it three more times with no response from above.

"Look out," said Farno, and he gently moved me to the side and scanned the names next to the buzzers. "I think Jenkins from our Life class lives here too." He must have found his name, because he pressed one of the buzzers and held it down.

Before long, a window opened two stories up and Jenkins stuck his head out. "Who's there?" he said, looking down.

Farno took a step back and looked up. "Hey man, it's me," he said and waved.

"Yo," said Jenkins.

"Pat Shay's here with me. We're going up to Esme's place but I think she's got her headphones on or something. Buzz us in, okay?"

I heard the window close, and a few seconds later the door buzzed. I grabbed the handle and Farno and I ran in. The door to the stairs was locked, so we had no choice but to take the elevator. The ascent was excruciatingly slow.

"Let's avoid fisticuffs and heroics," said Farno. "I want to get through this without anyone getting hurt, especially me."

When the elevator came to rest at Esme's floor, I pulled back the heavy door, and just as I got a view of her apartment and saw that its door was wide open, I saw someone bolt out of it and head down the short hallway. It could have been Dorphin, but all I saw was a blur. Stepping into the hall, I turned and saw the door to the stairway swing shut and lock. I bounded across the hall and into Esme's place. She was stretched out on the floor in the middle of her apartment, not moving. I dropped down next to her and took her arm to feel for a pulse, but as I groped along her wrist, I realized she was breathing.

"She's alive," I said over my shoulder.

Together we hoisted her up onto the couch where she'd be more comfortable. Farno went to get her some water, and I sat holding her hand and calling her name.

She eventually came around, shaking her head as if to clear it. When she opened her eyes, she saw me and said in a groggy voice, "Hey, Pat." A moment passed, and then she suddenly sat straight up and looked around nervously.

"Where is he?" she asked.

"Dorphin? He's gone," I said.

"He put this thing on my head, and then . . . everything went black."

Farno walked in with the water then. She looked up at him.

"What are you doing here?" she asked. "What are the two of you doing here?"

She held her head in both hands as we filled her in. "Are you getting this?" I asked.

She nodded.

Farno explained that the device Dorphin had used was something that helps them, whoever they are, to determine if you actually remember. According to him it was something new and it indicated some anomaly in the natural electromagnetic field emanating from the brain that was at the heart of the phenomenon.

"Did he have something like a television remote control?" asked Farno.

Esme nodded. "My god, it zapped me like an electric shock."

"He probably knows you don't have it, if he used that. That's a good thing," said Farno. "If he thought you had it, you might not still be here."

Esme took her hands away from her head and looked up. "Here's what I want to know," she said. "What is *it*?"

I turned to Farno and said, "Yeah, let's have it. We know too much already."

He got up, went over, and shut the door to the apartment. On the way back, he pulled up the chair from the computer desk and straddled it, crossing his arms over the back. "Okay," he said. "It's not like it's gonna change anything for you to know. Just, please, try to keep it a secret from here on out. Can you promise me that?"

Esme and I both agreed.

"There are some people—why these particular people and not others seems completely random—who are born with the ability to remember, after they are born, what it was like in the womb."

"Dorphin told me it was heaven—blue skies and dead relatives and omniscience, and that his device would allow me to see it," said Esme.

"Dorphin's an imposter. He's not even close to what the memory is. And, in fact, it's something that I truly can't describe to you. There just aren't words. It makes you different, though. It makes you experience the world differently than people without it. There's no special powers that come with it, no grand insights, but just a calm sense of well-being. All I can tell you is that you feel in your heart that you belong to the universe, that you know you have a purpose. That's it."

"What about the scribble?" I asked.

"I can make it automatically. I could make it ever since I could hold a crayon; perfect every time. It's a physical manifestation of the phenomenon. I don't understand it, only that it's a sign to others who have it that you also remember. There's something to knowing you're not the only one, and so we communicate this to one another. There's nothing more to it than that. There's no dark conspiracy. We're not out to take over the world or any of that silly shit."

"If it's so simple," said Esme, "then why keep it a secret?"

"First off," said Farno, "there's an understanding that comes with the remembering, sort of built in with it, and that is that it's better to keep it a secret from those who don't experience it. Look at Dorphin and the people he works for—the government; some pharmaceutical company, maybe, wanting to bottle and exploit that sense of purpose I mentioned; perhaps a vigilante group desperate to eradicate our difference from humanity. If you told people, they'd think we were talking about a memory of heaven, or the afterlife, or some realm in the course of reincarnation—start projecting onto it what they wanted it to be and become jealous they'd missed out. They couldn't be further off the mark. Think of how religious fanatics would abuse it. It has nothing to do with God in the pedestrian sense. The anti-abortionists would have a field day with it, never understanding the least bit of what it was.

The truth is, if you have it, you have it, you know, and if you don't, you'll never know."

I had a thousand more questions, but Farno said he had to leave. "She should probably stay somewhere else for a couple of days just in case they come again," he said to me. "If by then no one has broken into the apartment, it's probably a good sign that they know she's not authentic. No sense in calling the cops; they're not gonna believe you." He got up and headed for the door, and I thanked him for helping us. Without looking back, he simply waved his hand in the air. I thought Esme should also have said something to him, but she never opened her mouth. When he was gone, I looked at her and saw she was crying.

She remained silent while I helped her put a few things together and got her into her coat. It was as if she were drugged or drunk or sleepwalking. I told her I was taking her to my place, and I thought she would refuse to go, but she didn't. On the walk to my apartment, I kept my arm around her. She leaned against me, and I could feel her shivering. "Are you all right?" I asked her every couple of blocks, and instead of answering me, she'd put her hand on my side for a moment. The only sign that she was conscious at all was when we got to my apartment and climbed the impossibly long set of steps. I opened the door and flipped on the light switch, and when she saw it, she said, "Beautiful." I laughed, but she didn't.

She left my side and walked over to where the mattress lay on the floor. Unhitching the back of her dress, she let it drop right there, and wearing only a pair of underpants got into bed and curled into a fetal position beneath the blankets. She closed her eyes, and I turned the lights off so she could sleep. Instead of trying to find a place to sleep, I sat in the dark in front of my easel and had a beer, thinking through what had happened that night. She seemed so different, so beaten. The experience had changed her in some way, flipped a switch inside of her and turned off the manic energy. I pondered how and why, but it never came clear to me. Finally, I just lay down on the floor at the foot of the mattress and wadded a jacket up for a pillow. The floor was hard as hell, but I was exhausted.

My eyes hadn't been closed five minutes when I heard her voice, whispering. "Pat, come over here with me," she said. I didn't argue, but got to my knees and crawled over to the empty side of the mattress. Once I was under the covers, she turned to me and said, "Just hold me." So I did, and that's how we slept all night.

I was late getting up the next morning and had to rush to get ready for school. She was still asleep when I left. All day I wondered how long Esme would stay with me or if she'd be gone when I got home. I saw Farno in class and he completely ignored me. To show him I was true to my promise of secrecy, I also said nothing to him. When class was over, though, and we passed in the hallway, he subtly nodded and smiled at me. I took the first bus I could catch and stopped at the Chinese place up the street from my apartment, buying enough for two.

Esme was still there. She'd done the dishes and straightened the place up a bit—a very welcome sight indeed. Her demeanor was lighter, at least more cognizant. It wasn't that she no longer seemed changed, but at least she was talkative and smiled at the fact that I'd bought us dinner. Instead of my usual, eating right out of the white cartons, we cleared the table and she found a couple of plates I couldn't remember owning. She asked me what had happened at school, and I thanked her for doing the dishes and cleaning. After that, though, things went quiet.

Unable to take the silence, I asked her, "So, did you go out today?"

"No," she said, "but I'll show you what I did." She got up and walked over to an old drawing board I had set up by the window. She pointed down at the board.

On one side, taped to the slanted surface, was one of the day-care kids' drawings of the scribble. Lying next to them was a stack of drawing paper, the top sheet of which also had a scribble on it, but not *the* scribble.

"What are you doing?" I asked, smiling.

"I'm trying to draw the scribble freehand."

"Why?" I asked.

"I thought that if I could get it just right, I'd be able to remember. Sometimes things work in both directions," she said. Her smile became tenuous.

"Do you think that's a good idea?" I asked.

"It could work," she told me.

She seemed too fragile for me to try to talk reason to her, as if she'd implode if I called her process into question. Instead, I said, "Well, there's a lot of paper there," pointing to the five-hundred-sheet box of copier paper I'd ripped off from school that lay on the floor.

She nodded and sat down. Picking up a pencil, she leaned over and grabbed a new sheet of paper from the box. "I'll use both sides," she said.

"Thanks," I said and went back to the table to finish my dinner.

She worked relentlessly, attempting to reproduce the scribble. I sat, pretending to paint, and witnessed her mania, trying to decide what to do. Eventually, late into the night, she stood up, took off her clothes, and lay down on the mattress under the blankets.

The next morning when I awoke, she was already at the drawing board. I took a shower and got dressed for school, and when I told her I had to get going, she barely looked up. The sheets of paper holding the rejected scribbles had originally been neatly stacked, but now the stack was spilling onto the floor, and the chair she occupied was surrounded by scattered paper.

"How's it going?" I asked, trying to get a response from her before leaving.

"Good," she said, holding up her latest attempt. "Look, I'm getting really close." She laid the picture down next to the one taped to the board. "Don't you think?"

"Yeah," I said. "You're making progress." To be honest, it looked to me like she was even further from the mark than when she'd started. I said good-bye, but she was already beginning on her next scribble and didn't acknowledge my leaving.

That evening, when I returned home, I found a blizzard of copier paper covering the floor around the drawing table; the box was empty. The original day-care drawing and the small suitcase she'd packed the night she came to stay were gone and so was she. For the first time since I'd moved in there, the apartment felt empty. I left and ran over to her place. When she didn't answer, I buzzed for Jenkins. A minute later, he was sticking his head out the window above.

"What do you want, Shay?" he called down.

"Have you seen Esme?"

"Yeah," he said. "A few hours ago. She had a pile of suitcases, right there on the curb. A cab came and got her."

"Buzz me in, man," I said to him.

When I got to her apartment, I found the door unlocked. She'd left her computer and all of her books. I wondered if that meant she'd be back. Lying on the floor in the corner, I found the picture of her mother. It'd been taken out of its frame, which lay nearby in a pile of broken glass. I picked up the photo and brought it closer. Then I noticed that the face of the severe-looking woman had been covered with a scribble.

I went religiously to the Palace A every Sunday morning for a late breakfast, but she never joined me again. Later on, I learned from one of the professors that she'd dropped out. Making a phone call home, I told my mother to keep a lookout for her in town in case Esme'd decided to return to her father's house. Finishing that semester was one of the hardest things I've ever done. At the eleventh hour, when it looked like I wouldn't be able to come up with any new paintings for my final review, I had a breakthrough one night and dashed off a portrait of a little girl, sitting alone by an open window. Outside the sun is shining and the sky is blue. She's drawing at a table, and although the pencil in her hand is drawing a scribble on the paper before her, her eyes are closed. I called it *The Scribble Mind.* It was only one piece, but it was good enough to get me through the semester.

After graduate school I kept painting, year in and year out, with a show here and there but never to any great acclaim. When I was younger, that bothered me, and then I forgot about it, and the work itself became its own reward. Still, in all of those hundreds of canvases I'd covered not one ever gave me a hint as to what my true purpose was. Living without knowing was not so bad, especially after I'd married and had two daughters. I had all the purpose I needed in my family, and the art was just something I did and will always do.

I did see Esme one more time, years later. It wasn't that I'd forgotten her—that would have been impossible—but more that I'd packed that time away and painted through it. I was in a small gallery down in SoHo in New York City, where I had a few pieces in a show. I'd gone in that afternoon because the show was over and I had to take my work down. The owner of the place was back in her office, and the gallery was empty. I was just about to remove a painting from the wall when the door opened and in walked a woman with a young girl following. As I turned to see who it was, the woman said, "Hey, Pat." I noticed the black hair and her eyes and something stirred in my memory, although the expensive coat and boots weren't right. "Esme, what are you doing here?" I said.

She laughed. "I live uptown, and I saw an announcement for this show and your name and thought I'd come down and see what your paintings looked like. I never suspected you'd be here."

"It's great to see you," I said.

She introduced me to her daughter, who stood by the front window, looking out at the people walking by. Her name was Gina, and she seemed to be kind of a sad kid. I said hi to her and she turned and waved. She must have been about six.

I showed Esme my work and she praised it unconditionally; told me how glad she was to see I was still painting after all these years. We talked about a lot of things—the Palace A, our hometown, the university, the fact that she no longer bothered with her computer art—but neither of us mentioned the scribble or the night involving Dorphin or what happened afterward. It was strange dancing around those memories, but I was more than happy to do so.

Finally she said she had to go, and she leaned close to me and gave me a quick kiss on the cheek. "Thanks for coming," I said. Before she called to her daughter and they left the gallery, though, she made a kind of dramatic pause and brought her hand up to trace a quick scribble in the air. Then she winked at me and said in a whisper, "Pat . . . I remember." I put on a face of envy and excitement, though I felt neither. I knew she was lying, because the whole time she was there, the kid never came within eight feet of her. There are some mysteries in this world you can learn to live with and some you just can't.

THE
BEDROOM
LIGHT

They each decided, separately, that they wouldn't discuss the miscarriage that night. The autumn breeze sounded in the tree outside the open kitchen window and traveled all through the second-story apartment of the old Victorian house. It twirled the hanging plant over the sink, flapped the ancient magazine photo of Veronica Lake tacked to his office door, spun the clown mobile in the empty bedroom, and, beneath it, set the wicker rocker to life. In their bedroom it tilted the fabric shade of the antique floor lamp that stood in the corner by the front window. Allison looked at the reflection of them lying beneath the covers in the mirror set into the top of the armoire while Bill looked at their reflection in the glass of the hand-colored print, *Moon Over Miami*, that hung on the wall above her. The huge gray cat, Mama, her belly skimming the floor, padded quietly into the room and snuck through the partially open door of the armoire.

Bill rolled over to face Allison and ran his hand softly down the length of her arm. "Today, while I was writing," he said, "I heard, coming up through the grate beneath my desk, Tana's mother yelling at her."

"Demon seed?" said Allison.

He laughed quietly. "Yeah." He stopped rubbing her arm. "I got out of my chair, got down on the floor, and turned my ear to the grate."

She smiled.

"So the mom's telling Tana, 'You'll listen to me, I'm the mother. I'm in charge and you'll do what I say.' Then there was a pause, and I hear this voice. Man, this was like no kid's voice, but it *was* Tana, and she says, 'No, Mommy, I'm in charge and you will listen to me.'"

"Get outta here," Allison said and pushed him gently in the chest.

"God's honest truth. So then Cindy makes a feeble attempt to get back in power. 'I'm the mommy,' she yells, but I could tell she meant to say it with more force, and it came out cracked and weak. And then there's a pause, and Tana comes back with, 'You're wrong, Mommy. I am in charge and you will listen to me.'"

"Creep show," Allison said.

"It got really quiet then, so I put my ear down closer. My head was on the damn floor. That's when I heard Cindy weeping."

Allison gave a shiver, half fake, and handed Bill one of her pillows. He put it behind his head with the rest of his stack. "Did I tell you what Phil told me?" she said.

"No," he said.

"He told me that when he's walking down the street and he sees her coming toward him, he crosses over to the opposite side."

"I don't blame him," he said, laughing.

"He told you about the dog, right?" she said, pulling the covers up over her shoulder.

Bill shook his head.

"He said the people who live in the second-floor apartment next door—the young guy with the limp and his wife, Rhoda—they used to have a beagle that they kept on their porch all day while they were at work."

"Over here," he said and pointed at the wall.

"Yeah. They gave it water and food, the whole thing, and had a long leash attached to its collar. Anyway, one day Phil's walking down to the Busy-Bee to get coffee and cigarettes and he sees Tana standing under the porch, looking up at the dog. She was talking to it. Phil said that the dog was getting worked up, so he told Tana to leave it alone. She shot him a 'Don't fuck with me' stare. He was worried how it might look, him talking to the kid, so he went on his way. That afternoon the dog was discovered strangled, hanging by its leash off the second-story porch."

"He never told me that. Shit. And come to think about it, I never told *you* this. . . . I was sitting in my office just the other day, writing, and all of a sudden I feel something on my back, like it's tingling. I turn around, and there she is, standing in the doorway to the office, holding Mama like a baby doll, just staring at me. I jumped out of my chair, and I said, like, 'I didn't hear you knock.' I was a little scared actually, so I asked her if she wanted a cookie. At first she didn't say anything, but just looked at me with that . . . if I were writing a story about her I'd describe her face as *dour*—an old lady face minus the wrinkles. . . . Then, get this, she says in that low, flat voice, 'Do you Lambada?'"

"What the fuck?" Allison said and laughed. "She didn't say that."

"No," he said, "that's what she said, she asked me if I *Lambada*. What the hell is it anyway? I told her no, and then she turned and split."

"Lambada, I think . . . ," she said and broke out laughing again. "I think it's some kind of South American dance."

"What would have happened if I said yes?" he asked.

"Lambada," she whispered, shaking her head.

"Phil's got the right strategy with her," he said.

"But I don't like her coming up here in the middle of the day uninvited," said Allison.

"I'll have to start locking the door after you go to work," said Bill.

"This place . . . there's something very . . . I don't know." She sighed. "Like, you ever lean against a wall? It kind of *gives* like flesh. Almost *spongy*," she said.

"That's just the lathing. . . . It's separating away from the Sheetrock cause this building is so old. I know what you mean, though, with that eggshell smoothness and the pliancy when you touch it—like you said, spongy-weird."

"There's a sinister factor to this place. The Oriental carpets, the lion's-paw tub, the old heavy furniture—the gravity of the past that was here when we moved in. I can't put my finger on it. At first I thought it was quaint, but then I realized it didn't stop there."

"Like melancholy?" he asked.

"Yeah, exactly—a sadness."

"Just think about it. You've got Corky and Cindy down there, hitting the sauce and each other almost every night. They must have had to buy a whole new set of dishes after last weekend. Then you got the kid . . . nuff said there. What about next door, on the other side, the guy who washes his underwear on the fucking clothesline with the hose? That guy's also classically deranged."

"I forgot about him," she said.

"Well," he said, "let's not forget about him. I watch him from the kitchen window. I can see right down through the tree branches and across the yard into his dining room. He sits there every night for hours, reading that big fat book."

"I've seen him down there," she said. "Sometimes when I wake up in the middle of the night and go into the kitchen for a glass of water, I notice him down there reading. Is it the Bible?"

"Could be the fucking phone book for all I know."

"Cindy told me that when they got Tana that yippie little dog—Shotzy, Potzy, whatever—the kid was walking on that side of the house over by the old guy's property, and he came out his back door and yelled at her, 'If I find your dog in my yard, I'll kill it.' Now, I know Tana's demon seed and all, but she's still a little kid. . . . Cindy didn't tell Corky because she was afraid he'd Cork off and kick the crap out of the old guy."

"What, instead of her for once? Hey, you never know, maybe the old man's just trying to protect himself from Tana's . . . *animal magic*," said Bill. "You know, Cindy swears the kid brought a dead bird back to life. She just kind of slips that in in the middle of a 'Hey, the weather's nice' kind of conversation."

"Yeah, I've caught that tale," said Allison. There was a pause. "But do you get my overall point here?" She opened her hands to illustrate the broadness of the concept. "Like we're talking some kind of hovering, negative funk."

"Amorphous and pungent," he said.

"I've felt it ever since the first week we moved in," she said.

"Does it have anything to do with the old woman who answered the door with her pants around her ankles?"

"Olive Harker?" she said. "Corky's illustrious mom?"

"Remember, Olive hadta get shipped out for us to move in. Maybe she cursed the joint. You, know, put the Lambada on it."

"It wasn't her so much," said Allison. "I first felt it the day the cat pissed in the sugar bowl."

"Right in front of me—between bites of French toast," he said. "That cat sucks."

"Don't talk about Mama that way," she said.

"It baahhhs like a lamb and eats flies. I hate it," he said.

"She's good. Three whole weeks gone and she still came back, didn't she? You shouldn't have thrown her out."

"I didn't throw her, I drop-kicked her. She made a perfect arc, right over the back fence. But the question is, or at least the point is, if I follow you, how strange is it that she pissed right in the sugar bowl—jumped up on the table, made a beeline for it, parked right over it, and pissed like there was no tomorrow?"

"That's what I'm getting at," said Allison. "It fulfills no evolutionary need. It's just grim."

"Maybe it's us," he said. "Maybe we're haunting ourselves."

"I saw Corky digging a big hole out in the yard the other day," she said. "His back's full of ink—an angel being torn apart by demons. . . . I was more interested in the hole he was digging 'cause I haven't heard any yipping out of Potzy for a few days."

"Don't worry," he said. "I'm ready for him."

"How?" she asked.

"The other day, when I went out garbage picking, I found a busted-off rake handle. I wound duct tape around one end for a grip. It's in the kitchen behind the door for when Corky gets shit-faced and starts up the stairs. Then I'm gonna grab that thing and beat his ass."

"Hey, do you remember that guy Keith back in college?" she asked.

"McCurly, yeah," he said. "He did the apple dance. What made you think of him?"

She nodded. "Every time he flapped his arms the apple rolled off his head, remember?"

"He danced to Steve Miller's 'Fly Like an Eagle,'" Bill said. "What a fuckin' fruitcake. I remember O'Shea telling me that he ended up working for the government."

"Well, remember that time he was telling us he was reading *The Amityville Horror*?"

"Yeah," he said.

"McCurly said that one of the pieces of proof that the author used in the book to nail down his case that the house was really haunted was that they found an evil shit in the toilet bowl. Remember that?"

"Yeah."

"You said to him, 'What do you mean by an *evil* shit?' And McCurly looked like he didn't get your question."

"But what he eventually said was 'It was heinous.' I asked him if he could explain that and he said, 'Really gross.'"

They laughed.

She touched his face as if to make him quiet, and said, "That's the point. We paint the unknown with the devil's shit to make it make sense."

"Heavy," said Bill. A few seconds passed in silence.

"Right . . . ?" she said.

"Amityville was only like two towns over from where I grew up," he told her. "New people were in there and it was all fixed up. I'd go out drinking with my friends all night. You know, the Callahans, and Wolfy, and Angelo, and Benny the Bear, and at the end of the night we'd have these cases of empty beer bottles in the car. So around that time the movie came out. We went to see it and laughed our asses off—come on, Brolin? Steiger we're talking. One of the things that cracked us up big time was the voice saying, 'Get out. For God's sake get the hell out.' Steiger and the flies . . . baby, well worth the price of admission. So we decided we're gonna drive to the *Amityville Horror* house and scream, 'Get the hell out,' and throw our empties on the lawn."

"That's retarded," she said.

"We did it, but then we kept doing it, and not just to the *Amityville Horror* house. Every time we did it, I'd crack like hell. It was so fucking stupid it made me laugh. Plus we were high as kites. We did it to people we knew and didn't know and we did it a lot to the high school coaches we'd had for different sports. There was this one guy, though, we did it to the most—Coach Pinhead. Crew cut, face as smooth as an ass, googly eyes, and his favorite joke was to say 'How Long is a Chinaman.' He was a soccer coach, a real douche bag, but we swung by his house every weekend night for like three months, dropped the empties, and yelled 'Pinhead!!!' before peeling out on his lawn. We called the whole thing a Piercing Pinhead."

"Could you imagine how pissed off you'd be today if some kids did that to you?" she said.

"Yeah," he said. "I know. But get this. I was talking to Mike Callahan about five years later. When he was working selling furniture and married to that rich girl. I saw him at my mother's funeral. He told me that he found out that Pinhead died of pancreatic cancer. All that time we were doing the Piercing Pinheads, screaming in the middle of the night outside his house, tormenting him, the poor guy was in there, in his bedroom, dying by inches."

"That's haunted," said Allison.

"Tell me about it," he said and then rolled closer to kiss her.

They kissed and then lay quiet, both listening to the sound of the leaves blowing outside. She began to doze off, but before her eyes closed all the way, she said, "Who's getting the light?"

"You," said Bill.

"Come on," she said. "I've got an early shift tomorrow."

"Come on? I've gotten the damn light every night for the past two weeks."

"That's 'cause it's your job," she said.

"Fuck that," he said but started to get up. Just then the light went out.

She opened her eyes slightly, grinning. "Sometimes it pays to be haunted," she said.

Bill looked around the darkened room and said, as if to every-where at once, "Thank you."

The light blinked on and then off.

"Maybe the bulb's loose," he said.

The light blinked repeatedly on and off and then died again.

"That's freaky," she said, but freaky wasn't going to stop her from falling asleep. Her eyes slowly closed and before he could kiss her again on the forehead, she was lightly snoring.

Bill lay there in the dark, wide awake, thinking about their con-versation and about the lamp. He thought about ghosts in Miami, beneath swaying palm trees, doing the Lambada by moonlight. Fi-nally, he whispered, "Light, are you really haunted?"

Nothing.

A long time passed, and then he asked, "Are you Olive?"

The light stayed off.

"Are you Pinhead?"

Just darkness.

"Are you Tana?" he said. He waited for a sign, but nothing. Eventually he closed his eyes and thought about work. He worked at Nescron, a used bookstore housed in the bottom floor of a block-long, four-story warehouse—timbers and stone—built in the 1800s. The owner, Stan, had started, decades earlier, in the scrap paper business and over time had amassed tons of old books. The upper three floors of the warehouse were packed with unopened boxes and crates from all over the world. Bill's job was to crawl in amid the piles of boxes, slit them open, and mine their cargo, pick-ing out volumes for the literature section in the store downstairs. Days would pass at work and he'd see no one. He'd penetrated so deeply into the morass of the third floor that sometimes he'd get scared, having the same feeling he'd had when he and Allison had gone to Montana three months earlier to recuperate and they were way up in the mountains and came upon a freshly killed and half-

eaten antelope beside a water hole. Amid the piles of books, he felt
for the second time in his life that he was really "out there."

"I expect some day to find a pine box up on the third floor holding
the corpse of Henry Miller," he'd told Allison at dinner one night.

"Who's Henry Miller?" she'd asked.

He'd found troves of classics and first editions and even signed
volumes for the store down below, and Stan had praised his ef-
forts at excavating the upper floors. As the months went on, Bill
was making a neat little stack of goodies for himself, planning to
shove them in a paper sack and spirit them home with him when
he closed up some Monday night. An early edition of Longfellow's
translation of Dante, an actual illuminated manuscript with gold
leaf, a signed, first edition of *Call of the Wild,* and an 1885 edition
of *The Scarlet Letter* were just some of the treasures.

Recently at work he'd begun to get an odd feeling when he was
deep within the wilderness of books, not the usual fear of loneliness, but the opposite, that he was not alone. Twice in the last week,
he'd thought he'd heard whispering, and once, the sudden quiet
tumult of a distant avalanche of books. He'd asked down below in
the store if anyone else was working the third floor, and he was told
that he was the only one. Then, only the previous day, he couldn't
locate his cache of hoarded books. It was possible that he was disoriented, but in the very spot he'd thought they'd be, he instead
found one tall slim volume. It was a book of fairy tales illustrated
by an artist named Ségur. The animals depicted in the illustrations
walked upright and had distinct personalities, and the children,
in powder-blue snowscapes surrounded by Christmas mice, were
pale, staring zombies. The colors were odd, slightly washed-out,
and the sizes of the creatures and people were haphazard.

Without realizing it, Bill fell asleep and his thoughts of work
melted into a dream of the writer Henry Miller. He woke suddenly
a little while later to the sound of Allison's voice, the room still

in darkness. "Bill," she said again and pushed his shoulder, "you awake?"

"Yeah," he said.

"I had a dream," said Allison. "Oh my god . . ."

"Sounds like a good one," he said.

"Maybe, maybe," she said.

He could tell she was waiting for him to ask what it was about. Finally he asked her, "So what happened?"

She drew close to him and he put his arm around her. She whispered, "Lothianne."

"Lothianne?" said Bill

"A woman with three arms," said Allison. "She had an arm coming out of the upper part of her back, and the hand on it had two thumbs instead of a pinky and a thumb, so it wouldn't be either righty or lefty. The elbow only bent up and down, not side to side."

"Yow," said Bill.

"Her complexion was light blue, and her hair was dark and wild, but not long. And she wore this dress with an extra arm hole in the back. This dress was plain, like something out of the Dust Bowl, gray, and reached to the ankles, and I remembered my fifth-grade teacher, Mrs. Donnelly, the mean old bitch, having worn the exact one back in grade school when we spent a whole year reading *The Last Days of Pompeii*."

"Did the three-arm woman look like your teacher?" asked Bill.

"No, but she was stupid and mean like her. She had a dour face, familiar and frightening. Anyway, Lothianne wandered the woods with a pet jay that flew above her and sometimes perched in her tangled hair. I think she might have been a cannibal. She lived underground in like a woman-size rabbit warren."

"Charming," he said.

"I was a little girl and my sister and I were running hard toward this house in the distance, away from the woods, just in front of a wave of nighttime. I knew we had to reach the house before the darkness swept over us. The blue jay swooped down and, as I tried to catch my breath, it spit into my mouth. It tasted like fire and spread to my arms and legs. My running went dream slow, my legs dream heavy. My sister screamed toward the house. Then, like a rusty engine, I seized altogether and fell over."

"You know, in China, they eat Bird Spit Soup . . . ," he said.

"Shut up," she said. "The next thing I know, I come to and Lothianne and I are on a raft, in a swiftly moving stream, tethered to a giant willow tree that's growing right in the middle of the flow. Lothianne has a lantern in one hand, and in the other she's holding the end of a long vine that's tied in a noose around my neck. The moon's out, shining through the willow whips and reflecting off the running water, and I'm so scared.

"She says, 'Time to practice drowning' and kicks me in the back. I fall into the water. Under the surface I'm looking up and the moonlight allows me to see the stones and plants around me. There are speckled fish swimming by. Just before I'm out of air, she reels me in. This happens three times, and on the last time, when she reels me in, she vanishes, and I'm flying above the stream and surrounding hills and woods, and I'm watching things growing—huge plants like asparagus, sprouting leaves and twining and twirling and growing in the moonlight. Even in the dark, it was so perfectly clear."

"Jeez," said Bill.

Allison was silent for a while. Eventually she propped herself up on her elbow and said, "It was frightening but it struck me as a 'creative' dream, 'cause of the end."

"A three-armed woman," said Bill. "Rembrandt once did an etching of a three-armed woman having sex with a guy."

"I was wondering if the noose around my neck was symbolic of an umbilical cord. . . ."

He stared at her. "Why?" he finally said.

She was about to answer but the bedroom light blinked on and off, on and off, on and off, without stopping, like a strobe light, and from somewhere or everywhere in the room came the sound of low moaning.

Bill threw the covers off, sat straight up, and said, "What the fuck?"

Allison, wide-eyed, her glance darting here and there, said, "Bill . . ."

The light show finally ended in darkness, but the sound grew louder, more strange, like a high-pitched growling that seemed to make the windowpanes vibrate. She grabbed his shoulder and pointed to the armoire. He turned, and as he did, Mama the cat came bursting out of the standing closet, the door swinging wildly. She screeched and spun in incredibly fast circles on the rug next to the bed.

"Jesus Christ," yelled Bill, and lifted his feet, afraid the cat might claw him. "Get the fuck outa here!" he yelled at it.

Mama took off out of the bedroom, still screeching. Allison jumped out of the bed and took off after the cat. Bill cautiously brought up the rear. They found Mama in the bathroom, on the floor next to the lion-paw tub, writhing.

"Look," said Bill, peering over Allison's shoulder, "she's attacking her own ass. What the hell . . ."

"Oh, man," said Allison. "Check it out." She pointed as Mama pulled a long furry lump out of herself with her teeth.

"That's it for me," he said, backing away from the bathroom doorway.

"Bill, here comes another. It's alive."

"Alive?" he said, sitting down on a chair in the kitchen. "I thought it was a mohair turd."

"No, you ass, she's having a kitten. I never realized she was pregnant. Must be from the time you kicked her out."

Bill sat there staring at Allison's figure illuminated by the bulb she'd switched on in the bathroom.

"This is amazing, you should come see it," she called over her shoulder to him.

"I'll pass," he said. He turned then and looked through the open kitchen window, down across the yard toward the old man's house. For the first time he could remember, his neighbor wasn't there, reading the big book. The usual rectangle of light was now a dark empty space.

Later, he found Allison sitting in the wicker rocker, beneath the clown mobile, in the otherwise empty bedroom. The light was on, and she rocked, slowly, a rolled up towel cradled in her arms. "Come see," she said to him, smiling. "The first was stillborn, and this is the only other one, but it lived. It's a little girl."

He didn't want to, but she seemed so pleased. He took a step closer. She pulled back a corner of the towel, and there was a small, wet, face with blue eyes.

"Now we have to name it," she said.

IN THE HOUSE OF
FOUR SEASONS

At a large coffee table set upon a hillock within a grove of birch, Mrs. Gash, seated on the ground with her legs drawn up beneath her, pieced together a jigsaw puzzle depicting performers in a ring. Her concentration was such that she had obviously forgotten I was there, and holding in her fingers a piece that bore the image of a white horse's head in her fingers, she used the back of that hand to rub her nose as a child might, unthinking, as if lost in a game or being told a story. I leaned upon the arm of the divan, my elbow propped on two pillows, my legs curled up off the ground. After a sip of coffee, I watched a pale violet butterfly light upon a white branch. It was a perfect afternoon of serenity and the slightest breeze. That night, we were to set paper boats, holding lit candles, adrift on the glassy waters of the large pond, and again I would witness the miracle of constellations above from a cave at the bottom of the sea.

• • •

Spencer didn't see us in the driving snow. He expected us to be waiting for him at the dining table in the forest, and he trudged along through the drifts, pushing his silver cart. He hadn't a second to react when I leaped from behind a tree and smashed him across the head with a heavy branch. Both of his lightbulb eyes instantly shattered; there was a crackle of electricity, and black smoke billowed from the rectangle that was his mouth. "Treachery," he said in a manner devoid of urgency. He reeled away from my blow, head dented on one side, and then Andre came forward with his own branch. Being more powerful than I, he took what was left of the brass servant's head clean off. It hit the snow and rolled, shooting sparks.

Once the brass globe was cool enough to lift, Andre picked it up and carried it to the silver cart, where I'd cleared the bottom shelf of dishes. I helped him load it upon the conveyance and then pushed the cart toward the table in the forest where Lenice was waiting for us. While I labored through the gathering drifts, my hands freezing on the cold metal of the cart, Andre stayed behind to drag Spencer's body out of sight. By the time he caught up to me, I was sitting with Lenice and breaking the news to her that we'd done in the mechanical man. She began to cry, and I asked her if she wanted to escape the House of Four Seasons or if she would prefer to be buried alive beneath a slowly growing avalanche.

Andre lifted one of the platters off the cart and brought it to the table. "We'd better eat before we begin," he said over the wind. "We don't know when there will be another chance." The snow increased with every passing minute.

"Good idea," I said.

Lenice stopped sobbing, composed herself with a deep breath, and lifted the top of the large serving dish. I could tell by the smell before I even got a look that it was mutton again. And then Lenice let out a scream. I looked down at the platter and instead of the usual big roast leg of lamb we were usually served at lunch, there was a baby expertly carved, crafted, and created out of mutton. Pungent steam rose from it. Cloves for teeth and pearl onion eyes stared up. The action of lifting the lid had made its little legs kick and its arms reach up. The lamb baby was wrapped in a diaper of lettuce, and its hands were lobster claws, bright red.

"Dig in," said Andre and pulled off an ear.

Lenice gagged.

I covered the dish and took it away from the table to set it at the edge of the clearing. When I returned, I told Andre to fetch Spencer's head. He pulled the brass dome from the second shelf of the cart and laid it on the dining table. Tilting it to reveal an opening beneath the metal jaw, he reached in and said, "We need the brain. From that I can make a bomb."

Above the howling wind, sounds came from beneath the covered dish at the boundary of trees, and with each muffled cry, Mrs. Gash doubled over in pain as if something were breaking inside her.

The day Brown and I went fishing in the stream that ran from the bottom of Lookout Hill and snaked its way throughout the environs of the entire House to the sand dune at the farthest western extremity, he leaned very close after dropping a line baited with a bit of mutton and whispered, as if the very trees might be listening, "Denni, you know, I'll be honest, I find Ima quite an interesting lady. I dare say, if I may be somewhat base for a moment, I'd like to get my head up under her flowers and snowflakes and run riot in her most intimate of areas. But she is always with that damn fellow. My god, how do I get her alone?"

I laughed. "Are you serious, Brown?"

He stared at me strangely. "You won't tell him, will you?" he said. There was another pause, his voluminous visage went red, and he forced a laugh. "Of course, I'm joking . . . but . . . tell me that you, yourself, haven't envisioned an encounter with that generous breast."

I walked alone through the forest at sundown, the red and yellow leaves falling around me. A strong breeze blew from way off deep in among the trees where, no doubt, if I continued I'd come to the limit of the House of Four Seasons, where marvelous nature became a painting on a rock wall, a dark emptiness beyond which there was . . . what? An owl hooted in the distance, and I recalled what Ima had told me about his/her life in our session that afternoon—how when he was born she'd been sold by his parents to a traveling circus, billed as the Heshe from her tenth birthday and forced to endure the stares of strangers. I contemplated how difficult it must have been to rise to the level of distinction he had, world-renowned therapist and proprietor of the remarkable facility we now inhabited.

"How did you do it?" I'd asked her, thinking I might discover the secret to piecing together my own blasted self.

"Always being of two minds, I let them both work for me," she said.

An owl called again, and the distinctive sound brought another memory, one of fire and revenge, which was only quelled when Mr. Susan's voice summoned me back for dinner.

I had the others to my room, and we lay on our backs near the edge of the pond, staring into the perfect blue while Mr. Brown raised his voice just a notch above the tumbling waterfall and read to us from his book, *The Gilead*. It was the story of an immortal man and his search for Death. In this wretched character's second century, he'd lost the ability to fall in love. Trying to get the State to use the electric chair on him, a device he believed would circumvent the antique magic of his curse by dint of modern science, he murdered a young woman and her child in cold blood, bludgeoned them with a tree branch. He was tried and convicted. When they finally strapped him into the electric chair, put the bonnet on his head, and threw the switch, instead of scorching the life out of him, it blew up, starting a fire and killing all those who had sought to bring him to justice. He walked away without so much as a singed eyebrow.

"Time had made him a monster," said Andre.

"But you sympathize with him, don't you, even a little?" asked Lenice.

"The part about him killing the child?" asked Brown.

"No, his plight," said Lenice with a touch of exasperation.

"Hold on," said Mr. Brown, "how come you've got a waterfall in your room and I don't, Denni?"

I met my fellow patients, as Ima referred to us: Mrs. Gash, Mr. Susan, and Mr. Mutandis. With the dappled sunlight falling upon us through the thick green canopy overhead, we sat at the dining table in the forest and were served a lunch of soup, cold mutton, candied carrots, and tippers fried in wine sauce. The waiter, a mechanical man made of polished brass—large lightbulb eyes set in a round head with a seam of rivets from ear to ear across the crown and only three articulated digits on each hand—did the honors. Once we were seated, he came down the forest path, pushing a large silver cart on wheels, which held all the utensils and china and serving dishes. Mrs. Gash thought him a delightful novelty and clapped when he perfectly poured her a glass of wine. To this the metal servant bowed and said in a tin voice, "Spencer, at your service." Then he ambulated away, a cloud of blue smoke issuing from a small hole at the back of his head.

Over a long lunch, we made our introductions. Mr. Susan asked us to call him Andre. He was a somewhat older fellow with a sprinkling of gray in his mustache and sideburns, very fit and with an easy smile. When asked what he did, he let us know that he was in the chemical business.

The short, squat Mr. Mutandis, a man of many chins and a high red color in his face, asked us to call him Mr. Brown. It was an odd request, but the three of us agreed. Once he saw that we would honor his wish, he told us that he had been the proprietor of an orphanage, which had recently burned to the ground. I asked if anyone had been injured. He shook his head. "No," he said, "but many died." With this pronouncement, he checked the time on his pocket watch, which he kept on a chain in his vest pocket.

Mrs. Gash, or Lenice, as she let it be known was her first name, shook her head and said, "That's terrible." Mr. Susan winced, a candied carrot half in his mouth, half out, like a short orange cigar. "You know," said Brown, "when our metal man lifted the top off that mutton dish and the steam rose up, the aroma was near identical to that emanating from the ruins. Ghastly." With this pronouncement, he shoved a piece of meat into his mouth and began chewing.

Lenice Gash had very fine features, dark eyes, and short, light brown hair. My first impression of her was that she was as serious a woman as she was fetching. She told us that her husband was a man of God, and that she was a simple homemaker with a young child. "I miss my baby," she said to us, "but I'm delighted to be here. I feel better already." I told her we wouldn't be too long away from home. "That's right," said Andre. "Think of it as a vacation."

When it came my turn to divulge, I told them very little, and what I did give up was a sheer lie. "I'm a circus performer," I said. "I ride horses, standing on my head." Even Brown seemed impressed. "Please, call me Denni," I added.

After we'd finished with the food, we pushed our plates back and continued the conversation. We discussed our journey in the submarine, the natural beauty of the House of Four Seasons, and then in whispers we had our way with Ima.

"She seems very sweet," said Lenice, "if you're on the right side of her."

"And very gruff if you're on the left," said Brown.

Andre took a long toke of his cigar, nodded slowly, and, staring into the trees, said, "Oh, yes, she, he, whichever you prefer, is some grim business indeed."

"Whoever put the metal man together did a better job," said Brown.

"But perhaps she can cure us," I said.

"Why did you say she?" asked Lenice.

"I don't know," I said.

Of a dark, chilled afternoon, we stood at the bar to the left side of the path on the way to Lookout Hill. Mrs. Gash served as bartender. Andre had a whiskey neat, and Lenice and I sipped some dark red wine, slightly sweet and spiced perhaps with nutmeg and cinnamon. Looking back toward the forest, I saw a silver fox slip in among the trees and tried to point it out to the others but was too late.

"I smell snow," said Andre, resting his drink and turning up the collar of his long coat.

"I've not been able to get warm since autumn arrived," said Lenice. "I sleep with three sweaters on and two comforters. Do you think snow is possible here?"

"I smell a conspiracy," I said. "Do you notice how Brown rarely joins us now but for meals? On my way to the big pond yesterday, I saw him walking with Ima and he had his arm around him."

"I'll tell you," said Lenice, "from the very instant I saw the first yellow leaves begin to drop in the forest, I've experienced a growing sense of *something. . . .*"

"Doom?" asked Andre.

"Not doom," she said, shaking her head. "Definitely gloom, though. As though the charm of the House in spring and summer were a mere trick; a ruse or trap. I miss my child."

"Boy or girl?" I asked.

She was about to answer, but then she stopped and stared into the sky. I looked up, expecting to see the old turkey buzzard circling, but it was an empty gray expanse. The wind blew fiercely and threatened to steal our hats.

"Yes, I'm ready to return to the city," said Andre.

"Are we cursed and don't yet know it?" asked Lenice. "Is that what this is about?" There were tears in her eyes.

I put my arm around her and she turned and kissed me full on the mouth. We stayed pressed together for a very long time. When we broke apart, Andre lifted his glass and said, "To winter and Mr. Gash."

We were there, by the bar, drinking in silence, when the snow began to fall.

My bed has a canopy and the spring rains thrum upon it and run off all sides, creating a shimmering veil through which I view the day. The rain is strange here—wet yet unable to soak fabric. It splashes against my palm but dries immediately. Across a short stretch of wild grass (for my bed is positioned in a meadow) sit a desk, a chair, and, next to them, a dresser. There's a mirror atop the dresser in which I see the outline of my reflection made liquid by the rain as I sit, propped upon the pillows, writing this letter to you. In the bottom drawer of that bureau, a field mouse has taken up residence in a nest of dried grass and leaves.

There's no toilet to speak of here, but a short dash to a copse of trees will bring me to a rather crude hole dug into the earth and a little pine stump, upon which I can prop myself. The trees that aren't pines offer nice broad leaves, perfectly soft to the touch. If I were to quit my bed and travel in the other direction up over a small hill and then down, I'd come to a tall hedge, one part of which opens like a door and has a lock. The meadow that is my room is wide, and yesterday, I traveled back away from the bed and discovered a small waterfall with a pool beneath it with goldfish and lily pads. In the House of Four Seasons, everything outside is inside, and as old Ima, the hermaphrodite therapist—split straight down the middle so that one side is male and the other female—said upon our arrival, "May the therapeutic nature of this house drive those dark things within you . . . out."

The air was dense, weighted down by heat and high humidity. Even the butterflies and dragonflies by the pond had lost their frenetic flutter and moved as if swimming through water instead of flying in air. All of us, including Lenice, had stripped down to our underclothes and left our things scattered among the flowers in the meadow. Spencer arrived with glasses of lemonade on his silver cart.

"I'm going in," said Brown. He stood, removed his shirt to reveal his voluminous lard, and began stepping backward away from the pond. Then he yelled something incomprehensible and took off running, jiggling to beat the band. When he reached the water's edge, he leaped, made a meager arc, and came down flat on his stomach, water splashing outward in every direction. We laughed at his performance, but when the water was calm again, we noticed he had sunk out of sight. A small disturbance of bubbles broke the surface.

"For a man who oversaw the charring of orphans, he certainly has some fun left in him," said Andre.

"I find him quite handsome," said Lenice.

My attention was stolen by the recognition of an army of ants, marching single file through the grass beside my left arm. I called to the others to come and see. They knelt down beside me and put their faces close to the ground.

"The detail of the House is staggering," I said.

"Down to the last ant," said Lenice.

Andre stood up and looked toward the pond. "Hasn't Brown been down for quite a long time?" he asked.

"Yes," I said. But instead of diving in to find him, I ran to where he had set down the book Ima had given him. Opening it, I skimmed the pages. Every single one was perfectly blank.

Brown came up with a splutter and a splash of water, and I dropped the book. Before turning around, I heard Lenice ask him how the water was. "You must come in," said Brown. "I feel as if I've been reborn."

Mrs. Gash rose, walked slowly to the water's edge, and stepped into the pond. With slow grace, she lowered herself into the cool liquid, sighing in her descent.

"That does it," said Andre, "I'm going in."

"Me, too," I said.

At one point in the long hot day, while we were splashing one another and laughing, Ima appeared on the shore. He had his arms folded across his chest, the mustached half of his face turned to us and set in a grimace.

. . .

We boarded a stout, crystal submarine at the wharf in the city. I took one last quick glimpse of the spires and smokestacks, the soot falling like black snow, the pale faces of people trudging off to work past crumbling brick facades, and then the captain, a genial man with a beard and a peaked cap, sporting a blue uniform with gold epaulets, like someone from a children's adventure story, said, "All aboard." And we four passengers climbed down a crystal ladder into the clear belly of the ship as if we were stepping down instead into the dark brown water of the river itself. Once we were seated in our crystal chairs, more comfortable then you would imagine, the captain locked the crystal lid through which we had entered and took his own seat at the front of the ship, the crystal board of crystal levers and buttons spread out, nearly invisible, before him.

The propellers turned with a whisper-whirr and we descended, not so much diving as slowly falling, like in a dream, away from the dim sun and into darkness. The captain lit a single taper by which to see and called over his shoulder, "Make yourselves comfortable, my friends. I'll try to point out the sea life when we encounter it." We four passengers had been instructed not to speak while on this journey, but were assured there would be plenty of time to get to know one another once we had arrived at our destination. Before long, the brown harbor water gave way to a clear blackness, like a night sky. The sound of the propellers lulled me, and I half-dozed, studying the backs of the two men in front of me and the profile of the young woman to my left. Three men and one woman, I noted to myself, and then fell into a brief sleep.

When I woke, it was to the sound of the captain's voice. "To the starboard side, my friends. A perfect specimen of a *merillibus dachinasis.*" I looked, and there, swimming by, was a huge, brutish creature, whose body was clear as a jellyfish, like the submarine, but whose eyes and inner organs glowed brightly with a blue phosphorescence. Then I turned all around to see more glowing fish dotting the blackness like stars and planets everywhere and away into the distance.

It was Andre who found the skeleton buried in the sand of the dune where he often went to meditate in the mornings. It was dressed in a heavy coat and still wore galoshes. Its hat was attached by a chin strap and there must have been scalp upon that skull for many strands of long blond hair hung down below the brim. The day he brought us to see it a thick fog hung about the House.

When we notified Ima about Andre's find, he/she spoke from both sides of her/his mouth at once. The manly side said, "Eddings, Eddings, poor Eddings," and its feminine counterpart said, "I have no idea who it might be."

Brown stepped forward and said, "All right then, who's Eddings?"

Our therapist then turned his male side to us and, smoothing his mustache once and adjusting his monocle, said, "She was a spicy little dish." Then he smiled. "I thought she'd returned on the submarine," said Ima. "Some just can't bring themselves to leave." We gaped in awe at the impertinence of our keeper and had a few choice words for her rougher side when he left. Before long, Spencer came chugging along with the silver serving cart on wheels. It was a sin watching him try to get it up the dune, but eventually he managed and took the fetid remains away on the very cart that would that night ferry our mutton to the forest.

Birds flew overhead. Brown and I sat on a high-backed love seat in the middle of a field of yellow Johnny Bells, watching Andre fly a kite Ima had given him for admitting that his expertise in chemistry had to do with making explosives. The late spring breeze was cool and refreshing.

"Maybe a dream," whispered Brown.

"Huh?" I said.

"No, something about the kite, its image of an octopus, its snapping tail, reminds me of one of the children from the orphanage."

"They had such a kite?" I asked.

"No, this little boy, he had eight arms. Or eight half-arms, each with one fingernail on the end. He was a darling, but his parents, young as they were, would not keep him."

"What kind of orphanage was this?" I asked.

"Very, very cleanly. Fresh straw every other day, clean drinking water, cabbage soup with a gob of fat in it every third day and a slice of hard bread. Yeah, that boy was a whiz at putting together a puzzle."

One hot night right on the cusp between summer and autumn, I lay in bed and listened to the crickets sing and watched a lone firefly signaling to itself in my dresser mirror. There was moonlight but no moon. I'd just woken from a dream of the circus, watching a young woman fall to her death from the trapeze. The fact that I'd lied about being able to perform stunts on the back of a moving horse made me somehow culpable for her accident, and I was being pursued by clowns. I shook my head and got up. To drive off the heat, I went back to the pond with the waterfall in my own room and slipped out of my nightclothes and into the water.

Eventually I moved beneath the falling sheet of coolness, letting it splash upon my head in order to drive the bad dream away. When I opened my eyes, I found I had passed through the curtain of water and into a little tunnel that lay behind it. I saw the passage was not very long, for there was moonlight shining upon another cascade of water falling at the other end. I swam the secret passage, and once I reached the other end, moved through the refreshing veil only to find myself in a pool nearly identical to the one in my own "room."

Although I was naked, I crept out of the pool and looked around to see where I'd gotten to. There was a meadow, well lit in the moonlight, and off at not too far a distance, I saw a canopied bed. I crept closer, realizing I had infiltrated someone else's "room." I determined to, without waking the bed's occupant, simply take a peek and see who my next-door neighbor was. I inched toward the bed from behind the headboard.

It was everything I could do not to gasp upon finding Lenice, naked, in bed with another. Just as I hovered over them, Spencer's eyes lit up. I knew he knew I was there. His left hand's three articulated digits, which rested upon Mrs. Gash's creamy white breast, gave the slightest squeeze, and his lightbulb eye closest to me blinked on and off with a conspiratorial wink. As I backed away, a tiny blue cloud issued from the hole in the back of his head. I ran so fast through the moonlight beneath no moon, it was as if I were perched atop a charging horse.

I was up to my waist in snow, every step forward a great effort, and the ferocity of the blizzard nearly blinded me. I held the bomb in one gloved hand and Lenice by the other as we made our way through the forest toward the limit of the House of Four Seasons. It was farther than ever I could have imagined. I stopped and looked up, shielding my eyes, but could not find Andre anywhere around me. I called his name but could make out no reply above the shrieking of the wind. My arms and legs and feet and hands were numb, I could feel frostbite sinking its fangs into my face. Then I realized I no longer had Lenice by the hand. I turned around and saw nothing but white. The fact that I was trapped within an artificial world quickly filling with snow, in a cave at the very bottom of the ocean, made me know the absolute truth of loneliness. I wanted to stop and give in and be found, as Ima said, "in the spring when all this melts," just before she slammed shut and locked the door to her concrete bunker of an office. Instead I pushed forward, hoping to find the boundary so I might blow a hole in it and escape.

The submarine rose into a cave beneath the sea and finally surfaced in a subterranean grotto of stalactites and stalagmites and a small land bridge leading to a rock wall containing a metal door. "All ashore," said the captain. He opened the lid and climbed out to stand atop the crystal submarine and help us, one by one, step clear onto the narrow rock path. Once we were together in the dripping cave, he led us to the door. Two short knocks, three long, a short, and a long followed by a quick tapping of the fingernails, and the metal door creaked open. We were met by the startling figure of Ima, hunched and wrinkled, dressed in a colorful, billowing dress, bearing a pattern of flowers and snowflakes, and split down the middle with a line you could trace with your fingernail. On one side of her head, the gray hair hung long and was gathered in a pigtail with a piece of pink silk ribbon; on the other side his hair was trimmed short. One side a mustache, the other none. The male eye held a monocle. On the female side of the smile, gold teeth flashed. One arm was muscular and its opposite was delicate, tipped with red-painted cuticles.

"Very good, captain. They're mine now," Ima said, and the voice was coarse. "Come in," she then said, in a sweet grandmotherly tone, and turned that side to us as she pushed back the door and, leaving the captain behind, we entered a small, dim room made of concrete. Beneath one bare electric bulb that emitted a kind of muddy light, there were four chairs set up in a row, facing a single chair. We took the seats that were obviously ours and Ima took the other.

In the next few minutes, Ima told us in her sweetest voice all about the House of Four Seasons, and then assigned us each a daily task. Mine was to write myself a letter each morning of my stay at the house. I was told to relate to you all that went on the previous day. The young woman was to pray for an hour each morning. One of the other gentlemen was to meditate, and the other, the short, heavyset one, was handed a fat book titled *The Gilead* and told to read fifty pages of it each day before breakfast. "Back in your usual lives," said Ima, "your thoughts are scattered, your souls are shattered. Here you must piece yourselves back together. The cycle of the seasons will be the thread that holds the shards. From it, from them, you will create yourselves anew."

"I don't understand," said the young woman.

"You will, my dear," he said, and then our guide rose and went to a door situated directly behind his seat. "Follow me," he said, waving to us slowly with his feminine arm. We rose and followed. The door was pushed open and we entered into sunlight, blue skies, cotton clouds, and the sound of running water. "Spring," said Ima both harsh and soft, "like a sharp ache in the cranial country of joy."

"Brown is dead," said Andre, his words turning to steam in the cold. "I found him in a pile of orange leaves by the stream not far from Ima's office. From the look of the marks on his neck, he's been strangled. And this," he said, holding up a circle of glass attached to a string, "was lying next to his body."

"Did you report it?" I asked.

"Did I report it?" he said and smiled. "My friend, I believe the time has come to leave the House of Four Seasons."

We'd planned our secret rendezvous by communicating through a series of taps upon each other's feet beneath the dinner table earlier that evening. It was so late the crickets had gone silent by the time I went to meet Lenice under cover of darkness in the depths of the forest. She appeared seemingly out of nowhere, as if materializing like a ghost, wearing a sheer white sleeping gown. It had been hot that summer day, but the night had cooled and there was a layer of dew covering the ground. There was no conversation, but she put her lips to mine and her hand went directly for my belt. I could feel the warmth of her body, her fingers groping for my member, as my trousers fell to gather at my ankles.

Bats fluttered overhead, creatures scampered through their pitch-black tunnels in the underbrush. I heard the big clock above Ima's office door chime three a.m. And then we were on the ground; she on her hands and knees and me behind, a submarine in an undersea cave. For a time, I worked like I had stock in the company and then the fuse of my passionate release grew ever shorter. Still, I held out, thinking of our days and the implications of each passing hour, those gone and those still to come.

"More," she whispered, "more," moving forward and back with the precision and speed of a machine.

My fingers dug into the soft flesh at her hips, I gritted my teeth, I groaned like a man brought back from the dead, I did what I could, until everything suddenly went white. A chill struck my heart, a winter within, and then the world and Time exploded, shards of seasons flying everywhere, like leaves in autumn, rain and snow, like the miracle of stars in my skull.

THE
DREAMING
WIND

Each and every year, in that brief time when summer and autumn share the same bed—the former, sunburned and exhausted, drifting toward sleep, the latter, rousing to the crickets' call and the gentle brush of the first falling leaves against its face—the Dreaming Wind swept down from somewhere in the distant north, heading somewhere to the distant south, leaving everywhere in its wake incontrovertible proof of the impossible.

Our town, like the others lying directly in the great gale's path, was not exempt from the bizarre changes wrought by its passing. We prepared ourselves as best we could, namely in our hearts and minds, for there was no place to hide from it even though you might crawl into the space beneath your house and pull a blanket over your head. No manner of boarding up windows, stuffing towels beneath doors, turning out lights, or jumping into a lead-lined coffin and pulling shut the lid made a whit's worth of difference. Somehow it always found you and had its crazy way.

So it was that each year, often on a deep blue afternoon in late

August or early September, some of us noticed the leaves in the trees begin to rustle and heard amid their branches, just a whisper at first, the sound of running water. Then we knew to warn the others. "The Wind, the Wind," was the cry throughout the streets of town, and Hank Garrett, our constable, climbed up to the platform on the roof of his house and turned the crank handle siren to alert farmers out in the fields that the blowing chaos was on its way. The citizens of Lipara scurried home, powerless to effect any protection, but determined to share the burden of strangeness with loved ones and bolster the faith of the young that it wouldn't last forever.

In a heartbeat, in an eye blink, the wind was upon us, bending saplings, rattling windows, lifting dust devils in the town square, as though it had always been there, howling throughout our lives. Even down in a root cellar, thick oaken door barred above, hiding in the dark, you heard it, and once you heard it you felt it upon your face and the back of your neck, your arms, like some invisible substance gently embracing you. That's when you knew the wind was beginning to dream you.

Its name, the Dreaming Wind, was more indicative than you might at first believe. What is a dream, but a state founded enough upon the everyday to be believable to the sleeping mind and yet also a place wherein anything at all might and often does happen? Tomes of wonders, testaments of melancholic horrors wrought by the gale have been recorded, but I'll merely recount some of the things I, myself, have been privy to.

The human body seemed its favorite plaything, and in reaction to its weird catalyst I'd seen flesh turn every color in the rainbow, melt and reform into different shapes, so that a head swelled to the size of a pumpkin or legs stretched to lift their owner above the house tops. Tongues split or turned to knives and eyes shot flame, swirled like pinwheels, popped, or became mirrors to reflect the thing that I'd become—once a salamander man with an ibis head, once a bronze statue of the moon. In my wedding year, my wife Lyda's long hair took on a mind and life of its own, tresses grabbing cups from a cupboard and smashing them upon the floor. Mayor James Meersch Jr. ran down Gossin Street the year I was ten, with his rear end upon his shoulders and muffled shouts issuing from the back of his trousers.

Eyes slipped from the face and wound up in the palm, and mouths traveled to kneecaps—arms for legs, elbows for feet, a big toe nose, and wiggling index finger ears. Men became green monkeys and donkeys and dogs, and dogs sprouted cat's heads, whose legs became pipe cleaners and whose tails changed instantly to sausage links with tiny biting faces at their tips. Once three generations of a family's females, from little girls to wrinkled matrons, sprouted black feathers and flew up to circle the church steeple, croaking poetry in some foreign language. Pastor Hinch became part pig, Mavis Toth, the schoolmarm, became a chair with a lampshade head, yet this . . . this was not a hundredth of it, for there is no way to encompass in language the inexhaustible creative energy and crackpot genius that was the Dreaming Wind.

While our citizens suffered bodily these sea changes, bellowing with fear, crying out in torment at being still themselves inside but something wholly other outward, the landscape also changed around them. Monumental gusts loosened leaves that flew away from branches to become a school of striped fish, darting, as if with one mind, through the atmosphere, and trees turned to rubber, undulating wildly, or became the long necks of giraffes. Clouds slowly fell, wads of a violet, airy confection, and bounced off chimneys, rolled along the ground like giant tumbleweeds. Streets came to life and slithered away, windows winked, houses became glass bubbles that burst into thousand-petaled roses with doors and roofs. The grass never remained green, the sky never

blue but became other colors and sometimes different consisten-
cies like water, or jam, or once, a golden gas that coalesced our ex-
halations into the spectral forms of dead relatives who danced the
Combarue in the town square. And all of this was accompanied
by a discordant symphony comprised of myriad sounds: breaking
glass, a tin whistle, a sneeze, a hammer claw ripping nails from
green board, the sighs of ancient pachyderms, water swirling down
a drain. . . .

Chaos and jumblement, the overall discombobulation of
reality—the effect lasted two or three hours, and then, as quickly
as it came, it went. The force of the gale decreased incrementally,
and as it did, so did its insane changes. People slowly began to reform into themselves as they'd been before the wind. The streets
slunk guiltily back to their normal paths, the houses re-achieved
their household, the clouds blanched to their original puffy white
and ascended as slowly as they'd fallen. By night, the wind had
moved on to disrupt the lives of the good citizens in towns to the
south of Lipara.

Some might ask, "Well, why did your ancestors stay in that spot
and not move after they saw it was a yearly event?" The answer was
simple. Come to Lipara and see for yourself that it's the most beautiful spot in the world: wide blue lakes, deep green forests teeming
with game, and farmland of rich, loamy soil. Besides, to escape the
wind's course one would have had to move west, to the desert, or
east, where lay the ocean. Hearing this, some might say, "Well, all's
well that ends well, and once the wind had passed, all was guaran-
teed to return to its former state." Yes and no. What I mean is most
of the time this was true, and besides the upset of having yourself stretched or shrunk or turned temporarily into a nightmarish
creature for a few hours, the entire rest of the year was very good
living. Remember, I said, *"Most of the time."*

There were instances, exceedingly rare, mind you, wherein the

Dreaming Wind's mischief remained behind after the wind itself had blown south. There was an old oak tree at the edge of town that never lost its ability to—at mid-summer—bear a strange yellow fruit, the fragile consistency of fine china and the size of a honey-dew melon, that upon ripening, fell off, broke against the ground, and hatched small blue bats that lived for two weeks and feasted upon field mice. And Grandmother Young's talking parrot, Colonel Pudding, once touched by the wind's fickle finger, had its head replaced with that of her great-granddaughter's baby doll—a cute little bisque visage, whose blue glass eyes had lids that winked and closed when it lay down. The bird still spoke but prefaced every screeching utterance with a breathy, mechanical rendition of the word "Mama."

Perhaps the parrot was somewhat put out, but no terrible harm was done in these two incidents. Still, the possibility of unremitting permanence represented by their changes stayed alive in the minds of the citizens of Lipara, its threat continuously resurfacing and growing to monstrous proportions in all imaginations as each summer neared its end. It was one thing to be a goat-headed clown with feather-duster arms and carrot legs for a few hours, but to remain in that condition for a lifetime was something else entirely. The Dreaming Wind was playful, it was insane, it was chaotic, and it could be dangerous. Little did any of us suspect for generations past and for most of my long life that it could be anything else.

Then, a few years ago, the strange wind did something so unusual it shocked even us veterans of its mad work. It was nearing the end of a long lazy summer, memorable for its blue days and cool nights, and the leaves were beginning to curl on the elm trees, the first few early crickets were beginning to chirp their winter's tales. Each of us, in our own particular way, was steeling himself for the yearly onslaught of the mischievous event, offering up prayers to God or reassuring ourselves by reassuring others that as certain as the wind would come, it would pass, and we would again enjoy the normal pleasures of life in Lipara. Constable Garrett did as he had always done, and chose three reliable children, paying them a dime a day, to go to the edge of the forest and listen intently for a few hours after school for the sound of water running through the treetops. Everywhere, families made plans as to where they would meet up, what room they would weather the storm in, what songs they would sing together to quell their collective fear.

The end of August came and went without incident, and the delay heightened the apprehension of the arrival of the Dreaming Wind. We older folks reminded the younger that it was known to have come as late as the middle of the second week in September and that it was to be remembered that the wind could not be dictated to but had a mind of its own. During these days, every curtain lifting in a breeze, every gust dispersing the gossamer seed of a dandelion skeleton, caused blood pressures to rise and neck hairs to stand on end. By the middle of the first week in September the alarm had been falsely raised four times, and Constable Garrett, whose bad knee was beginning to protest the long climbs to his roof, jokingly said he might just as well set out a sleeping bag up there.

By the end of the second week in September, nerves were frayed, tempers flared, and children cried at the slightest provocation. The aura of anxiety produced by the anticipation of the wind had begun to make Lipara a little mad even before its arrival. Miss Toth, standing in front of her class one day, could not remember for the life of her what fifty-seven divided by nineteen was, no matter how many times she tapped her ruler against the blackboard. She had to have Peggy Frushe, one of the older girls, run across the square to the apothecary's shop to inquire as to the answer to the problem.

Beck Harbuth, the apothecary, couldn't help out just then even though he knew the answer was three, for he had absentmindedly filled a prescription for Grandmother Young with a bottle full of laxative pills instead of her usual heart medicine, and had to brush past Peg and chase the old woman down the street. In his pursuit, he collided with Mildred Johnson, who was bringing her eggs to the market in the basket on the front of her bike. Sitting in the road amid the cracked shell and splattered yoke debris of their sudden meeting, Harbuth apologized to Mildred for the accident and she merely replied in a loud disgusted tone, "Don't worry, Beck, it's all the fault of the damn wind."

Grandmother Young was only a few paces ahead of the collision of the apothecary and the egg woman, and because her hearing was weak, she never noticed a thing, but Colonel Pudding, who was riding his usual perch atop the left shoulder of his owner, did. He lit into the sky, carrying with him the last phrase he'd heard, which was "The damn wind," and, as was his practice when he heard a phrase that caught his fancy, began screeching this alarm in the mimicked voice of she who had uttered it. Constable Garrett, sitting in his office with the window open, heard someone cry, "Mama, the damn wind," sighed, slowly rose from his chair, and started for a fifth time up the steps toward his roof.

And so it went, a comedy of errors caused by troubled minds—but no one was laughing. Things got worse and worse, until the start of October when the last squadrons of southbound geese passed overhead. The collective worriment of the citizens of Lipara reached a crescendo, nerves snarling like balls of twine in the paws of kittens, and then all fell into a kind of blank exhaustion. Still the wind had not come. A few weeks later, when the first snow fell, blowing down from the north on a mundane autumnal gale, we knew for certain that the Dreaming Wind had done something undreamed of. The realization came to all of us at once that our strange visitor from the north wasn't coming this year, and in that instant we froze for a moment, wondering what would become of us.

The sky grew overcast and stayed muskrat gray for days on end, the temperature dropped to a bitter low, and the lake froze over as if the absence of the wind had plunged the world itself into a sodden depression. Cows gave half their normal measure of milk, roosters didn't bother signaling the dawn, dogs howled at noon, and cats were too weary to chase the mice that invaded Lipara's houses. The citizens, who had always surmised that the elimination of the Dreaming Wind would fill them with a sense of relief that might border on a kind of spiritual rebirth, now went about their daily tasks as if in mourning. Woven in with the gloom was a pervasive sense of guilt, as if we were being punished for not having appreciated the uniqueness of the blowing insanity when it was upon us.

The winter, with its blanket of snow and immutable coat of ice, presented in its seemingly static freeze the very opposite of change. Grandmother Young took to her sick bed, complaining she no longer had the energy to go on. Colonel Pudding was beside himself with concern for his owner, and stayed all day in her room with her, pacing back and forth along the headboard of the bed, his fixed-fast bisque lips repeatedly murmuring the word "Mama." Constable Garrett's bad knee was now worse than ever, or so he claimed, and instead of going out on his daily rounds, making sure the town was safe, he stayed at his office desk, playing endless losing rounds of solitaire. Pastor Hinch preached a sermon one Sunday in the midst of Lipara's rigor mortis that exhorted all of the town's citizens to wake up and effect their own changes, but when it came time for his congregation to answer him in a prayer, two-thirds of the response he received was unbridled snoring. Lyda and I sat at the kitchen table, sipping tea, staring just past each other, each of us waiting for the other to begin a conversation and listen-

ing to the wind that was not a Dreaming Wind howl outside our
door.

Eventually, with the spring thaw, things picked up somewhat.
There was a rote, joyless, humdrummery to life, though. Everything seemed drained of interest and beauty. I think it was actually
Beck Harbuth, the apothecary, who first mentioned to a customer
that he no longer dreamed at night. The customer thought for a
moment and then nodded and said that he also could not remember having dreamed since the end of the summer. This observation
made the rounds for a week or two, was discussed in all circles, and
agreed upon. Eventually Mayor James Meersch III called an emergency town meeting, the topic of which would be the epidemic of
dreamless sleep. It was to be held in the town hall on the following
Thursday evening at seven p.m.

The meeting never took place, because in the days following
the mayor's announcement many people began to realize, now
that they were concentrating on the matter, that in fact they were
dreaming. What it was, as articulated by Beck Harbuth—the one
who started it all—is that nothing unusual was happening in their
dreams. The dreams that were dreamed in the days following
the failure of the wind were of a most pedestrian nature—eating
breakfast, walking to work, reading yesterday's newspaper, making
the bed. There were no chimerical creatures or outlandish hap-
penings to be found in the land of sleep anymore.

The second reason the meeting was canceled was that Grandmother Young passed away on the Tuesday before the meeting,
and although she had grown very frail of recent years, the entire
town was surprised and saddened by her passing. She was Lipara's
oldest citizen, 125 years old, and we all loved her. True to her no-
nonsense approach to life, her last words spoken to my wife, who
was among a group of neighbors who were taking shifts watching
over her in her final hours, were "Death has got to be less dull than

Lipara these days." Her funeral was as grand as we could muster in our downtrodden condition, and the mayor allocated funds so that a special monument to her memory could be erected in the town square. As her coffin was lowered into the ground, Colonel Pudding, sitting on a perch we'd positioned near the grave, shed baby-doll tears and uttered his one-word eulogy: "Mama." Then he spread his wings, took off into the sky, and flew out of sight.

The days passed into summer and we dreamed our dreams of eating peas and clipping our toenails. It seemed nothing would break the spell that had settled upon the town. We sleepwalked through the hours and greeted one another with half-nods and feeble grins. Not even the big fleecy clouds that passed overhead took on the shapes of dragons or pirate ships as they had once upon a time. Just when the stasis became almost intolerable, something happened. It wasn't much, but we clung to it like ants on a twig being swept downriver.

Mildred Johnson was sitting up late one night reading a new book concerning the egg-laying habits of yellow hens. Her husband had already gone to bed, as had her daughter, Jessica. The reading wasn't the most exciting, and she'd dozed off in her chair. Some time later, she woke very suddenly to the sound of low murmuring coming from her daughter's room. She got up and went to the half-open door of the bedroom to check on the girl, but when she peeked in she saw, in a shaft of moonlight, something moving on the bed next to Jessica's pillow. Her first thought was that it was a rat and she screamed. The thing looked up, startled, and in that moment, before it flew out the window, she saw the smooth, fixed, baby-doll expression of Colonel Pudding.

The parrot's return and the unusual particulars of the sighting could not exactly be classified as bizarre, but there was enough of an oddness to it to engender a mild titillation of the populace. Where had the bird been hiding since the funeral? What was its midnight message? Was it simply lost and had wandered in the open window or was there some deeper purpose to its actions? These were some of the questions that set off a spark or two in the otherwise dimmed minds of Lipara. As speculation grew, there were more reports of Colonel Pudding visiting the rooms of the town's sleeping children. It was advised by the pastor at Sunday service that all windows of youngsters' bedrooms be kept closed at night, and the congregation nodded, but just the opposite was practiced, as parents and children alike all secretly wanted to be involved in the mystery.

Beyond his nighttime visits, the parrot began to be spotted also in broad daylight, flitting here and there just above the rooftops of the town. One afternoon during the first week of summer vacation, he was seen perched on Mavis Toth's left shoulder, yammering into her ear as she walked to the bank. Something was going on, we were sure of it, but what it was, no one had the slightest idea. Or I should say, none of us adults had a clue. The children of Lipara, on the other hand, took to whispering, gathering in groups and talking excitedly until a grown-up drew near. Even usual truants of the school year, like the master of spitballs, Alfred Lessert, began spending vacation days at the schoolhouse under the pretense of doing math problems for fun. It was the belief of some that a conspiracy was afoot. Parents slyly tried to coax their children into divulging a morsel of information, but their sons and daughters only stared quizzically, either pretending not to know what their folks were getting at or really not knowing. Miss Toth came under scrutiny as well, and instead of really answering questions, she nodded a great deal, played with the chain that held her reading glasses, and forced a laugh when nothing else would do.

The intrigue surrounding the schoolhouse and the town's children remained of mild interest to the adults throughout the summer, but as always, the important tasks of business and household chores took precedence and finally overwhelmed their attention, so that they did not mark the vanishing of old newspapers and cups of flour. As the first anniversary of the wind's failure to appear drew closer we tried to pull tight the reins of our speculation as to what would happen this year. In our private minds we all wondered whether the present state of limbo would be split by the gale again howling through town, or if the time would again pass without incident and give further proof that the dreaming weirdness had run its course for good, never to return.

One Friday morning in late August, I went to the mailbox and found a piece of folded paper, colored green, and cut into the shape of a parrot feather. I opened it and read: COLONEL PUDDING INVITES YOU TO THE FESTIVAL OF THE DREAMING WIND. The date was the very next day, the time, sundown, and the location, the town square. It went on to proclaim: BRING ONLY YOUR DREAMS. I smiled for the first time since the end of the previous summer, and I was so out of practice that the muscles of my face ached slightly. As old and slow as I was, I ran up the path, calling to Lyda. When she saw the invitation, she actually laughed and clapped her hands.

Late the next afternoon, just before twilight, we left the house and walked to the town square. It was a beautiful evening—pink, orange, and purple in the west where the sun had already sunk half below the horizon. The sky above was dark blue and a few stars were beginning to show themselves. A slight breeze blew, enough to keep the gnats and mosquitoes at home. We held hands and walked in silence, joined along the way by other townspeople heading in the direction of the festival.

The town square had been transformed. Streamers of gold paper were draped upon the picket fences and snaked around the light posts. In the southern corner, rows of folding chairs had been set up facing a slightly raised, makeshift stage that had been formed from wooden pallets. Two tall poles on either side supported a patchwork curtain comprised of a number of old comforters safety-pinned together. Six lit torches had been set up around the performance area, casting a soft glow that became increasingly magical as the sky darkened. Constable Garrett, big cigar in the corner of his mouth, dressed in a colorful muumuu and wearing a bow in his hair, acted the usher, making us form a line a short distance from the seating. We complimented him on his outfit, telling him how lovely he looked, and he nodded wearily as usual and answered, "What did you expect?"

All around the festival area, Lipara's children moved busily, with purpose, and in the middle of this bustle of activity stood Miss Toth, her skin blue, her hair a wig of rubber snakes, whispering directions and leaning down to put her ear closer to the ideas and questions of her students. Suddenly all was quiet and still but for the flickering of the torch flames. "Please have your tickets ready," said Garrett, and he held his hand up and waved us on. Before taking our seats, we were directed to three long tables upon which lay painted papier-mâché masks of animal heads, household items, seashells. The masks could be affixed to one's head by wire ear loops. Mixed in among the masks were newspaper hats, and at the end of each table was a stack of cardboard fans.

I settled on a mask that made my head a can of beans, and Lyda adopted the visage of a barnyard chick. Mildred Johnson's face became a bear paw; her husband's a bright yellow sun. Beck Harbuth chose a dog mask, and Mayor James Meersch turned away from the table a green monkey. Once everyone was something else, we put our newsprint caps on our heads, took our fans, and went to sit before the stage. The show started promptly. Miss Toth appeared from behind the curtain, carrying a hat rack, which she set down next to her. She welcomed us all and thanked us for coming, introduced Colonel Pudding—creator and founder of the Festival of the Dreaming Wind—and walked off the stage. A moment later, from over our heads, there came the sound of flapping wings, and Colonel Pudding landed on the top of the hat rack. He screeched three times, lifted his wings, bobbed his head twice, and said, "Mama, *The Tale of the Dreaming Wind*. Once upon a time . . ." before flying away. Jessica Johnson ran out from behind the curtain, whisked the perch off the stage, and the play began.

The play was about a great wizard who lived, with his wife and daughter, in a castle way up in the mountains. He was a good wizard, practicing only white magic, and for anyone who made the arduous journey to see him, he would grant a wish as long as it benefited someone else. The only two wishes he would not grant were those for riches or power. A chorus of younger children sang songs that filled us in on the details of life upon the mountain. White confetti blew across the stage, becoming snow, to mark the passage of time.

Then the wizard's wife, whom he loved very much, caught a chill that progressed into pneumonia. It soon became clear that she was dying, and no matter what spells of enchantment he tried to work, nothing could cure her. When she finally died, he was deeply saddened, as was his daughter. He began to realize that there were things in the world his magic couldn't control, and he became very protective of his daughter, fearing she would succumb to the same fate as her mother. He had promised his wife that he would always love the girl and keep her safe. This responsibility grew in his mind to overshadow everything, and the least little cut to her finger or scrape on her knee caused him great anguish.

Time passed and the girl grew older and developed a mind of her own. She wanted to go down the mountain and meet other people. The wizard knew that there were all manner of dangers waiting for her out in the world. Before she got to the age where he knew he could no longer stop her from leaving, he cast a spell on her that put her into a profound sleep. To protect her, he encased her in a large seed pod with a window so that he could see her face when he needed to. There she slept, her age unchanging, and he finally felt some relief.

He noticed at the end of the first year of her protective sleep that she must be dreaming, because he could see through the window the figures and forms of her dreams swirling around her. It became clear to him that if he didn't find some way to siphon out the dreams, they would eventually fill the seed pod to bursting, so, using his magic, he cast a spell that added a spigot to the top of the structure. Once a year, as summer turned to fall, he'd climb a stepladder, turn the spigot, and release her pent-up dreams. They sprayed forth from within like a geyser, gathering themselves up into a kind of cloud that, when fully formed, rushed out the castle window. The mountain winds caught the girl's dreams and drove them south, where their vitality affected everything they touched.

As the story unfolded on the stage before me, I was amazed at the quality of the production and how ingenious the props were. The seed pod that contained the wizard's daughter was a large luggage bag covered with glitter, with a window cut to reveal the girl's face. Her dreams swirling within were colored paper cutouts of small figures—different animals and people and objects—attached to thin sticks that the daughter, played wonderfully by the beautiful Peggy Frushe, controlled with her hands, hidden from sight, and made sail gracefully before her closed eyes. When the dreams were released by the turning of the spigot, they took the form of younger children in colorful costumes, who whirled madly around the stage and then gathered together before blowing south. And what was even more amazing was that the errant Alfred Lessert, with his freckles and shock of red hair, played the troubled wizard with a pathos that transcended drama and stepped neatly into reality.

While I sat there, noting the remainder of the play, wherein a youth comes to the far north to beg for a wish to be granted, discovers the girl and frees her, does battle with her father, who just before killing the lad with a deadly spell, succumbs to his daughter's pleas and spares him, letting the young couple flee down the mountain toward freedom, I was preoccupied, seeing my own years in Lipara unfold on a wooden-pallet stage in my mind. Before I knew it the action transpiring in front of me had rushed on, and the wizard was delivering his final soliloquy, a blessing for the couple, amid a blizzard of falling snow. "Out there in the world, my dear," he said, calling after his daughter, and scanning the crowd to look at each of us, "the wind will blow both beautiful and bitter, and there's no telling which it will be whenever the boughs bend and the leaves rustle. There is no certainty but that there is no certainty. Hold tight to each other and don't be afraid, for sometimes, in the darkest night, that wind may even bring you dreams."

At the end of the production, the players bowed to thundering applause. We were then instructed to hold high our fans and to wave them as hard as we could. Everyone in the audience and onstage paddled the air with all they had, creating two hundred small gusts of wind that joined together to form a great gale that gave comfort and left no one unchanged. Afterward, some danced the Combarue to the sound of Constable Garrett's harmonica while the children played hide-and-seek in the dark. We all drank punch and talked and laughed late into the night until the torches burned out.

On our walk home by the light of the stars, Lyda turned to me and divulged how, when she and some of the other neighbors were clearing out Grandmother Young's house, she'd discovered, beneath the bed, a set of loose papers that held the plans for the festival and the outline of the play. "By then the Colonel was putting the scheme she'd taught him into action, and so I kept it a secret from everyone so as not to ruin the surprise," she said. I told her I was glad she had, just as we passed the bench in the shadow of the strange old oak that gave birth to blue bats, and we caught sight of Alfred Lessert and Peggy Frushe sharing a kiss. "Some things never change," I whispered.

Wearily, we crawled into bed that night, and I lay for a long time with my eyes closed, listening to Lyda's steady breathing and the sound of a breeze sifting through the screen of our open window. My thoughts, at first, were filled with the sights and sounds of the festival—the glow of the torches, the masks, the laughter— but these eventually gave way to the sole image of that old wizard, alone on his mountain in the far north. Through the falling snow, I noticed his beard and recognized his wrinkled face. Murmuring some incantation, he lifted his wand. Then he nodded once, granting me my wish, and I realized I must be dreaming.

THE
GOLDEN
DRAGON

It was a few months after Lynn and baby Jack and I moved into the left half of a ninety-year-old duplex on Harris Avenue that I met Gil. He came to the front door one night—a medium-built, dark-haired guy with a face that had definitely been punched more than once. Pointing over my shoulder, he told me his house was the one behind mine. "I'm your neighbor," he said, and I shook his hand. He laughed and asked if I wouldn't mind giving him a ride down into Camden. "I don't have a car," he said. I hesitated a minute, because Camden wasn't the safest place at night. "I just have to pick something up at a friend's place," he said. "Five minutes, no longer." His smile seemed genuine, so I agreed, wanting to act the good neighbor. I told Lynn I'd be back in a few minutes. On the way to the car, I noticed he limped.

Driving down Harris, Gil told me about how he'd gotten his house with the money that came to him from a job-injury claim. "My back," he said, smiling. I nodded while out the windshield I could see the neighborhood getting shittier. "I worked sanitation for the state," he said. Eventually, he had me turn off Harris and onto a backstreet. A few seconds later, by his instruction, I pulled up in front of a big dilapidated place. All the lights were out inside and the front porch sagged. "One minute," said Gil before he left the car. The instant he was gone, I knew the trip was a bad idea. A lot of the other houses on the street were boarded up and falling apart. There were no working streetlights. More than ten minutes passed, and I started to get nervous. Eventually I saw him through the passenger window, hobbling toward the car. "Let's get out of here," he said as he got in.

"Did you just score weed?" I asked as I pulled away.

Gil laughed and nodded.

Before I went home, I stopped over at his house. As we passed through the doorway, I noticed that there were two live parrots on perches on the porch of the other half of his duplex. They whistled in unison. "I hate those two fucks," said Gil. "When the big, crazy kid from down the block gets them going, they don't shut up for hours."

There was a guy sitting on the couch in his living room, staring at the television, which wasn't on. "This is the guy I share the house with," said Gil, and he introduced us. Ellis seemed shy and had kind of pointy ears, and looked like he'd just finished weeping. I thought he might be brain-damaged. Then we all smoked, and just as I caught the first inkling of a buzz, Gil said, pointing at his friend, "This guy knows everything about vitamins."

"Yeah," said Ellis as he took a hit and nodded. As he passed me the joint, Gil said to him, "Go get your supply and show him."

"Okay," said Ellis, and he went into the back of the house somewhere.

Gil finished off the weed and while he stubbed the roach in the ashtray he laughed. "He's got a case of vitamins in there," he said. "He spends a fortune on the shit. Takes them three times a day, a dozen at a clip."

"Is he sick or something?" I asked.

"He tells me it's going to increase his mental capacity."

We couldn't laugh because Ellis was back, carrying a red suitcase. He laid it on the coffee table and unzipped it. As he lifted the flap, a few brown bottles rolled out onto the floor. It was a king's ransom in vitamins. He picked up one of the escaped bottles and read the label. "Essential Oil of Sea Arrow," he said. Looking at me with his droopy eyes, he added, "It activates the pineal gland." We heard the parrots whistle and Gil and I laughed. Ellis gathered his bottles and zipped up his case.

Two days later, I was in the park, pushing baby Jack in his stroller, when I saw this guy running in the afternoon heat, shirtless but wearing jeans and work boots. As we headed across the sunburned lawn toward the pond, I saw him dashing beneath the trees all along the perimeter of the park. Otherwise, it was high noon and the place was deserted. I sat on my usual bench, Jack next to me in the stroller, beneath a giant oak that could catch a breeze even on the hottest days.

We sat there in silence for a long time and I told Jack to watch the sunbeams on the pond. I closed my eyes for a second, feeling as if I could just doze off, but then felt something move on the bench beside me. I opened my eyes and saw the runner. He was sitting there lighting a cigarette. He had curly hair and his muscled arms were loaded with tattoos. When he saw I was awake, he put his hand out toward me to shake. "You met my cousin the other day," he said.

I shook his hand. "Who?" I asked.

"Gil," he said.

"Oh, yeah," I said. "He lives right behind me."

"He told me you took him down into Camden the other night."

"I did."

"Don't ever do that again," he said. "I know where you went. On that street, you're lucky somebody didn't walk up behind you and put one in your skull."

"It didn't look so great," I said.

"Yeah, don't go back there. That house is a meth lab run by bikers."

"Thanks," I told him.

He crushed out his cigarette and stood up. "Back to work," he said.

"It's a hot day to be running," I said.

"I'm trying to get clean," he said. "I need to sweat." He took off, jogging at first, and eventually broke into a full run.

Thursday night, I went over to Gil's to play poker. When I arrived, Gil let me in and put a beer in my hand. His cousin Bobby was there and Ellis was sitting on the couch.

"I heard you met Bobby," said Gil.

"Yeah," I said, nodded, and waved to Ellis. Bobby came up beside me and pointed to an elderly Asian gentleman, sitting in the corner. "That's Ming the Merciless," he said. The old man laughed and made his big cigar into a smoking middle finger. He wore suspenders and a rumpled white shirt.

We got down to playing cards at the dining room table. Gil dealt first. I was good at drinking beer but lousy at cards. Before the deck made the rounds twice, I was out a pocketful of nickels.

During a beer break, Gil had gone to the bathroom and Bobby was in the kitchen. Ellis sat on one side of me and the old man on the other. Ming asked me for a light, and I asked him what his name was. "It's not really Ming, is it?" He smiled and shook his head, but at the same time told me, "What difference does it make?"

I broke a dollar bill and lost it all, a nickel at a time. Ellis told everybody about a dream he'd had a lot recently.

"Every night almost, a winged creature," he said.

"A winged creature?" said Bobby and laughed.

"I heard there's a vitamin you can take for that," said Gil.

"Fuck you," Ellis said.

Ming smiled and laid out a full house like he was opening a fan.

Bobby told Gil about an old friend of theirs, Pussy, who was in some motorcycle gang called the Grim Business. He'd recently been shot dead in a tattoo parlor in South Philly. Ming folded for the night, and as we played on, quietly told us a story about his restaurant, the Golden Dragon, which stood across the street from the house Lynn and I rented. He swore that Marilyn Monroe had stopped there one night for dinner.

"Ming, come on," said Gil, smiling. "Wasn't she dead before you opened that place?"

"His bullshit is merciless," said Bobby.

The old man smiled and continued describing Monroe's yellow dress with the plunging neckline and how her breasts had hypnotized him. "She ordered the moo goo gai pan," he said. I pictured her on the wide sidewalk in front of the restaurant, oak roots rumpling the concrete and leaves shading the place. She smoked a cigarette, standing beneath that painting of a dog-headed dragon in gold leaf and fire-engine red.

The restaurant was boarded up now, but Ming said he and his wife still lived there. The fancy red lacquered architecture had rotted and every now and then a chunk of the facade would just fall off onto the sidewalk. Since the beginning of the warm weather, wasps had invaded the rotting beams, and I could hear them buzzing all the way across the street through the screen of my bedroom window.

I lost about eight bucks that first night of cards, drank too much, and smoked too much weed. After Bobby and Ming left and Ellis went off to bed, I said to Gil, "You mean to tell me that guy Ming and his wife live over there in that fuckin' restaurant?"

Gil nodded. "He doesn't even have electricity. I'm not sure if they have water."

"That's messed up," I said. "He's no spring chicken. How do they get by?"

"I don't know," said Gil. He took a drink of beer and then told me, "Things went in the toilet when Mrs. Ming got some weird virus. Ming doesn't know what to do. In the beginning when she wasn't completely out of it, she'd whisper orders and recipes from a cot in a back room. Me and Bobby'd go over there for dinner occasionally. After a while, though, she just shrieked in pain and that's when the workers split on him. The customers never came back."

That night I awoke around three a.m. and went downstairs for a glass of water. When I returned to the bedroom, I looked out the window and saw a shadow across the street, pacing slowly back and forth in front of the boarded-up entrance to the Golden Dragon. Every now and then, the glowing cherry of a cigar ash flared.

I made the mistake of telling Lynn that Bobby and Gil used to be heroin addicts. She said she didn't want either of them around the house and wished I wouldn't go over there on Thursday nights. I told her both of them were clean and weren't using. She didn't look convinced. "You have responsibilities," she said, referring to the fact that it had fallen to me to watch baby Jack because she had to go to work. "Hey, I'm on it," I said. I spent my days pushing a stroller, doling out the oatmeal and mashed peas, and playing a game Jack and I made up called Paradise Garden. I'd shown Jack the sign above the restaurant on one of our walks, and we pretended that there was a golden dragon that owned the garden.

One night, after Lynn got home from work, put a chicken in for dinner, and was playing with Jack on the living room rug, a call came through from the hospital. There'd been a big accident on

Admiral Wilson Boulevard and they needed extra nurses. I told
her I'd take her, worried about her driving through Camden alone
in the dark. She had a glass of wine and then went to put her uniform back on. A half hour later, we got in the car, baby Jack in his
car seat in the back. There was a traffic jam where Harris Avenue
met Route 130, detour traffic from the big accident. We sat in that
for a long time before things started moving.

Jack and I finally arrived back home after dropping Lynn off.
As I opened the front door, I could see all the way into the kitchen
through living room and dining room, where Bobby and Gil were
sitting at the table. When they saw me, they waved. I walked back
there, wondering how they'd gotten in with the doors locked. I was
a little scared. On the way, I put Jack down near his toy box in the
dining room. When I hit the kitchen, Bobby said, "Dinner time."

"What do you mean?" I said.

"There was a chicken in the oven," said Gil and they both
stood up.

I then noticed a faint smell of smoke and saw the open oven
door and window.

"We were sitting over at Gil's and saw the smoke coming out
from under the door," said Bobby. "We ran over, but your door was
locked. So we broke in through the window. Check it out," he said,
and waved over his shoulder for me to follow him out the back
door. On the little metal table where Lynn kept her gardening tools
sat a roasting pan with a perfectly blackened chicken in it.

Bobby stuck his finger into the bird and it shattered. "I think
it's done," he said.

After Lynn heard about the chicken incident, Thursday night
poker was no longer an issue. It was a good respite for me from the
parenting life, interacting with adults for a few hours each week. It
didn't hurt anything. I usually won a little money, had a few beers,
smoked a joint, and stumbled home before 1:30.

Gil came to the back fence one afternoon when Jack and I were outside, and asked me if I'd hold the extension ladder for him so he could pull some bird's nests down from the eaves of his house. The sound of their chirping was freaking Ellis out. I put the baby in his playpen near the garden, straddled the low picket fence, and grabbed the rungs of the ladder. He hobbled up thirty feet with his bum leg and started dislodging handfuls of hay and twigs, shredded cigarette filters, and bits of string. The detritus rained down, dreamlike. But right in the middle of the slow falling— *plop, plop, plop*—three sightless baby birds hit the ground like ripe fruit.

I took Jack inside, but watched from the open kitchen window as Gil dug a hole. I couldn't see because of the fence, but I knew when he scooted them, writhing and chirping, into their grave.

"This is really fucked," I heard him say to himself. He shook his head, and then he put the dirt in. We heard them from underground for the rest of the afternoon and so did their mother, who landed in the lilac and frantically called. "I oughta kill her too," he said to me later as we had a cup of coffee in my kitchen, "but then where would it end?"

The next night, the old man Ming came late to the poker game. He remained standing quietly by the door in his overcoat and hat. One by one, each of us at the table stopped talking and drinking and looked over at him. There was a long silence, and then he said, "Would one of you accompany me back to the Golden Dragon? I believe my wife has died."

"Why don't you call the cops?" said Gil, pointing to the phone.

"I don't want the cops," said Ming.

"I'll go," said Bobby. "Let me just get the flashlight."

"My wife's a nurse," I said.

"Okay," said Ming. "Meet us."

Trying to explain the whole thing at once to Lynn wasn't easy, but luckily baby Jack was asleep in his crib, and she didn't mind running across the street to check things out. She knew Ming from occasionally talking to him on the sidewalk, and he'd always been nice to her.

Bobby signaled to us with the flashlight from the alley between the Golden Dragon and a defunct dance studio. He was holding the black metal side door open. We stepped in.

He said, "Check this out," and put the light up to a giant glass globe that was the top of a penny gum ball machine. I noticed that it was a beautiful antique, and then I saw what he meant. Within the bubble, a thousand roaches scurried away from the light, around and between faded gumballs.

"That's gross," said Lynn.

Bobby laughed. "This way," he said.

It was pitch-black inside, and we had only the single beam of light to guide us. From the little I saw of the painted Buddhas, silent fountains, and empty fish tanks, it was clear that the Golden Dragon had once been an opulent place.

We went through a hallway, and then Bobby said, "Okay, watch your step, we're going down." He showed us to a set of metal stairs that descended into the basement. At least down there I could see a little light shining. In the corner of a large dark expanse, Mrs. Ming lay on a kind of army cot with small tea candles set on stands at each of the four corners. She was emaciated, her skin stretched taut across her ribs and skull. Her complexion was silver and her naked body was contorted so that she looked as if she'd been frozen in the act of falling. Her hair had shed off all over the pillow. Ming stood next to his wife and swept his hand in front of him, indicating that Lynn should approach.

To Lynn's credit, she didn't flinch but stepped right up and leaned over the body.

I gagged.

"Has she expired?" asked Ming, holding his hat in his hand and turning it by the brim.

"Definitely deceased," said Lynn, still bent over the body. Abruptly, she stood up, turned to Ming, and put her hand on his shoulder. "I'm sorry," she said. He nodded. "You're going to have to call an ambulance or at least the police," she said.

I was surprised when Ming returned to the poker game the following Thursday night. We avoided the subject of Ming's dead wife, and I talked about my mother-in-law for comic effect. Somewhere around eleven p.m. the cards lost their luster. We switched over to just drinking. Ellis rolled a fat joint and we burned it. When things got so quiet we could hear the parrot on the front porch next door imitating the sound of a ringing phone, Ming shook his head and told us that his wife had come back from the dead to haunt him.

"What are you talkin' about?" said Gil.

"Shit, my ex hasn't even died and she haunts me," said Bobby.

Ming's hands were trembling and there was sweat on his razor mustache. "She gets in bed beside me. The covers move and then she's there. Her touch is so cold. All night long she whispers through my dreams a story about her and me setting sail on an ocean liner made of ice. The captain gives us a tour all the way down to the very bottom of the ship. Then a man enters the chamber, screaming, frantic to tell us that the ship is sinking and water is coming down the passageway. In the morning . . . "

"B complex to counteract depression," said Ellis.

Ming made no reply but, out of the corner of his eye, nervously studied the stream of smoke curling up from the tip of Gil's cigar.

"She's cursed me," said the old man.

"Why would she do that?" asked Bobby.

"There was another woman, some years back," he said. "I saw her until my wife found out, and then I broke off the affair. Out of spite, my lover put a spell on my wife. And now that she's passed on, my wife haunts me." Ming looked exhausted, on the verge of some disease, himself.

"Vitamin B," said Ellis. "And some fish oil."

Ming sighed.

"Are we on the verge of some ancient Chinese secret?" asked Bobby.

Ming cracked a smile. "I'm not Chinese," he said.

"How can you have a Chinese restaurant?" asked Ellis.

"Around here?" said Ming. "Think about it."

"Is this more psychological or like physical stuff?" I asked.

"Last night," said Ming, "while I was sleeping, she materialized and stuck her finger up my ass. Like a crooked icicle. The cold scorched me to my heart."

"What kinda deal is that?" said Gil.

"That's pretty psychological," said Bobby.

"As usual, I dreamed we were on a cruise," said Ming and tears formed in his eyes.

"Easy, easy," said Gil.

"You know it all comes out of your head," said Gil. "You're getting over on yourself."

"Don't tell me about ghosts," whispered Ming.

"Here's a proposition," said Bobby. "I'll play you in a game of cards for your ghost. A hand of poker, five cards, suicide jacks wild."

Ming grinned and dismissed the idea with a wave of his hand.

"Say he wins and you get the ghost?" asked Ellis.

"He wants the ice finger," said Gil.

"We should play," said Bobby. "As an experiment, that's all."

"Oh, it's real," said Ming, and his grin disappeared. He held his empty glass out to me. I filled it with beer from the quart I was working on.

"Humor me," said Bobby.

Ming finished the beer in two long swallows. He finally nodded. "If you lose, you get my ghost," he said. "If I lose, what do you get?"

"If you lose, you get to whip us up a batch of Chinese food next Thursday night. Moo goo thy pants, a platter of it," said Bobby.

"In other words, there's no way you can win," said Ming.

Gil dealt. It took only minutes and Bobby's three queens lost to Ming's royal flush. The second he saw that he'd lost, Bobby suddenly raised his eyebrows and said, "I feel a draft in my asshole." Ming laughed harder than anyone.

Ming never came back for poker. I saw him on the street one day and called over to him. He waved and said hello. Then he was gone, somehow leaving a message for us with the parrots. "Going home," the birds repeated in the old man's weary voice.

"Where's home?" asked Gil when we discussed the whole saga on the following poker night.

I guessed Korea, Gil guessed Japan, and Ellis was sure it was Mongolia. Bobby said, "Where the heart is."

When the ghost grabbed Bobby it had nothing to do with his job, which was snorkeling in the Delaware River, cutting brass off sunken ships with an acetylene torch. How fitting would it have been, keeping in mind the dream that Ming's wife had spun for her husband, if Bobby'd drowned? He didn't, though. What he did was fall off the wagon.

When I asked Gil where his cousin was, he told me, "He's living in a trailer down by the river. I went to see him the other night."

"How's he doing?" I asked.

"He's speedballing," said Gil, shaking his head. "He's the walkin' prince of Death."

Bobby attacked an old woman—busted her in the face and stole her purse. He got caught, was sentenced to ten years as a repeat offender, and got sent to prison. The night that Gil told us about it, we didn't play cards but just sat in the living room and drank. On the next Thursday, when I went to Gil's the lights were out and no one answered the door. After that, on Thursday nights, I'd sit out back by the dying garden, smoke, and drink a few beers by myself. Summer slipped into autumn, but until it got too cold for them to be outside, I'd hear those parrots, in the distance, still channeling Ming.

During the first snowstorm of that year, the Golden Dragon caught fire, and from the front window, Lynn and baby Jack and I watched the old restaurant turn to ash. I noticed a figure standing outside on the sidewalk also watching the blaze. The strobe from one of the fire engines passed over him, and I recognized Gil, momentarily bathed in red. I hadn't seen him in weeks. I went out to the porch and called to him. Gil waved, came over, and climbed the steps, and I let him in.

The instant I saw him in the porch light, I could tell he'd followed Bobby off the wagon. He was pale and thin and his hands shook badly when he lit a cigarette. A sharp smell of gasoline came off his coat.

"You don't look so good," I said.

"I went back to it after Bobby got busted."

I almost asked, "Why?" but realized how stupid a question it was.

"Me and Ellis split," he said. "I showed him an article in the paper one day by a famous doctor that said that taking vitamins was useless."

"Are you kidding?" I asked.

"He said I was too negative, and he left me. My using again didn't help either."

"Do you hear from Bobby?" I asked.

He took a drag of his cigarette. "Yeah, he called once for a minute. He sounded fucked-up, not high but shaky. Right before he hung up I asked him what the joint was like, and he told me, 'Like an ocean liner made of ice.'"

I shook my head.

"You've gotta stay away from me now," said Gil, staring out the window. "Keep your doors locked, day and night. If you see me, don't talk to me. Make like I don't exist. I'll let you know if I kick it again."

"Okay," I said.

Without another word, he left. I never saw him again.

PERMISSIONS

P.S.

Insights,
Interviews
& More...

Meet Jeffrey Ford

Lynn Gallagher-Ford

I WAS BORN IN 1955 and grew up in the town of West Islip, on Long Island, in New York State. We lived in a development on Pine Avenue around the corner from the local grade school, South Gate. I have one older brother and two younger sisters. In addition to my immediate family, my maternal grandparents also lived with us, first upstairs and then in an apartment that had once been the garage.

My father was a gear cutter, and my older brother is now also a machinist. My grandfather had been a professional boxer and a hard-hat deep-sea diver in the merchant marine during the Second World War. My grandmother read people's fortunes with an ordinary deck of playing cards. She had seen more ghosts than Hans Holzer and told tales of banshees, clairvoyance, death fetches, and prophetic dreams. My mother did not go to work until the mid-seventies and then took on various office jobs. She was also creatively inclined, spending her private time painting, writing, playing the piano, the guitar, and making Super 8 movies that she wrote, cast with family members and neighbors, and directed. She read constantly and eclectically, everything

About the author

from *The Letters of Tchaikovsky* to Harry Crews to Sherlock Holmes, and my father read to me—Rider Haggard, Kipling, Stevenson, Tennyson, Wilde, etc. My love of stories and fiction came primarily from these people I grew up with.

I didn't do very well in school. I spent my entire educational career between kindergarten and my sophomore year of high school either on the verge of failing or failing. It didn't help (or it did) that my mother's policy was that if you didn't want to go to school, you didn't have to. I'd stay home and read. One year I missed fifty-four days.

Then I woke up and passed a few classes in my last two years of high school. I took the Regents Scholarship exam and scored high enough on it to get free books and tuition at the local community college. I went for one semester and then had to drop out because I'd failed every subject. I had majored that semester in drinking beer and smoking dope. After that, I worked in various machine shops, department stores, and warehouses in order to save up to buy a clam boat. This allowed me to become a clammer on the Great South Bay, one of the best jobs in the world when you're eighteen.

During this time of work I continued reading and writing and still wanted to be a writer of stories and novels. So after a few years of working the flats, I saved up money to go back to school. I returned to the same community college and did two years straight while working at night loading trucks for Roadway and as a stock boy in Sears's garden department. There's nothing like a few years of real work to make you appreciate school. My grades were excellent by the time I finished my two years at Suffolk County Community College.

In my final year at community college, I read a novel, *Grendel*, by John Gardner, and thought it was a terrific book. The next year, I transferred to SUNY Binghamton in upstate ▶

> 66 It didn't help (or it did) that my mother's policy was that if you didn't want to go to school, you didn't have to. I'd stay home and read. One year I missed fifty-four days. 99

New York. I was there only one semester before the university hired John Gardner to teach fiction writing. By the time I found out he had been hired, I had missed the cutoff date to sign up for his classes. I went to see him anyway and told him I wanted to take his classes. At first, he dismissed me. As I was walking away from his office, though, he came out into the hallway and called me back and said, "Okay, I'll give you a chance." I took classes with him the rest of my undergraduate years and also for two years of a master's degree. I admired a lot of his later fiction, but as good a writer as he was, he was an even better teacher. He published some of my first short stories in his magazine, *MSS*.

I got married in 1979 to Lynn Gallagher and graduated with my master's degree in 1981. After that I worked as an adjunct teacher in various colleges around the Philadelphia area. We wound up living in a row house in South Philly. I also attended Temple University on and off for four years in pursuit of a Ph.D. in literature. My first son, Jackson, was born in 1988. I had finished all the course work for my Ph.D., passed my prelims, passed my oral exams, and written a draft of my dissertation, which had been approved by my advisor, but I had to make a decision as to whether I wanted to be a scholar or a fiction writer. With a son and a family to support, I felt I couldn't do both. I dropped out of the Ph.D. program and took a full-time, tenure-track job at Brookdale Community College in New Jersey. Twenty years later, I still work there and am now a full professor. It's a great job. In 1988, I also published my first novel, *Vanitas*, with Space & Time Press in New York, and this helped me decide to dedicate more time to writing. My other son, Derek, came along a few years later, and I quit writing novels for a while and concentrated on writing short fiction. We

66 I admired a lot of his [John Gardner's] later fiction, but as good a writer as he was, he was an even better teacher. He published some of my first short stories in his magazine, *MSS*. 99

moved to South Jersey, first to Collingswood and then to Medford Lakes.

My stories started appearing in obscure "literary" and genre publications pretty regularly. My writing time was at night, after everyone else in the house was asleep. I'd stay up until two or three in the morning. Those were fun times. For all of the new writers out there who are publishing in journals and zines, don't believe it when the naysayers tell you that nobody reads them. In 1996, an agent from New York read a story, "Grass Island," I had published in *Puerto Del Sol*, the literary magazine of the New Mexico State University. He told me that if I had a novel, I should send it to him. I happened to have a piece of a novel, the first four chapters of *The Physiognomy*. I sent it, he sold it, and I was on my way.

The Physiognomy won the World Fantasy Award for Best Novel of 1997 and was a *New York Times* Notable Book of the Year. In the years that followed, I published four more novels and two collections of short stories. I've published more than seventy short stories in anthologies and magazines. My fiction has garnered three more World Fantasy Awards, a Nebula Award, an Edgar Allan Poe Award, and the Grand Prix de l'Imaginaire in France.

I still do most of my writing late at night when everyone is asleep, even though I have to be up early to take my younger son to high school. Those dark, quiet hours are a beautiful time. When I get too tired to stay awake, I hear voices in my ears, and very often they speak pieces of stories to me. Sometimes I remember them and write them down. When I write, I have the feeling that the stories and novels already exist somewhere in my head, or out there somewhere in another dimension, and the process of writing them is the process of merely discovering them. ❧

> ❝ For all of the new writers out there who are publishing in journals and zines, don't believe it when the naysayers tell you that nobody reads them. ❞

The Metaphysics of Fiction Writing
An Anecdote

A FEW WEEKS AGO I got an invitation to give a talk to a group known as the Garden State Horror Writers. I said sure, since the place where they meet is up around where I teach in Monmouth County, so I figured it wouldn't be too hard to find. Eileen Watkins, who is a member of GSHW, told me she was putting together a press release for the event and she needed me to come up with a topic on which I'd be speaking. I told her that I was hoping I wouldn't have to do anything formal but just engage the membership in a casual discussion and Q & A. Eileen told me that's what it would basically turn into, but she needed a subject for the press release. "Pick anything," she said, "it doesn't matter." So, off the top of my head, I immediately came up with the Metaphysics of Fiction Writing. I think what happened was, since the topic title was to really remain just a title, I figured I'd reach for the brass ring and in the process punched through stratospheres of the pontifical. At the time, I thought it was an amusing title, but later on, when Eileen sent me an e-mail with a link to the press release at their site, I realized I might just as well have punched myself in the head.

Of course, the first thing I did about it was nothing. A couple weeks went by, and I gave it nary thought. The morning of the talk, I got up with a bad feeling. Once I'd gotten in the car and was on my way, I started frantically thinking about the Metaphysics of Fiction Writing, and what I could possibly say about it. . . .

I've always been fascinated with the phenomenon of how a story plays out in a reader's mind when reading and a writer's

About the book

mind when writing. I'm not sure it's the same for everyone, but I'm talking about the little "movies" behind my eyes when I'm involved in either process. I put quotes around the word "movies" because, although they're visually like a film, I can also sense the emotions of each character, so in a way they are a deeper experience than watching a film. Do you see pictures when you write and read fiction? The thing that always amazed me about this phenomenon is that these streams of imagery are initiated by nothing more or less than wiggles of ink on sheets of paper. I scan my eyes over these symbols and an entire world blossoms in my mind. And there are characters there, I see, who look nothing like the people I know in life. Incredible.

For example, back in 1985, say, Stephen King could have written a book—a collection of wiggles of ink on paper. It was published. Someone bought a copy and read it. When they were done, they gave it to a friend. The friend read it and then sold it in a garage sale. Over the years, the book changed hands two dozen times until this woman, in the summer of 2005, buys the copy from a used bookstore and takes the volume on vacation with her to Long Beach Island in New Jersey. She sits down beneath her umbrella, facing the breakers, and begins to read. The book scares the crap out of her.

King's wiggles of ink have transferred the emotion of fear across Time and Space—twenty years and from Maine to New Jersey. While the woman on Long Beach Island reads, she sees in her mind imagery of the drama of King's story. A book is a time machine of our intentions, our ideas, our emotions; the alchemy of ingredients psychological, physical, and experiential, which have coalesced in the form of the words we choose.

What fascinates me about this process the most is that in the creation of the manuscript, as a fiction writer caught up in the vision of ▶

> **❝** Do you see pictures when you write and read fiction? The thing that always amazed me about this phenomenon is that these streams of imagery are initiated by nothing more or less than wiggles of ink on sheets of paper. **❞**

The Metaphysics of Fiction Writing
(continued)

the fiction he or she is trying to relay to paper
through the selection of the appropriate wiggles
of ink and their strategic placement, he or she
must choose which images at play in his or her
own mind he or she will transfer symbolically
through words to another's mind. In other
words, I see a scene—

A guy and a girl are sitting in a diner. She's
wearing a black leather jacket and smoking a
cigarette. Her hair is blond, tied in the back
with a green rubber band, and she has a tooth
missing on the right side of her smile. He's
wearing a white undershirt and jeans. He's
speaking in a whisper and at the end of each
statement he taps the edge of his car key against
the top of the table. His eyelids indicate he is
either tired or completely stoned. She's got a
half-cup of coffee. He's got coffee too, but
there's also a plate with smeared yolk and
two crusts of toast in front of him. The benches
of the booth they are sitting in are old green
vinyl, cracked in places and sometimes repaired
with duct tape. They sit next to a window, and
between them and the window is one of those
little silver jukeboxes where you can flip
through the selections. They're the only
customers in the place with the exception
of an old Chinese gentleman, wearing a brown
sports jacket and hat, sitting on one of the
stools at the counter near the cash register,
drinking coffee. There is a sizzling of burger
meat from the grill, but the cook is nowhere
in sight. A fan turns slowly, suspended from a
pressed tin ceiling that has gone to grime. The
girl takes a drag, flicks her ash, and says, "No."

In your mind's eye can you see the scene I'm
describing? If you do, I'll bet if I ask you to tell
me whether it is day or night outside that diner
window while the couple is sitting there, you
can. What did you see? I, of course, don't

describe what time of day it is, but when *you* look it is filled in. The writer can't give you words for everything he is seeing, because then the writing would be overloaded and we'd never get to the plot. The reader, in the process of reading the fiction, is confabulating at least half of the imagery of the "movie" he or she will see upon reading, just as you were kind enough to fill in daytime or nighttime outside the diner's window, as well as the young man's hair color and style, perhaps the old calendar on the wall near the register or the cup full of pens, the style of hat on the old man at the counter, how many cars are in the parking lot outside the window, what the girl is wearing beneath the black leather jacket, which songs are available on the jukebox.

Here's what it comes down to—when we really enjoy a piece of fiction, very often it's because the vision the writer's words transfer to our minds is so vibrant. We can become invested in the story. How does a writer know which pieces of the waking dream and in what combination will be the most effective in channeling his or her vision to the reader? Remember, this stuff has to go from the writer's mind to the page to then be read and interpreted by the reader. Plenty of room for mess-ups, it would seem. My feeling is, I don't think you can consciously decide this kind of stuff. The process of choosing imagery to carry your story must be intuitive in some way, not intellectual. . . .

Right about here this whole twenty-mule-team string of hoo-ha I was building unraveled and dripped out my ear when I came to the part of the drive where I was called upon to turn onto Route 9, a road I'd not driven on before. There were a couple more sparks of ideas for other metaphysical stuff in writing ▶

66 The writer can't give you words for everything he is seeing, because then the writing would be overloaded and we'd never get to the plot. 99

The Metaphysics of Fiction Writing
(continued)

in addition to the continuation of the web of
confusion above, but they came and went like
ghosts more tired than angry; one quick jingle
of the chains followed by snoring.

When I got to the library where this event
was supposed to take place, I was sweating.
I still wasn't sure what I was going to talk about,
and I could readily see myself burbling and
blithering, my revelations more underwhelming
than a bucket of lime Jell-O, in front of a room
packed with embarrassed silence. Once inside
the library, I searched around for the GSHW,
but couldn't find anyone from that group.
The librarian looked up the meeting schedule
and told me she had nothing on the schedule
for that day. I went on one of the library's
computers and checked the GSHW site and
read the press release for my event. I had the
wrong day. I was a whole week early.

I cracked at myself for being such a pile.
Then I got back in the car and drove home.
On the journey, I didn't think about the
Metaphysics of Fiction Writing for a second,
but listened to the radio—a show about truffle
hunters, their dogs, and the fierceness with
which they protect their stands of oak. ❧

An Excerpt from Jeffrey Ford's *Shadow Year*

On New York's Long Island, in the unpredictable decade of the 1960s, a young boy laments the approaching close of summer and the advent of sixth grade. But when a night prowler is reported stalking the neighborhood, he and his brother, Jim, appoint themselves ad hoc investigators, and set out to aid the police— while their little sister, Mary, smokes cigarettes, speaks in other voices, and moves around the inanimate clay residents of Botch Town, a detailed cardboard replica of their community they've constructed in their basement. Ensuing events add a shadowy cast to the boys' night games: disappearances, deaths, and spectral sightings capped off by the arrival of a sinister man in a long white car trawling the neighborhood after dark. Strangest of all is that every one of these troubling occurrences seems to correspond to the changes little Mary has made to the miniature town in the basement.

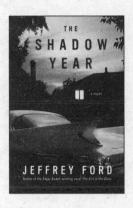

Not since Ray Bradbury's classic Dandelion Wine *has a novel so richly evoked the dark magic of small-town boyhood.* The Shadow Year *is a masterful re-creation of a unique time and place, and a hypnotically compelling mystery. Now available in hardcover from William Morrow, an imprint of HarperCollins.*

IT BEGAN IN THE LAST DAYS OF AUGUST when the leaves of the elm in the front yard had curled into crisp, brown tubes and fallen away to litter the lawn. I sat at the curb that afternoon, waiting for Mister Softee to round the bend at the top of Willow Avenue, listening carefully for that mournful knell, each measured *ding* both a promise of ice cream and a pinprick of remorse. Taking a castoff leaf into each hand, I made double fists. When I opened my fingers, brown crumbs fell and ▶

scattered on the road at my feet. Had I been waiting for the arrival of that strange changeling year, I might have understood the sifting debris to be symbolic of the end of something. Instead, I waited for the eyes.

That morning, I'd left under a blue sky, walked through the woods, and crossed the railroad tracks away from town, where the third rail hummed, lying in wait, like a snake, for an errant ankle. Then along the road by the factory, back behind the grocery, and up and down the streets, I searched for discarded glass bottles in every open garbage can, Dumpster, forgotten corner. I'd found three soda bottles and a half-gallon milk bottle. At the grocery store, I turned them in for the refund and walked away with a quarter.

All summer long, Mister Softee had this contest going. With each purchase of twenty-five cents or more, he gave you a card: on the front was a small portrait of the waffle-faced cream being pictured on the side of the truck. On the back was a piece of a puzzle that, when joined with seven other cards, made the same exact image of the beckoning soft one but eight times bigger. I had the blue lapels and red bow tie, the sugar-cone-flesh lips parted in a pure white smile, the exposed, towering brain of vanilla, cream-kissed at the top into a pointed swirl, but I didn't have the eyes.

A complete puzzle won you the Special Softee, like Coney Island in a plastic dish—four twirled Softee loads of cream, chocolate sauce, butterscotch, marshmallow goo, nuts, party-colored sprinkles, raisins, M&M's, shredded coconut, bananas, all topped with a cherry. You couldn't purchase the Special Softee, you had to win it, or so said Mel, who, through the years, had come to be known simply as Softee.

Occasionally Mel would try to be pleasant, but I think the paper canoe of a hat he wore

every day soured him. He also wore a blue bow
tie, a white shirt, and white pants. His face was
long and crooked, and, at times, when the
orders came too fast and the kids didn't have
the right change, the bottom half of his face
would slowly melt—a sundae abandoned at the
curb. His long ears sprouted tufts of hair as if
his skull contained a hedge of it, and the lenses
of his glasses had internal flaws like diamonds.
In a voice that came straight from his freezer,
he called my sister, Mary, and all the other girls
"Sweetheart."

Earlier in the season, one late afternoon, my
brother, Jim, said to me, "You want to see where
Softee lives?" We took our bikes. He led me way
up Hammond Lane, past the shoe store and the
junior high school, up beyond Our Lady of
Lourdes. After a half hour of riding, he stopped in
front of a small house. As I pulled up, he pointed
to the place and said, "Look at that dump."

Softee's truck was parked on a barren plot
at the side of the place. I remember ivy and a
one-story house, no bigger than a good-sized
garage. Shingles showed their zebra stripes
through fading white. The porch had obviously
sustained a meteor shower. There were no lights
on inside, and I thought this strange because
twilight was mixing in behind the trees.

"Is he sitting in there in the dark?" I asked
my brother.

Jim shrugged as he got back on his bike.
He rode in big circles around me twice and
then shot off down the street, screaming over
his shoulder as loud as he could, "Softee sucks!"
The ride home was through true night, and he
knew that without him I would get lost, so he
pedaled as hard as he could.

We had forsaken the jingle bells of Bungalow
Bar and Good Humor all summer in an attempt
to win Softee's contest. By the end of July, ▶

though, each of the kids on the block had at least two near-complete puzzles, but no one had the eyes. I had heard from Tim Sullivan, who lived in the development on the other side of the school field, that the kids over there got fed up one day and rushed the truck, jumped up and swung from the bar that held the rearview mirror, invaded the driver's compartment, all the while yelling, "Give us the eyes. The fuckin' eyes." When Softee went up front to chase them, Tim's brother, Bill, leaped up on the sill of the window through which Softee served his customers, leaned into the inner sanctum, unlatched the freezer, and started tossing Italian ices out to the kids standing at the curb.

Softee lost his glasses in the fray, but the hat held on. He screamed, "You little bitches!" at them as they played him back and forth from the driver's area to the serving compartment. In the end, Mel got two big handfuls of cards and tossed them out on the street. "Like flies on dogshit," said Tim. By the time they'd realized there wasn't a pair of eyes in the bunch, Softee had turned the bell off and was coasting silently around the corner.

I had a theory, though, that day at summer's end when I sat at the curb, waiting. It was my hope that Softee had been holding out on us until the close of the season, and then, in the final days before school started and he quit his route till spring, some kid was going to have bestowed upon him a pair of eyes. I had faith like I never had at church that something special was going to happen that day to me. It did, but it had nothing to do with ice cream. I sat there at the curb, waiting, until the sun started to go down and my mother called me in for dinner. Softee never came again, but as it turned out, we all got the eyes. ∾

Have You Read?
More by Jeffrey Ford

THE GIRL IN THE GLASS
(Edgar Award Winner)

The Great Depression has bound a nation
in despair—and only a privileged few have
risen above it: the exorbitantly wealthy . . .
and the hucksters who feed upon them. Diego,
a seventeen-year-old illegal Mexican immigrant,
owes his salvation to master grifter Thomas
Schell. Together with Schell's gruff and powerful
partner, they sail comfortably through hard
times, scamming New York's grieving rich with
elaborate, ingeniously staged séances—until an
impossible occurrence changes everything.

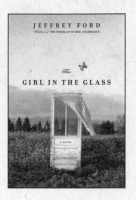

    While "communing with spirits," Schell
sees an image of a young girl in a pane of
glass, silently entreating the con man for
help. Though well aware that his otherworldly
"powers" are a sham, Schell inexplicably offers
his services to help find the lost child—drawing
Diego along with him into a tangled maze of
deadly secrets and terrible experimentation.

    At once a hypnotically compelling
mystery and a stunningly evocative portrait
of Depression-era New York, *The Girl in the
Glass* is a masterly literary adventure from a
writer of exemplary vision and skill.

"Ford has written a book that features a dog
  man who impersonates a dog and a snake that
  dies of a broken heart. That, for the record, is a
  winning combination."
              —Chelsea Cain, *New York Times*

THE PORTRAIT OF MRS. CHARBUQUE

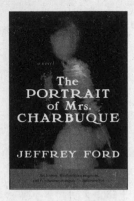

A mysterious and richly evocative novel, *The Portrait of Mrs. Charbuque* tells the story of portraitist Piero Piambo, who is offered a commission unlike any other. The client is Mrs. Charbuque, a wealthy and elusive woman who asks Piambo to paint her portrait, though with one bizarre twist: he may question her at length on any topic, but he may not, under any circumstances, see her. So begins an astonishing journey into Mrs. Charbuque's world and the world of 1893 New York society in this hypnotically compelling literary thriller.

"A strange and affecting tale of obsession, inspiration, and the supernatural, with a dash of murder thrown in. . . . The twists and turns of Mrs. Charbuque's commission keep the pages turning." —*New York Times Book Review*

"Art history, Hitchcockian suspense, and Pynchonesque augury." —*Baltimore Sun*

Don't miss the next book by your favorite author. Sign up now for AuthorTracker by visiting www.AuthorTracker.com.